Angel in My Fingers

(Frieda's Story)

By

Julie Poole

Copyright

Angel in My Fingers (Frieda's Story) First Published 2015
Published by J.P. Publishing
Cover Design by Rebecca Poole from Dreams2Media
Editing by Elizabeth H. O'Reilly
Proofing by Harriette H. Charbonneau
ISBN – paperback – 978-0-9933522-5-6
ISBN – ebook - 978-0-9933522-4-9

Acknowledgements

Acknowledgements are made to the following, whose work I have mentioned in this novel:

The Butterfly Effect: Written and directed by Eric Bress and J. Mackye Gruber: BenderSpink (co-production), FilmEngine (co-production), Katalyst Films (in association with), Province of British Columbia Production Services Tax Credit (with the participation of) (2004).

Alice's Adventures in Wonderland: Lewis Carroll. Oxford University Press (2009). First printed (1865).

Guide to Tarot: Sarah Kettlewell, Caxton Editions: London (2000).

Universal Waite Tarot Deck: Conceived by Stuart R. Kaplan, Colouring by Mary Hanson-Roberts, Drawings by Pamela Colman Smith: Stamford CT (1990).

Messages from Your Angels: Doreen Virtue, Hay House Inc.: California (2002).

It's a Wonderful Life: Frances Goodrich, Albert Hackett, and Frank Capra: Liberty Films, (1946).

The Godfather: Written by Mario Puzo, directed by Francis Ford Coppola and produced by Albert S. Ruddy (1972).

Shawshank Redemption: written and directed by Frank Darabont (1994).

Citizen Cane: produced, co-written and directed by Orson Welles. Also written by Herman J. Mankiewicz (1941).

Special Thanks

I would like to thank the following people for their help with the development and production of this book:

Dreams2media - thank you Rebecca Poole for the fabulous book cover.
Betsy and Hatsie - for your wonderful proofing and editing.

To my children, Tom, Chris, and Charlotte; I love you all dearly and am so grateful for you being in my heart and part of my life.

To my readers, who have asked for more - I thank you from the bottom of my heart for your support and kindness.

And finally, of course ... to the angels; I thank you.

Julie Poole

Dedication

***

*Your task is not to seek for love,
but merely to seek and find
all the barriers within yourself
that you have built against it.*

***

Rumi

Books by Julie Poole

Angel on My Shoulder (Sarah's Story)
Book 1 in the 'Angel' series

Angel in My Heart (Clarabelle's Story)
Book 2 in the 'Angel' series

Angel in My Fingers (Frieda's Story)
Book 3 in the 'Angel' series

COMING SOON
Angel in My Paws (Fred's Story)
Book 4 in the 'Angel' series

Contents

Prologue

Cassie watched the woman approach the door with a knowing smile, examining her carefully from head to foot. *Yes, she was definitely nervous… a first timer then*, she nodded to herself thoughtfully. They were always nervous the first time, although Cassie had no idea why. *Was it Ma they were scared of, or just the cards?* There was nothing in either Ma or the cards to be scared of, but she could feel the woman's nervousness emanating down the path and through the closed front door of the old cottage like little tidal waves of panic. *Bless her*, she thought. She smiled reassuringly at the woman from her seat in the window, making sure that her smile went all the way up to her emerald green eyes and smiled the biggest smile she could find inside her, but it did not register to the visitor. The woman's sad eyes were fixed so intently on the heavy wooden door at the end of the gravel path that she failed to notice either the huge smile or the twinkling green eyes that shone warmth and reassurance to her through the glass. Cassie felt sorry for the woman who clearly had the weight of the world on her shoulders, poor thing! Her head was drooped heavily as she walked down the path, her shoulders hunched, her worries prematurely aging her, so much so that she looked more like someone of Ma's age than the middle-aged woman that she clearly was.

"Don't panic, my dear, Ma will sort you out," Cassie said confidently, looking over at Ma with adoration.

The old lady sat quietly at the small round table waiting. Her gnarled ancient hands rested gently in her lap holding the crystal ball lovingly as she gazed at the cards on the table before her. Her grey eyes focused on her prayers and the cards simultaneously as she waited for the bell to ring. If she heard the logs crackling in the hearth or noticed the fragrance from the incense burning in its stand she did not show it, so intent was she on her mantra. Soft light bounced off the faded walls of the old stone cottage from the many candles lit throughout the room as she repeated her words, "Mother, Father, God Creator, help me to help this woman to find her way," she whispered softly, stroking the clear quartz crystal ball in her hands. "Fill these cards with love, with healing, with inspiration, with knowledge and with guidance, to help this lady, within her highest good. Thank you."

Cassie watched quietly, knowing not to disturb Ma when she was working. She was often working, but never seemed to tire despite her advanced years and increasingly frail body. She didn't know how old Ma was, or how long she had been helping people, but she knew that it was a *very* long time indeed! She'd been with Ma some years now, and in that time she had seen hundreds, if not thousands of people like this one, come and go. The new ones always came nervous, and left smiling. The old ones, the ones who came time and time again, came and went with a smile, but always went with a bigger smile than when they arrived. Ma was a wonder!

The doorbell rang loudly, making them both jump, even though it was expected. Ma quickly placed the crystal ball on its stand in the centre of the table, picked up her cane resting by her side and stood up slowly, giving her old bones time to shift position as she went from a sitting to a standing position. She shuffled slowly to the door, her old feet not quite lifting as they should as she manoeuvred herself down the hall, leaning on her trusty cane for both balance and support.

"Coming, my dear," she called brightly, in a voice stronger than a woman her age had a right to have. She shuffled down the hall towards the door. "Nearly there," she called again, reaching the door with a bright smile. She shuffled her weight onto her left leg, adjusting her cane, allowing her to balance her weight onto it as she reached for and opened the front door with her right hand. "Good morning, my dear," she beamed brightly at the woman standing nervously on the door step. "You must be Jane. I'm Ma." She saw the woman's hesitation and quickly added, "Everyone calls me Ma, my dear. Do come in, come in." Ma showed the woman in, beckoning her to take a seat in the chair opposite her own at the round table. Shuffling around to her own chair, she sat down carefully, gently placing her cane to the side of the table, resting it against the old china pot stand in the corner of the room with great care. Having satisfied herself that all was right and well with her cane, she looked up, smiling gently at the woman in front of her. Kindness and reassurance shone out from Ma's eyes as she picked up the Tarot deck on the table in front of her. Shuffling the cards slowly she handed them to the woman with a smile; a smile that said, 'trust me.'

Cassie beamed happily as she made herself comfortable on the window seat. It had begun! She loved watching Ma work! The old lady's eyes twinkled with love and compassion as she set about helping the woman to find her way. Her soft white curly hair framed her old and withered face with a gentleness that befit her. She bent over the cards, concentrating intently, talking gently; explaining, helping and guiding the woman in front of her. Over the next hour Ma worked her magic as Cassie watched enthralled. She saw with glee the light come back into the sad woman's eyes, noticing how her back straightened gradually and her shoulders lifted from their hunched stance as the confusion and fear were lifted out of her by Ma's words; as if by magic, that somehow, in some way, Ma was making it all better. Cassie knew exactly how Ma did this. She'd watched enough of these readings to understand the power to heal and help that these Tarot cards had, as did the other Angel cards that Ma sometimes used. She could feel their energy, their vitality and their power. Sometime later, money was exchanged, a hug was given, and Ma was seeing the woman out; a much lighter, brighter and stronger woman, that much was clear. There was no doubt about it, Ma was an angel in human form! She was a miracle worker and Cassie absolutely, totally, completely adored her.

Cassie heard the door close and watched with pride as Ma shuffled back into the room and settled into her chair with a contented sigh. A serene smile on her face, she beckoned to Cassie to come closer. "Where are you, Cassandra Alexandra the Third?" Ma called playfully. "My eyes are tired and I can't see you so well over there."

Cassie smiled, moving gracefully from the window seat, she took her place next to the old lady. Ma rarely used her full given name, but Cassie loved it when she did. It made her feel very grand!

"Oh, there you are! Well that went well, Cassie, don't you think, dear?" Ma grinned happily. Cassie nodded her agreement emphatically. "Need to clear up, must always clear up!" she smiled, picking up the pack of cards from the table, she shuffled them thoughtfully, but, just as she was about to put them back in the pack, she hesitated. Suddenly she pulled three cards from the pack and laid them face up on the table. She examined them, smiled and sighed. "Enough for today, Cassie, I'm feeling rather tired. I think I shall have to take a little nap. Keep an eye on things would you, there's a love."

Ma's eyes closed and within seconds, the old lady was breathing heavily, the smile still on her lips as she drifted into a deep sleep. Her energy spent, the concentration of the last hour had taken its toll and she was exhausted. Cassie watched over her, examining her closely. Ma's body was slim, as it always had been, but now the skin was loose and wrinkled, increasingly so every day it seemed. Her frame, delicate and frail as she slept in the chair. Cassie was sure that she was getting more frail and more delicate, almost by the day, but Ma would have none of it.

"Oh, Ma, you need to slow down. Look at you, fast asleep within seconds! You're doing too much!" Cassie sighed, knowing that she was wasting her breath. Ma loved her work, and Cassie loved Ma, so it was the way it was, and that was that! She turned her attention away from Ma and looked at the cards on the table, focusing on the brightly coloured major arcana card that was staring up at her, demanding her attention. The card stared back. 'Death' it said; 'endings' it called. Cassie knew the card didn't mean *actual* death, it meant merely the ending of something that needed to end, in order to make way for a new beginning. The card sat next to two Aces from the minor arcana; the Ace of Cups overhung the Ace of Wands, indicating new beginnings in both career and emotions. *Hmmm, how interesting! Work is changing, security and stability increasing. Well that's a massive change, huge! I wonder how that's going to unfold,* she puzzled. She didn't have to wait for very long to have the answer! As if on cue from her very thoughts, suddenly the room filled with light. A warmth washed over Cassie with such intensity that she felt quite dizzy. She blinked several times, allowing her green eyes to adjust to the brightness and, as they did, she watched with horror as the spirit of Ma rose up from the chair, right in front of her; floating out of her body and serenely walking into that very light; a light in which a man stood, his arms outstretched, a smile of pure love on his face. *Pa?* Cassie wondered, but she knew it could only be Pa that Ma would walk to like that! And not walk, she was half skipping, half running to this man with a look of sheer joy on her radiant and beautiful face. The years had fallen away from Ma and her body seemed renewed. Cassie had never met Pa, so she looked at the family photographs on the dresser to check, and yes, it was definitely him. He'd been gone some ten years now, but it was clear that he'd come back to fetch Ma and take her home; home to 'upstairs.' Cassie felt the love, the light, and the rightness of it all - Ma had gone out the way she wanted to; peacefully - in her sleep, surrounded by her beloved Tarot cards, her crystals, her candles and love, having helped yet another person to find their way.

Her body sat motionless in the chair, her head drooped onto her chin; she was still, lifeless, but incredibly peaceful. Cassie let a tear slide down her face. She'd miss her, she'd miss her so much, but it was clearly Ma's time, and Cassie just couldn't feel sad for Ma as she watched her walk away into the light, holding tightly onto Pa's hand. Ma turned silently in the light, smiled at Cassie and waved goodbye, blowing her a kiss, then she was gone. "Goodbye, Ma, and thank you. Be happy, Ma," Cassie called, curling up in a tight, black ball of sadness on Ma's lap. She gently stroked her still and silent face with her paw. "Bye, bye, Ma, I love you," she meowed, as she heard a distant voice call back from the light,

"I love you too, Cassandra Alexandra the Third. You're the best cat, the most beautiful cat, the most magical black cat I've ever had, and I will miss you too!"

Cassie sat on Ma's lap until they came. She didn't know how long it was, but she thought it was the next day that Ma's son came and called the doctor, and the funeral parlour. He cried a lot, she noticed, but he smiled a lot too.

"You're with Pa now, and that's where you need to be,"

he whispered, stroking Ma's face gently. Cassie looked up at him from Ma's lap. She hadn't moved in what seemed like days and she was stiff and sore. She meowed quietly. The man looked down at the cat with understanding in his eyes and compassion in his heart. "It was her time, Cassie, her time. Come on now, come away," he said, lifting her gently away from Ma's lap.

Cassie allowed him to move her, watching as the men took Ma away. He was right, it was time. It was time for her to move on too. She'd been here for ten years and they'd been good years, but it was time now for new starts, new beginnings. The cards had said endings, and they'd said new beginnings; new career, new emotions. The ending was now clear - Ma was gone, new beginnings meant new starts. Cassie pondered the meaning of the cards, and then she understood. It was time for her to find a new Ma; a Ma to whom she could teach the Tarot cards - a Ma who would keep their joint legacy alive. It was time for Cassie to share what she knew from her old Ma and adopt herself a new Ma, but first she had to find her!

Cassie ran quickly and quietly to the cat flap and jumped through it, running full speed away from the cottage as fast as her legs would carry her. She looked behind her to make sure that she wasn't followed; she didn't want the man to catch her and take her back with him. He was nice, but he wasn't Ma, and he definitely wouldn't understand, she just knew that he wouldn't! She ran and ran, for mile after mile; for hour upon hour, and eventually, came to a stop on the outskirts of a village, a village that her instincts told her would be right for her.

Cassie sat under a tree and rested while she pondered

the problem that was finding 'the new Ma' and searched for a solution. "Time for manifestation," she declared determinedly, and began to draw up the job description for the very special person whom she would deem to adopt, although a probation period would be wise, she felt. Cassie visualised the paper, the pen, and then began the words. "She will, of course, have to be very sensitive and intuitive, with an open loving heart. She'd have to believe in energy, and the magical power of the universe to guide, create, heal and inspire. And she would absolutely *have* to know that animals can talk, and if at all possible, be able to *speak* C.A.T. - that's 'Cassandra Alexandra the Third,' or CAT for short, of course! Now then, what else do we need?" Cassie concentrated hard as she manifested her wish list of other essential criteria. "1 - No other pets, that's non-negotiable, cats don't share!" she declared emphatically. "2 - No small children! That's non-negotiable too; I cannot possibly have young sproglets pulling on my whiskers and tail, no Sir! 3 - A single older lady I feel would be best for all concerned, to ensure that she can have my undivided attention, which she will, of course, need in order to complete her training, and I, of course, will have hers. Again, as in 1 above, cats do not share! Definitely needs to live alone!" Cassie gazed at the sky for any further inspiration, but none came. "Oh well, that's it then? No more to add? We have our wish list?" Again, she looked up at the sky, and this time, she seemed satisfied that an answer was given of confirmation as a big black raven flew overhead with a loud squawk. "Perfect!" she declared to the sky, adding, "which way?"

The raven flew around in circles and then disappeared,

not really hugely helpful, so Cassie stayed put, waiting to be shown the way. It was simply a matter of patience, a sign would come. She curled up in the morning sunshine and went into a deep sleep, recharging her energy in readiness to continue her mission, after a brief respite of sun and snooze, and the wait for the obligatory sign.

Standing precisely two feet away from Cassie, and totally invisible to her, stood Clarabelle, grinning happily from halo to feather. "Older lady, no young children, no dog, no husband? Sadly not, but I can assure you that your other criteria will be met and met very well, my dear, C.A.T." Clarabelle giggled happily, just picturing Fred's face when Cassie turned up. "Oh my, there will be some fireworks in the Brown house tonight! Smashing!" she beamed. "Just perfectly smashing! It's been far too quiet, for far too long! Time to shake it up a bit, aye team?"

Nat, Sephi and Elijah grinned the grin of the naughty and the wicked, with great difficulty, of course, being the perfectly 'almost perfect' and 'nearly there / doing our best' Guardian Angels that were allocated to the various members of the chaotic Brown household - angels that were determined to create a stir in more ways than one!

"Are you really sure about this, my dear sister?" enquired a doubtful Clarence from the side lines. "You really think this is a good idea?" he worried.

"Clarence, now what have we agreed? You know how much I appreciate all your help and mentoring over the years, but it's time for you to trust me a little now, and let me do things my way!" She beamed happily at the team of angels; a team standing ready, willing and able! "Smashing! Just perfectly smashing!"

Chapter 1

"No, Angelica, you cannot wear your fairy costume to school! Now take it off, put your uniform on and do as you're told!" Sarah stood, hands on hips, doing her best to manage her daughter's tantrum without causing any further chaos in an already chaotic household.

David stood quietly watching the on-going argument from the door and scratched his head in confusion. *What's her problem?* David didn't get it at all. He couldn't wait to start 'big school' today. He'd been trying on his new school uniform when he got home from nursery every day for weeks now, despite Mum telling him daily to leave it alone. He stood admiring his reflection in the mirror that hung opposite the door in Angelica's bedroom. He turned to the left and then the right, admiring the view from both sides, before admiring the front view, again! He smiled happily at the new red jumper, which sported the school badge lovingly sewn on by Mum, albeit rather wonkily. He grinned at the smart black trousers and shiny black shoes, all worn proudly by the five year old boy, who wondered precisely how long he was expected to keep them looking that smart and shiny! "Mum, just tell her! We're gonna be late!" he groaned in frustration. "Anj, just DO it! Please?" he begged. *God, I hate my sister sometimes! HATE her! Girls! Pah!*

Angelica Brown glared first at her mother, then at her twin brother in defiance. "But, Mum, WHY can't I wear my fairy outfit to school? It's so pretty!"

"Because you can't and that's an end to it! Put your uniform on right now or there will be trouble, madam, got it?" Sarah glared her most stern glare at her defiant five year old daughter, crooked her head to one side and plonked her hands on her hips determinedly. "GOT IT?" she said again. The warning stance and tone said 'do not mess with me lady!'

Angelica got it. With a deep sigh, to evidence clearly to all concerned, that it actually *was* the end of the whole, entire world that she hadn't got her own way, she pulled off the fairy costume and reluctantly picked up the red school jumper, pulling it over her head with annoyance. "Fine! I'm doing it! See? I'm doing it!" she screeched, frustrated at the loss of the battle; although to be fair, she had thought it was a tad unlikely that she'd get away with the fairy costume on the first day of infant school, but you never know! Always worth trying! She pulled on her little black pleated skirt, yanking the red jumper down over the skirt's waistband firmly. Sitting down heavily on her bed still glaring at her mother, she pulled on the white socks that came right up to her knees and stepped into her new smart black shoes. She looked at herself in the mirror and glared. "There! Ready, see! Didn't take long did it! Don't know what the fuss is all about!" Taking another quick look at her appearance, she had to admit, the whole outfit together was surprisingly rather fetching, although she wasn't sure if red really was her colour!

Glaring at her mother with as much pure hatred as she could muster, she stomped out of her bedroom and flounced down the stairs dramatically, flicking her hair as she flounced. It didn't have quite the desired result that she'd hoped for, on account of her long blond hair being pulled back and platted by her mother before breakfast, thereby disabling her from the essential 'hair flick' that was necessary when showing extreme annoyance, but she did her best at a good sulk. She picked up her new satchel from the hall peg and glared up the stairs to her mother and brother disparagingly. "Well?" she demanded, "Are we going then or what?"

Sarah looked at her daughter and smiled sweetly, determined not to allow Angelica to receive the attention that she was clearly demanding from her appalling behaviour, and upset everyone on the twins' first day at the village infant school. "Yes, dear, let's go. You ready, David?"

"I was born ready, Mum!" came the reply, as the whirling dervish that is normal for the average five year old boy, flew down the stairs beside her, making as much thunderous noise as possible on his bumpy way down; doing a wonderful impression of a herd of elephants banging down the stairs rather than one small child.

"Don't run, David!" she scolded, but smiled at his enthusiasm. She knew what this was *really* about. Angelica was nervous. She'd never admit it, of course, being the diva that she was; but there was no doubt about it, her darling daughter, who had the confidence of a Hollywood starlet on an average day, was scared to death!

"Yeah, crapping it baby!" shouted Fred from the front door with a grin. His lead hung from his mouth in preparation for the short walk to the school. David and Angelica's 'his and hers' lunch boxes, side by side at his furry golden feet, were ready to go. "Anytime today, lady! Hurry up!" he moaned, "Have I got to do everything around here?"

Sarah grinned at Fred with relief and gratitude. *He really is a God-send, bless him, and he's right about madam; she is 'crapping it'!*

"Totally crapping it, lady, as well you know!" he grinned, "unlike this one! Hang on - where's he gone?" Fred stared at the open door and the broken speed record that the young master of the house had left in his wake as he'd legged it halfway down the lane in his excitement to start his first day at school. "Wait!" he shouted, dropping his lead in panic, "wait for me, David!"

Sarah grabbed the lunch boxes, keys and the dropped dog lead and followed Fred through the door, whilst somehow managing to push Angelica through it without too much protest.

Fred was very much aware of Angelica's nerves; he'd listened to her cry half the night. No one else knew, of course. She'd be mortified if she found out that even Fred knew, and being the loyal dog that he was, he would, of course, keep her secret to the grave. Not much got past Fred's ears; there were no secrets in the Brown house, not from Fred anyway. He knew everything, absolutely totally bloody everything, and therefore was The Boss, Head of House, being the genius that he was, of course. He wouldn't tell Mum or Dad that mind, but HE knew, oh yes indeedy!

Fred's ears lolloped as he ran down the lane; finally catching up with David, he barked instructions as clearly as he could. "Wait!" he woofed, in his sternest bark. "Wait right there, young man! Where do you think you're going!" he growled crossly.

David stopped instantly, knowing not to argue with Fred. "Sorry, Freddie. I'm just excited! Can't wait, mate, just can't wait!"

"Yes well, waiting is what you are going to have to do, young man, if we are to get you there in one piece. What have I told you about that road? Well? Huh?"

"Sorry, Freddie. I know; the road nearly killed you and Dad and we gotta be real careful… It's 'dainjruss'!" David solemnly recited, having heard this from Fred on a regular basis for the last four and a half years.

"Indeed." Fred nodded, happy with the response. "Very dangerous!"

"Well actually it isn't!" corrected Clarabelle, two steps behind them; appearing suddenly perched on Sarah's shoulder. "It's only 'dainjiruss,' David, if it is *run* across instead of *walked* across, and run across *without* looking; as Fred here well knows!"

"Yeah, yeah, that's right; start the day with having a go, Mrs.! Never mind a 'good morning' or a 'hello,' just jump right in to the 'dig a dog day'!"

Clarabelle smiled at the dog lovingly, a twinkle in her blue eyes. *Really, Fred could be sooo dramatic sometimes!*

"Just trying to keep 'em safe, is all!" Fred sulked. Snatching his lead out of Sarah's hand, he sat down heavily and dramatically on the gravelled lane waiting for her to clip it to his collar. "Come on, come on!" he moaned, "haven't got all day! They're gonna be late!"

Seraphina and Elijah grinned, watching the argument. *Really, would those two ever stop arguing? It had been like this for months now, Fred arguing with Clarabelle!* There was clearly a battle going on for 'top dog/boss,' and, of course, it was completely fruitless! Clarabelle was, and always would be, in charge of this house, no matter how much Fred tried to usurp her! He'd accepted his position in the 'Brown Pack' of third place for nearly five years, but this last year he'd started thinking he was above everyone, even Clarabelle! Really it was so silly! So, the pecking order, or pack order, was Sarah and Simon Brown; happily married, nay 'blissfully' happily married, for six years, who were, of course, numbers one and two in the pecking order; followed by Fred, the family dog. Then there was Angelica and David Brown; twins, and daughter and son of said Sarah and Simon. That was the human pack, of course, with Fred coming in the middle, a very respectable third place for a dog; who was more like the nanny to the twins than the family dog, as well as being best friend to Simon, and confidant and mentor to Sarah. He could speak three languages; dog, human and angel and was a genius! He should be more than happy with third place! Dogs usually came last in human households! Only he wasn't! He wasn't happy, and he wasn't third! Because above Sarah and Simon was, of course,

Clarabelle, Sarah's GA (Guardian Angel); followed closely by Nathaniel, Simon's GA. Then there was Elijah and Sephi, the twins' GA's (equal status), and THEN the humans! So Fred really was seventh; and this last year, at the age of six years old - which in dog terms is positively middle-aged - Fred had decided that he really should have more power than seventh place, being the genius that he was. Sephi shook her head in amusement. Oh, the battles! Fred really had caused so much trouble this last year! Rather than try to work his way up the pecking order, as in dog fashion, he had just decided, in his wisdom, to take on the Boss, Clarabelle, and kick her off her spot! Silly boy! As if!

Sephi grinned at Elijah, a knowing grin, a grin that said 'here we go again!'

"I know, mate, I know!" Elijah smiled. "He's not going to know what's hit him!" he whispered.

"What? What was that? What are you two whispering about?" demanded a suspicious Fred. He *knew* he was winning the war with Aunty Clarabelle. It was only a matter of time before she gave up the throne as 'head of house' and gave the crown over to Fred, he just KNEW it! "Come on then!" he barked sharply, ordering his motley crew along. "Let's go before this lot are late for their first day!"

Fred pondered his crown as he lolloped down the lane towards the school, wondering how he could wear it. There were practicalities to work out, but he'd figure it out. Aunty Clarabelle's crown was a beautiful golden halo, and being an angel of some quite high standing, she wore it well; he'd give her that much. That being said, as a Golden Retriever with a magnificent thick golden coat himself, Fred had decided that the golden halo would go with his coat rather nicely and look rather fetching! He'd have to work something out; attach it to his collar or something. How? Fred pondered some more... He may have to have a word with his mate Frank again. Yes! Frank was a Saint and mixed with the angel crew upstairs - Saint Francis of Assisi, always a help to animals, and in particular Fred - and they were great mates! He may be able to get him some angel yarn or angel string or something similar; something to attach his soon-to-be new halo to his collar. Yes, Frank would know! He'd help him sort it! Fred was determined to find a way that much was certain. It was just a matter of time before she gave it up, he was sure!

Clarabelle smiled quietly to herself, knowing perfectly well that Fred was daydreaming of having his own halo as he led them all down the lane. She really couldn't work out where this obsession had come from! A dog having a halo? Ridiculous! "Must have a word upstairs and find out what's going on!" she decided, "Someone upstairs must know where all this has come from!" Clarence didn't know either, and Clarence knew everything! Her angelic brother had mentored her for eons and it had been his suggestion to take this tack with Fred. "Yes, time to put our little Freddie back in his place!" Clarabelle grinned to herself at her little plan, nearly in place now. "Usurp my position, Freddie?" she beamed happily. "First? I don't *think* so! You'll soon be wishing for that seventh place that you have, my dear; yes indeed! Eighth place I think, oh yes indeed, eighth place is just perfect! And if you don't behave yourself soon Frederick, I may even go for tenth place for you; bring you in *after* the twins even! I shall win this war, and you WILL know your place, and peace WILL return to the Brown household! Now, Cassandra Alexandra, are you ready? Smashing!"

Chapter 2

From her spot under the bushes, Cassie watched the group in the lane pass by her with interest. *That dog was a menace, an absolute menace! Fancy arguing with an angel, and a Guardian Angel at that!* Cassie was bewildered. Still exhausted from her journey, she shook her head in disgust and went back to sleep.

***

Sarah stood nervously with the other mums waiting for the bell to ring in the school playground. She looked around her at the twenty nervous new faces - and that was just the mums!

Children stood nearby, sizing up each other; comparing shoes, satchels, lunch boxes, as well as the obviously varied levels of terror. David would be fine, she was sure, but Angie? She really could be such a diva, especially when she felt nervous or threatened, which she most definitely did today, that much was clear. She looked over at Fred, tied to the railings just outside the school gates, with a nervous smile.

"They'll be fine, Mum, nothing to worry about!" he barked, with as much reassurance as he could manage.

"Sarah, she will be fine, my dear, you know she will!" whispered Clarabelle in her left ear, perched on her shoulder watching the proceedings. "Really, child, do you think Sephi is going to let Angelica get into grief?" She patted Sarah's shoulder reassuringly, injecting calm and warmth simultaneously into her nervous ward. Smiling over to Seraphina, perched on Angelica's shoulder, and Elijah, perched on David's, she had no doubts whatsoever. The children's angels had their instructions - get their wards through their first day without drama, help them settle and make friends, keep all calm and generally be the God-send they were meant to be. "It's all going to be just smashing, Sarah, just smashing!" she chirped. But before Sarah had a chance to reply, a loud ringing vibrated across the playground as the school bell sounded.

"Year 1's, this way please!" yelled a young girl who'd suddenly appeared out of nowhere, waving her arms in the air theatrically. "This way, children! Year 1's, this way."

"Blimey, is that the teacher?" Sarah asked Clarabelle in shock. "She looks about twelve!"

"Miss Jones is, in fact, twenty-four years old, Sarah, and I promise you that she is absolutely lovely! An excellent teacher, a complete natural! Don't panic!"

Grabbing both children's hands, Sarah walked

nervously over to the waiting Miss Jones. She was suddenly terrified! *Handing her babies over to this stranger? Blimey!*

"Ah, the twins!" the teacher smiled, bending down to child height as Sarah approached; Miss Jones shook their tiny hands. "You must be David; very handsome and grown up you are too, young man," she beamed, smiling right into his eyes. Sarah could feel David positively glowing with the praise from this young woman. "And Angelica; what a beauty you are! My, my, and how very lucky we are to have you in our class! I'm sure we're going to be great friends." Angelica smiled shyly at the pretty lady and decided immediately that she liked her. "And don't you both look smart in your uniforms?" she beamed at the pair, then added quietly, whispering in Angelica's ear, "Although, not quite as smart as in a fairy costume, aye, Angelica?" Angie shook her head solemnly, wondering quite how this lady knew about her current obsession with fairies!

Miss Jones proceeded to move from child to child as they cautiously approached, each of them clutching their parent's hand tightly. She shook every tiny hand in turn, saying something personal and complimentary to each and every one of them. She had learned each child's name, studying their files and photographs for a week before, until she had them all memorised. Her work and diligence had paid off! She had remembered everyone correctly, including, it seemed, their personality types and idiosyncrasies, playing to each perfectly. Finally she stood up straight, calling them into line, and line up they did! Sarah was gobsmacked!

"Blimey do you think we could get her home to train Fred?" she giggled to Clarabelle.

"Indeed!" came the laughing reply. "I told you she was good, didn't I?"

The pair, along with the other mums, stood in awe of this seemingly magical young woman, watching with admiration and not a little disbelief, as she took complete control of twenty, previously nervous five year old infants in a matter of seconds. They watched her gaze down at the incredibly straight line of waiting children with such warmth and charm that Sarah could physically feel the twenty sets of nerves dissolve from the waiting class. "Come along then, children, off we go!" sang the teacher, looking over her shoulder at the bewildered mums behind her. "Three-thirty on the dot mums, not a minute past! Ta-ta for now!" And then she was gone. Like the Pied Piper of Hamlin, without question or hesitation, all twenty children filed after her into the abyss that was Redfields Infant School without a second glance back at their shell-shocked mums.

"Well!" breathed Sarah, not realising she'd been holding her breath.

"Well!" giggled Clarabelle.

"Wow!" all twenty mums said (or thought), simultaneously! And then they dispersed.

***

Fred led Sarah back down the lane quietly as he pondered his new crown.

He and he alone had controlled that situation in the

school yard, he was sure of it! He had sent signals to the teacher to tell her what to do, so it was down to him that it had been such a roaring success.

"You are kidding me, Fred! Really, you do take the biscuit!" Clarabelle scolded, reading his thoughts as usual.

"Intrusive you are, Miss!" he moaned. "Bit of privacy here wouldn't go amiss! Bloody cheek! Humph!"

"What's he moaning about now?" questioned Sarah. She was getting fed up with the arguments between these two, only most of the time she wasn't fully up to speed on what it was that they were arguing about, not being able to read thoughts herself. She had managed to learn to speak dog, which was an achievement in itself for a human, but reading thoughts wasn't in her repertoire, just yet!

"Fred thinks he was the one who created such calm in that playground just now, getting all the children to respond to Miss Jones. Ridiculous!" Clarabelle explained. "That dog is way too big for his boots if you ask me, Sarah!"

"Yeah, yeah, babe, don't get your knickers in a twist!" cheeked Fred.

Clarabelle glared at him. "That teacher spent most of last week studying, Fred, STUDYING! She learned their names, their likes, their little personalities! She had all the mums fill in a questionnaire about their children; a questionnaire that she designed, in her own time. She asked them to attach a photo and send it in, weeks ago! She, and she alone, is responsible for the success that just happened, not you!"

"Yeah okay, well maybe she did, but it was me that

helped!" Fred just wouldn't back down, not an inch!

Sarah looked at them both in alarm. *What on earth was going on with these two? They used to be such good friends!*

"Don't you worry about a thing, Sarah dear. It's all in hand, all in hand. ..." Clarabelle trailed off, a huge smile appearing on her face as they turned into the lane and she spotted Cassie under the bush. "Oh look, Sarah! Isn't that a cat there under the bush? Do you think she's alright? I think she's hurt!"

Sarah looked over to the bush as Clarabelle fussed and sure enough, there was a cat under the bush. It didn't move, not a muscle!

Cassie lay still, deathly still. She really couldn't figure it out! She'd been fine just a second ago... She'd stretched, she'd had a wash, she'd rolled over... And now for some strange reason, she couldn't move... not a single muscle... she was paralysed! "Oh my God, I can't move!" she meowed loudly, panic and fear in her cry. "What's wrong with me? Why can't I move?" Her cries increased in volume and panic, creating an avalanche of emotion in the concerned Sarah, who bent over immediately and stroked the distressed Cassie soothingly.

"What's wrong, little girl? What have you done? Here, let me help." Sarah scooped the cat up into her arms and held her gently.

"I can't move, I can't move!" yelled Cassie.

"There, there," soothed Sarah. "I'll take you home and we'll get the vet and help you, I promise."

"Home? Home? Your home? I don't think so! You have a dog and kids and noise and yuck, and you've probably got a man too, for those noisy kids. No, no, this isn't right! I don't want your home, I want a quiet home! Put me back under the bush, immediately!" But although Cassie's mouth was open and she appeared to be talking, and talking complete sense as far as she was concerned, nothing was coming out! Just loud meows! Even her speaking voice was paralyzed! She watched with horror as Sarah proceeded to carry her down the lane and into her home.

Clarabelle giggled. It was only temporary, this little bit of paralysis, and she'd lift it, just as soon as Cassie realised that she was onto a good thing with Sarah.

Fred could not believe his eyes, or his ears! He hadn't moved a muscle either! He was frozen in shock! Suddenly his legs worked and so, unfortunately did his mouth! "You have got to be kidding me! No bloody way, lady! No, no, NO! I refuse, I absolutely bloody refuse, to have this mangy, scrawny CAT in 'MY HOUSE'! A *cat* I ask you! A bloody *cat!*"

"Yes, Fred, a cat! A cat who is unwell, in pain and frightened and you can moan all you like, but this is my house and I am bringing this cat home, end of!" Sarah marched down the lane, cat in arms, leaving Fred to march himself and his lead (which he'd picked up in his mouth), and march he did. In total disgust, he marched himself straight to bed, where he decided that he would stay until this intruder was removed! "A cat, a bloody cat!" he spat, in total abject horror, "A CAT! ARGHHH!"

And Clarabelle grinned, wondering quite how long she would need to leave the paralysis in place. ...

"Yes indeed I did, Frederick, and I can do it to you too if you don't quiet your mouth and attitude!" Clarabelle grinned, delighted with herself and her little miracle.

"But you heal people, not paralyse them! How is that allowed? I'm gonna report you, report you I will, get you sacked!" he argued, still not quite believing the turn of events that had happened today.

"I had it sanctioned upstairs as well you know! Now, stop arguing and go and make friends!" she ordered.

"Will not!"

"Will too!"

"Won't!"

"Will!"

"Will you two shut up!" yelled Sarah, watching the pair from the kitchen door with frustration. "I don't know what's got into you two lately, arguing like this all the time! It's driving me nuts!"

"It's her fault, Mum, it's her! She paralysed the moggie and made you take it home, to MY house!"

"Fred, this is MY house not yours, best you remember that, Mr.! And Cassie is not a moggie; she is a very beautiful black cat, with a gentle loving soul, and she needs looking after. I like her, and the children will adore her, and she's staying, so that's that!"

"But. ..."

"No buts, Fred."

"But. ..."

"Enough, Fred!" And with that, Sarah was gone, again! Back to the bloody cat, Dog-damn-it! And then he could hear her, on the phone to Dad. *Good old Dad, he'll sort it. He won't let that moggie stay in my house! But wait, what was this?* Fred crept closer to the living room door and watched with horror the scene in front of him. There was 'Mangy Moggy,' laying on the sofa... the *bloody sofa! He*, 'Fred the Fantastic,' wasn't allowed on the sofa! Never had been, and here was this upstart, this mangy moggy, laying happy as you like, on his bloody sofa; being petted and stroked by Mum. How could she! Fred let out a howl, like the end of the world was nigh, and collapsed onto the floor in floods of tears. "How could you?" he howled, "How bloody could you?"

"Shush, Fred," was the only response.

Fred howled louder. And louder. Nothing! *Bit louder then?* Fred howled the loudest, most hurt, betrayed, disgusted howl that he could manage.

Sarah simply shut the door in his face.

Fred fainted!

"Yes, Si, I will, darling ... Yes, I'll take her to the vet right now ... Yes, dear, you're right, she probably will have owners. The microchip will tell us who and we can contact them. Yes, my love, I'll go now." And then she was gone, cat and all!

Fred sat by the front door and waited. With any luck the mangy moggie would die on the way to the vet, or at the very least be put down. "Please make it painful, as painful as possible," he prayed.

"Fred! That's not nice!" a shocked Clarabelle declared.

"Death to cats, do you hear me! Death to bloody cats!"

"Tsk!"

And then Clarabelle was gone too, with Mum, off to

'Terry the Terrible,' down at the vets.

***

"No, Mrs. Brown, there doesn't appear to be a microchip on this cat I'm afraid to say." Terry, the vet, shook his head sadly. *What is wrong with people that they don't microchip their pets?* He really didn't understand it. "All you can do is put an advert in the local shops, on line, you know, that sort of thing. Are you okay to keep her for now?"

"Yes, yes, of course, that's fine. I'm happy to help. She is a beautiful cat, don't you think?" Sarah smiled at Cassie, who purred back in response. Somewhere between the house and the vets, she had begun to be able to move again, but only a little. As the paralysis began to lift, she had felt Sarah's warmth, her care and she knew that she liked her very much. She reminded her of Ma in many ways. Her home, for one, was very similar. It had a big open fire, which Cassie loved. The sofa was very comfortable, though not quite as much as Ma's, it would do, for now. She would give it a few days and see. She couldn't possibly make a decision yet, she still had to meet the man of the house, and Cassie really didn't like men much; didn't rate them at all in fact. And as for the children, well, she would hold judgment on that, for now. It very much depended on whether she could train them not to pull her tail or her ears, to be able to hold her properly and to behave appropriately with her. That just left the dog. Cassie sighed. The dog wasn't an issue really. She could soon sort him out! He had one mouth with a set of average teeth. Pathetic as a weapon really! Just the one end to defend the whole self? Ridiculous! She herself, of course, had the mouth and teeth, similar to the dog, but her teeth were far sharper than his, of course, and then there were the four (yes four!), lots of feet; each with razor sharp claws, times five, so that was twenty claws, plus the teeth - twenty-one weapons, as opposed to his one. It was no contest! She felt sorry for him really, bless! No defence at all in comparison to the master race - cats! And then there was the attitude - so subservient! Dogs have masters - pathetic! Cats have servants... everyone knows that! Yes, maybe she would stay, maybe she would.

All was quiet in the Brown house when Cassie returned. Fred was sulking in the back garden, talking to his favourite tree, moaning the unfairness of life as he chewed old faithful - his eternal bone. Cassie watched him from the window and pitied him. So stupid these dogs! Everyone knows trees can't talk!

"Well actually, my dear, that is where you are quite wrong!"

"What! Who said that? Who's there?" Cassie stood up, arching her back, hairs standing on end, ears back, ready to fight.

Clarabelle glowed her glow, lighting up the room and Cassie stood in wonder. Wow! Where did you come from? she wondered silently.

"Hello, Cassandra Alexandra. I am Clarabelle. Welcome to the Brown family, and to our little angel family," Clarabelle beamed. "I did not want to show myself to you earlier for fear of frightening you, little one. I am glad to see that you are feeling better."

Clarabelle stood in front of her, at about six inches tall, she was dressed in a long, white gown and had long, white, sweeping feathers draping down to the floor behind her. There was a light of gold above her, and Cassie could see that it was a halo! The angel's hair was golden, too, curling just past her neck and onto her shoulders in soft waves; her eyes, the clearest and brightest blue that Cassie had ever seen. She looked about thirty, but Cassie reckoned that she was probably ageless. She was incredibly beautiful! Cassie was delighted! How very wonderful, an angel living here. Maybe she would stay!

"Several angels actually, my dear!" Clarabelle began to fill Cassie in on the Brown household members and their respective angels. She reassured Cassie that despite her aversion to the male version of the human species, Simon was actually very nice! And that, yes, of course, the children would be kind to her. Cassie was delighted to discover on the briefing that both children, and indeed even the mother Sarah, could speak dog, and if they could speak that stupid language, she just knew there'd be no issues with them learning to speak C.A.T.! She was even more shocked to discover that not only could Sarah and both the children talk dog, but they could also see and talk to their angels! Well, fancy that! She was definitely staying now! She had things to teach, to share, to inspire, and it seemed that Sarah may well be the recipient of that teaching.

Cassie looked around her for the first time properly. She noticed the incense burning in its holder, the crystals and candles dotted around the room, the light and balance that created such warmth and harmony, and her decision to stay was solidified.

"I have informed Sarah that you do not have an owner and that you will be staying. She is quite in agreement with this, I am happy to say. You see, I have been teaching Sarah for many years now, Cassandra, and she does follow my advice, for the most part, but I do feel that there is room for new inspiration," Clarabelle explained. "There has been little opportunity for development over the past few years with the twins at home, but now, oh yes indeed, now it is time for her to move forward into her role, now that the children have started school. I shall let you settle in for a little while and then we shall begin, yes?"

"Is she my new Ma then, Clarabelle? May I call you Clarabelle?" Cassie shyly asked. She was rather overwhelmed with this turn of events, having never spoken with an angel before. Oh yes, she'd been around the block, more than once in fact, being a black cat and incredibly knowing, with several lifetimes behind her, but this ... this was new!

"Yes, my dear, she is your new Ma. But first we must sort out Fred. He will not be happy with this arrangement; you do know that don't you, dear?"

Cassie smiled. Sort out a dog? Oh yes, bring it on!

Chapter 3

"Oh, Mum, it was brill!" David bounded down the lane, swinging his satchel happily. "Ben says, an' Greg says, oh, an' Will says, that Miss Jones is '*The* Best Teacher' in the whole, wide, world!" Sarah smiled at her son, relieved that he'd enjoyed his first day, and that he'd clearly made lots of new friends. She noticed the new shoes, scuffed and marked already; his new trousers, mud splattered - she knew they'd be going through several pairs of each over the coming school year. Boys! Angelica, on the other hand, looked pristine, as if she'd just stepped off a catwalk!

"And how was your day, Anj?" she asked gently, nervously awaiting the response.

"Well, Mum, it was really quite good, surprisingly enough, especially considering all the boys in the class! So many!" Angelica sighed. *I hate boys, totally hate them! So noisy, so dirty, so chaotic! What is wrong with them? Why do they have to be so loud and boisterous?* "But I made lots of new friends with the girls. There's umm, thingy, and umm, wass-her-name, umm, dunno! And umm, her with the red hair, and her with the nice shoes - oh yes, Megan with the shoes, she was nice. Umm, can't remember the other names - but they was nice, Mum!"

"They *were* nice, Angelica."

"Yes, Mum, that's what I said, they *was* nice!"

"*Were!*" Sarah shook her head in despair. Continually correcting grammar from her children was the only way to teach them, but God, she felt like such a nag! She smiled to herself about Angelica's comment about Megan. So typical of her clothes-obsessed daughter to only remember one name of all the friends she had met and made, and only because this Megan had nice shoes!

"Black shiny ones they was, Mum, real shiny!" she fawned, dreaming of Megan's shoes. "Patent they're called, I fink! Can I have some? Please, please, Mum, can I have some?"

"*Were* nice and, no, Angelica, you can't have some, and yes they are called 'patent,' but patent, whilst they look very nice when they're brand new out of the box, they do scuff very easily, hun, and they don't stay looking nice for very long. They're 'for best' really, for parties and things, Anj. For school and running around you're much better off with your black leather ones that I bought you, darling. They'll look smart for ages! You know how you hate to look scruffy!"

Angelica pondered this new information, agreeing with her mother that maybe her shoes were actually *the* best ones in the whole, entire class! *Yes, stick with what I have. Megan will be looking scruffy before you know it and I shall be the prettiest and best dressed of them all!*

"How was your day, Mum?" David asked politely,

changing the subject away from Angelica and her shoes. *My sister is such a prima donna!*

Sarah smiled at her son. "Well, David, it was rather interesting as a matter of fact. We have a new guest. It's a surprise. You'll see in a minute."

"Where's Freddie, Mum?" Angelica asked, suddenly noticing the lack of the family dog's presence on the short walk home from school.

"Ah, well Fred is sulking, my dear. He's refusing to come out of his bed. He'll get over it I'm sure."

***

Fred was indeed sulking. Apparently the 'Mangy Moggie' was staying! He just couldn't get over it! As soon as he'd found out, without a word, he'd collected all his toys from all over the house: bones, chews, his squeaky rabbit, his rubber balls, his lead and his bowl, and he'd taken to his bed - and that was precisely where he was going to stay until this upstart was removed! He had sent the entire family to Coventry and was determined that he wasn't going to speak to anyone, or anything, until she'd gone - that damned CAT! He was also on hunger strike, hence the removal of his bowl - although to be fair, he wasn't sure how long he'd last on that one! "I'd rather die that live with a mangy moggie!" he announced dramatically, forgetting that he was on silence mode. "Die, do you hear me!"

Of the two children, it was Angelica who took to Cassie the strongest. Upon entering the living room where Cassie lay sprawled on the sofa, she ran immediately to the black cat, sitting down gently beside her. "You're so pretty!" she crooned. "May I?" she asked, looking at the cat and waiting for a response. Cassie looked at her warily, then seemed to nod her ascent, allowing Angelica to slowly and very gently stroke her.

Sarah was gobsmacked! Unlike David, her daughter was not renowned for either her consideration or for her manners, but there was just something about Cassie that commanded respect, and Angelica seemed to know it. She stroked Cassie gently, almost purring along with her, so delighted was she with the new pet. Cassie responded by climbing onto Angelica's lap and rubbing herself against her, bonding them quickly and firmly. Sarah watched them thoughtfully. Cassie was almost regal; feminine, dainty, refined - not unlike Angelica. The black fur of the cat contrasted vastly against the pale skin of the small child as they cuddled. Cassie began to chew Angelica's long blond hair, still tied in its plait; her green eyes sparkling as they connected, whilst Angelica's turquoise blue eyes twinkled at the play. *Yes, that cat is going to be good for her*, Sarah decided, *soften her a little*. The two were an instant success!

David, on the other hand, watched this bonding briefly, stroked the cat half-heartedly for a millisecond, then went to find Fred, worrying about him. The small boy plonked himself on the floor in front of the dog's bed, and cocked his head. "You alright, Freddie?" he asked kindly. Fred let out a tear, milking this attention as much as possible. David immediately reached forward, wrapping his little arms around the disgruntled Fred, cuddling him as if his life depended on it.

Boys together! thought Sarah as she watched.

Cassie was watching too. She liked the little boy immediately; he had a sweetness about him, and looked very similar to the little girl stroking her at that moment. *Same colouring, same size, not identical but definitely a strong bond there between these two, yes definitely a strong bond.* Their eyes were identical, but that was all. David was strong, she could feel it; confident, relaxed. Angelica on the other hand, was not. She could feel the little girl's tension and was immediately aware of her need to be the centre of attention. Her bossiness was palpable; *this need to control, and gosh, such a huge lack of compromise in this one! Wonder where that came from?* she wondered. *David didn't seem to have that at all.* She watched him some more with interest. He had an instinct, an intuition, an awareness that Angelica did not. She watched him soothe the dog and was impressed.

"Don't worry, Freddie; you will always be my best boy, promise!" declared David emphatically. "You and me, buddy, best pals! Never mind them two, aye?"

"She's allowed on the sofa, David! The damned sofa I tell you! It's a disgrace!" Fred cried. "And she's staying!" he howled.

"I know, Fred, I know," David soothed. "Let's go upstairs and play, mate; leave them to it, aye? ... I've got doggie-chocs..." he added, persuasively... "Lots!"

Forgetting all about his determined vow not to leave his bed, *and* that he was meant to be on hunger strike, at the word doggie-chocs, play and bedroom, Fred bounded out of his bed and followed David up the stairs two at a time. *I'll deal with the mangy moggie later! Oh yes, indeed I will! And as for Queen Clarabelle, it's her fault the mangy moggie is there in the first place. Once I've got that crown off her, I'll get rid of that damned cat for good!*

Cassie watched the two go upstairs. *I'll explore up there later*, she decided. Curling up with Angelica, she felt for her energy. *Yes there is definitely something amiss here,* she decided. She has the same instincts as her brother, the same awareness, but hers is blocked. *Too worried about attention, yes that's it! Oh my, I have some work to do here to sort this lot out, and that's before I even begin to train the Mrs.!*

***

"So it's all going beautifully, Clarence, just beautifully!" declared Clarabelle excitedly. "She's settled in so well, so well!"

They were sitting on their usual Cloud 322 chatting, high above in the stratosphere above Redfields, planning and plotting as per usual. They looked down at the sleepy small town far below, delighted with themselves. Sarah and Simon's house was a hive of activity as the children set off for their second week at school, chattering ten to the dozen as they walked/ran down the lane with their lunch boxes, Sarah running behind with Fred. Clarabelle smiled at Fred's presence on the walk to the school. It had only taken two days for Fred to re-join the school run after his tantrum. Once he'd realised that Cassie wasn't allowed to go, and that he was, he'd felt a little appeased and gradually, over the week, the sulks had reduced - a little! So far, the two pets had not spoken nor had they had any direct contact, staying firmly out of each other's way; but sooner or later, they would have to meet, and Clarabelle knew that when they did, sparks would fly.

"How bad do you think it's going to get, Clar?" Clarence asked gently, "Once they do the 'face-off'?"

"Oh, they'll rip each other apart for about a month, I would guess," she replied without any concern. "Cassie, of course, will win, and Fred will finally accept defeat; although knowing our Freddie, it will be later rather than sooner, bless him!"

"Healing at the ready then?" Clarence grinned.

"Indeed!" smiled Clarabelle.

"So when are you going to introduce Sarah to the cards then, my dear? After the fireworks are over between those two, I assume?"

"Oh yes, Clar, definitely after! There'll be far too much disruption until the war has been won, to do any learning of cards."

Brother and sister sat pondering the levels of fur-flying that would be occurring over the coming weeks - the scratches, bites and fights - and smiled. They knew it would settle and that eventually, the pair would make friends. Cassie was an important part of Sarah's journey, and progression, as was Fred. They'd just have to smooth it out a bit for them to help them along, *but maybe not just yet,* thought Clarabelle with a wry smile. *Fred needs to calm down a bit and get back in his place - eighth place!* she giggled. "Clarence, where does this obsession of Fred's come from? You know, the thing he has about a crown? Any clue?" she asked, not for the first time.

"Nope, no idea, my dear!" Clarence was bemused. He'd been watching Fred for a while now, particularly when he was sleeping. The angel had been entering Fred's dreams quite regularly and knew that Fred was having many, repeated dreams about having a crown of golden feathers, not dissimilar to their own halos in fact, but he had no clue why! *Most unusual behaviour for a dog!* It had simply started, a few months ago, right out of the blue one sunny afternoon, whilst Fred was asleep under the apple tree in the garden. He'd been twitching away in his sleep, paws up by his ears, pulling his imaginary crown onto his head then grinning inanely. *Most peculiar!* "I'll have a word again upstairs, see what I can find out," he replied. "Try to get to the bottom of this madness!"

Just then Frank flew past, on his way to 'downstairs' to collect another soul. His black shadow darkened the cloud they were sitting on as he passed, not noticing the pair as he focused on his mission.

Hospital, home, nursing home or accident? Clarabelle wondered, knowing she wouldn't have long to find out. Sure enough, a few seconds later, Frank was returning; retrieved soul wrapped up in his black arms, carried safely back to 'upstairs' from the motorbike accident that had just happened in the nearby town of Redville, eight miles away. The Grim Reaper had done his job; collected the departed soul from the mortal plane that is humanity, and returned him to the light. The pair watched with a smile as a host of angels hurriedly flew down to the scene of the accident, shining their light and healing energy across the area; helping those left behind to deal with the trauma of the smash. Blue healing light, invisible to those on the ground, but very clear to both Clarabelle and Clarence from above, shone around the ambulance crew, the other driver and the nearby gathered crowd, then it dispersed into the road itself to neutralise the dark energy of the fatal accident.

"He's slowed down a lot these last few years, don't you think, Clarence? Frank, I mean. Hasn't had a speeding ticket for years!" Clarabelle chirped. "I think Fred going missing for so long has made him think. Or was it all the tickets he used to get? Do you think he finally got the message?"

"No doubt about it, it's because of Fred," Clarence replied. "Misses him terribly Frank does! Those two worked together as a team for eons, and Frank still refuses to work with anyone else. Misses his partner he does, aye, and that's a fact!"

"I wonder where he went, don't you, Clarence? One day Fred was here, the next day he was gone! I mean, I know he said the Boss had a mission for him, but no one thought he'd be gone for this long! It's been more than six years! Very strange indeed - must be a very important mission to be gone for so long!"

"He'll turn up when the Boss has finished with him, Clar, and then we'll find out." Clarence smiled. He was perplexed though. "Do you know what's weird though, Clar? Even the Archangels don't know where Grim-Reaper-Fred is! I know, I've asked! No one upstairs has a clue, so it must be a secret mission from the highest level, maybe even as high as Metatron level. This mission must be an important one, too, to leave the Grim Reaper

41

department short-handed! Mind you, I heard on the grapevine that they'd replaced him, so maybe he isn't coming back at all!"

Just then Clarabelle noticed Simon coming home. *Hello, what's going on here? He's meant to be at work!* "Must go, Clar, something's afoot! Tata for now." And Clarabelle flew back down to 'downstairs' in a rush to check on things in the Brown household. Fred the Grim Reaper and his mysterious disappearance from The Angelic Realms forgotten, for now!

***

Nathaniel was perched on top of Simon's head as Clarabelle rushed into the Brown's living room wearing her 'concerned hat.' His hair, as usual, was doing 'its thing'; sticking up to its full six inches of orange 'Gonkness'!

"What's up, Nat?" she asked quickly. "What's he doing home in the middle of the morning?"

"Oh, nothing to worry about, mate, just a bit of 'man flu.' You know what they're like these chaps, bit of a cold and that's it! Gone off sick, just like that!"

"Why's your hair sticking up then? It only does that when you panic!" she asked worriedly.

"Oh, you know men and colds! He's going to be a nightmare till he shifts it and I just can't take the stress!" he screeched, pulling his cap out of his robes and covering the offending hair quickly.

Clarabelle examined Simon carefully. *Yes, just a bit of a cold*, she decided. *Nothing more.*

Simon sat in his favourite chair, practically in the foetal position. His handsome face was pinched and sad, his eyes watery and his nose, a brighter red than Rudolph's as he rubbed it, sniffing theatrically. "I'm dying!" he lamented, to a devoted and worried Fred, sitting at his feet who was doing his best to sympathise. "Totally dying! Sarrrr, is that hot lemon ready yet?" he shouted through the open door to the kitchen, wiping his nose for the hundredth time that morning.

"You are not dying, Si, you have a bit of a cold, darling, that's all," smiled Sarah, handing him his mug of hot lemon, and another box of tissues, as she came back into the room for the tenth time in as many minutes. *Men! Really, they were such babies at times!*

"Am, too, dying! Even the Boss said I look awful!" her husband defended. "And I didn't ask to go home, hun, he sent me home! So I must be ill - really, really ill!"

"Clarabelle, is he 'really, really ill'?" Sarah asked the smiling Clarabelle.

"Not at all!" she scoffed. "He has a cold; that is all. He'll be fine, I promise."

"There you go, Si, you're fine. Clarabelle says so!" Sarah said happily, confident in her angel's prognosis.

"Oh, I dunno, mate," Nat chipped in, "Man flu is really, really bad!" he argued, defending his man against this onslaught of unsympathetic females. His defence, however, was not about the flu though. He knew Simon only had a cold - his worry was about the energy of continued complaining that Simon would be giving off for the coming days whilst he recovered. "Really bad!" Nat added for emphasis, moving from Simon's head over to the mantelpiece where he could survey the damage properly.

"If it's any consolation, darling, Nat agrees that you are very, very poorly, alright?" Sarah smiled, stroking her husband's hair soothingly, whilst at the same time, rolling her eyes to Clarabelle and winking. "Very poorly indeed, poor baby!"

Simon felt better immediately, knowing his angel was there to stick up for him. He'd never seen him, but he knew he was always there and had his back. Ever since his accident five years ago, Simon had believed in angels whole-heartedly, particularly in view of the fact that he had seen many of them when he was in his coma!

"Thanks, Nat, you the man!" he said in a gravelly voice, directing his comment towards the fireplace, where Nat was perched precariously on the edge of the mantelpiece. Simon coughed dramatically to prove to all just how very ill he was. Clarabelle and Sarah smiled discretely.

"They don't believe you, Dad, they don't believe you!" barked Fred, disgusted at the lack of solidarity from the family for his poorly hero. "I believe you, Dad, I do!" he promised, laying down heavily across Simon's feet in a show of support.

"Ow, Fred, too heavy!" Simon squeaked, before coughing again. "Everything hurts, Buddy; even my feet! Get off, Fred, go lie down there's a good boy, aye?"

Cassie watched from the sofa, wondering just how loud the coughing was going to get. It really was most disturbing! So noisy! "Can't he cough quieter?" she asked the fussing crew, wondering if she should remove herself to Angelica's room for a bit of peace and quiet. *This was why I don't like men! So dramatic and noisy!*

"You are so catty!" Fred defended. "Catty! Yeah, baby, do us all a favour and sod off upstairs!"

"Fred! Language!" Sarah scolded.

Clarabelle sighed. There'd be no learning of cards this week, that much was certain, but this may be an opportunity to bring things to a head between Fred and Cassie. With Simon too ill to shout at them and keep them separated, as he had been doing all week, and with Sarah busy nursing Simon, she could bring things to a head nicely between the pets downstairs, whilst the grown-ups were out of the way and busy 'dying' and 'nursing.' "Why don't you take him up to bed, Sarah?" she suggested. "Tuck him in and let him rest up. I think that will be best, don't you? Stay with him a while maybe? Give him some T.L.C., bless!" She eyed Fred carefully. *Yes, let's bring things to a head. Smashing!*

Chapter 4

As soon as Sarah had left the room with a weak and wobbly Simon leaning on her for support, Clarabelle closed the door firmly and quietly. "Right, you two, let's sort this out then shall we?" she commanded, sealing the room in a bubble of light. "Sound-proofing!" she grinned. "So that you can scream at each other as loud as you like and no one will hear!"

Both Cassie and Fred looked at her warily, and then at each other... It had begun!

***

Sarah gazed at her sleeping husband and grinned.

He really was such a baby when he was ill, bless! She stroked his blond hair softly, not wanting to wake him. He snored loudly, his breathing noisy from his blocked nose. She felt his forehead and was pleased to feel that his temperature had fallen, from the hot lemon cold remedy she had made for him earlier. His long, lean, 6'4" body was curled up on his side, head resting gently against her arm as he slept; his arm flopped over her belly. Wobbly belly now, she thought. Mind you, to be fair, after having the twins at nearly forty I didn't expected it to go back flat and firm, as it may have done if I'd have had the children in my youth. Sarah examined herself, reasonably pleased with her figure. Not bad for middle age, she thought, still a size twelve. Her hair was longer now than it had been when she'd met him, nearly down to her elbows now. It suited her, she decided. There was the odd touch of grey coming through her thick, chestnut locks, but nothing the hairdressers couldn't get rid of with a bit of colour! Its waves curled over her shoulders and she focused on the length, examining it for split ends. Nope, all good!

She moved her gaze to her husband, comparing him now to the man she had met seven and a half years before. God, he's so beautiful! She was still amazed that she had found such a wonderful and loving man, not to mention bloody gorgeous! He really was her dream come true, even now after all these years. Soulmates, best friends and lovers (and passionate lovers at that!), they really were the dream couple! Sarah sighed contentedly, wrapping her arms around him tightly. You may be the biggest baby on God's planet when you're ill, but you'll always be my hero, darling! she thought happily, dozing off with him in the quiet of the house.

***

Whilst it may have been quiet in the house thanks to

Clarabelle's sound-proofing spell, it certainly wasn't quiet in the living room ... it was far from quiet!

Cassie's back arched again to its full extent. Her fur stood on end as she pounced yet again, all twenty claws at their full stretch; the front five on her right paw aimed squarely for Fred's nose. "Strike Twenty-one!" she hissed, digging her razor sharp claws into his tender, moist nose, pushing each and every one in, mercilessly deeper, before going in for her fifteenth bite of his floppy left ear. "Strike twenty-two!" she spat, blowing out the torn-out golden fur from her mouth. She hissed and growled at the panting, bleeding Fred, "Ready to surrender yet, stupid?" she screeched, striking yet another blow, perfectly aimed and attached firmly, now just under Fred's right eye.

"Never!" he screamed, blood pouring down his face. "We will never surrender!" he panted, yelping at the sudden pain that came from his rear end as Cassie bit down hard on the tip of his tail. How the hell did she get round there so quick? he wondered. God, she's fast! She's like bloody lightning! And those claws are lethal; talons they are, bloody talons! Bloody hell! He was losing, and he knew it. There must be a way, there has to be a way! Fred turned quickly, fangs at the ready to pounce down on her scrawny neck and snap it in half, but Dog-damn-it, before he'd got half way round, she was on top of him again, biting down hard on the middle of his back, before spinning herself around like a bloody acrobat again, launching herself full pelt at his bum! She bit hard, digging in all ten front claws either side of the bite to ensure victory. Fred howled like a banshee, collapsing on the floor in a heap.

"Give it up, stupid!" she hissed, spitting out another mouthful of golden fur. "You can't win, you will never win! Cats are supreme, the master race, and the sooner you get it, the easier it'll be on you!" And then she was pouncing again, and again, and again. ...

Clarabelle watched happily from her perch on top of the mantelpiece, preening her feathers and fluffing up her halo as the battle raged. Really, so much blood to clean up, when will he give it up? she wondered.

Fred fought and fought, but no matter how hard he tried, he didn't manage to land one bite. Not one bloody one! He couldn't believe it! He was in shock! Okay, so he'd never actually had a real fight before, only play fights, and they were with his toys, or the children - hardly the same thing as fighting this killing machine of meanness! Fred was confused ... He had no idea what to do!

"I suggest, Frederick ..." smiled Clarabelle from her perch, "that you surrender magnanimously to Cassandra; and the sooner the better!"

"Never!" he screamed, shaking at the very thought of it.

"Are you sure you don't want to review that answer?" hissed Cassie, pointing her bloodied claws at him with relish. "I am actually beginning to feel quite sorry for you now, so if you admit defeat, and say the words, 'Cats are the master race,' I shall let you live!"

"Sod off!"

"Okay then, stupid, don't say I didn't give you a chance for mercy. Die then, as you clearly have a death wish!" she hissed, and launched yet again at the stubborn and battered Fred.

And the battle continued, and continued, and continued.

Clarabelle looked down at the cream carpet with concern, deciding that she'd better work up a magic miracle to get all the blood stains and fur out of the soft wool before Sarah woke up! Actually, Nat is better at the magic if I'm honest, she decided. "Nat? Oh, Nathaniel?" she called out gaily, in a sing-songy voice.

"Wassup? I is here!" shouted Nat, as he flew into the room. He surveyed the chaos with alarm. "What on earth? Clarabelle! Aren't you going to stop this blood bath?" he screeched.

Clarabelle simply smiled, continuing to preen her feathers.

"Oh, mate, we can't be having this!" he yelled, hair on full alert. He couldn't believe that she was just sitting there, watching, and without a care! His cap, as ever, 'boinged' up and off his spiked-up-hair like a rocket. Nat spun around with alarm, grabbing the falling cap before it fell onto the carpet and got trampled in the battle that raged a few feet below them.

"Stay out of it, Nat!" Clarabelle's tone was warning, but Nat simply could not stand back and do nothing. He pulled out his magic wand and pointed it at the warring pair.

"Cease immediately!" he shouted.

Cassie and Fred froze suddenly, stopped in their tracks by the power of the magic being directed towards them.

"Peace!" shouted Nat, "now!"

Both animals dropped to the floor, rolled onto their backs; all eight legs in the air, and surrendered.

"There! That's better!" exclaimed Nat. "Enough, do you hear?"

"Oh, alright, Nat; enough's enough." agreed Clarabelle, although she herself firmly believed that it would have been much better if they'd been allowed to continue until Fred had surrendered.

"Mate, you know that's never gonna happen!" Nat said to a disappointed Clarabelle. "Fred's far too stubborn to surrender - not without losing face! You need to create something where he can lose and still save face!"

Clarabelle nodded thoughtfully. "Yes, I guess you're right. Let's clean him up then, Nat. I think it's going to take two of us to sort him, and then there's the carpet!"

"And the broken furniture, Clar; look at the state of that lamp!" Nat pointed at Sarah's favourite blue china lamp, laying on the floor, broken and trampled from where Fred had knocked it over in the heat of the battle.

"Actually, you focus on the furniture and the carpet, Nat. Leave Fred to me - it's important." Clarabelle instructed, flying down to Fred's side. "Now, Freddie, would you like some healing, my dear?" she asked gently. "Let me help you?"

Fred glared at Clarabelle. Let her help me! I don't bloody think so! This is all her fault anyway! If she hadn't brought the mangy moggie into my house I wouldn't be in this state! "Sod off!" he mouthed, or tried to, but his lip was so swollen he couldn't speak! Bugger it! He was stuffed! He'd have to let her help him. Poo! "Go on then, do your thing!" he reluctantly acquiesced, immediately feeling the heat from the healing energy that she was now pouring into him. Dog-damn-it! He'd forgotten how lovely her healing was, it had been so long!

Fred relaxed and let go, and as he did, he remembered back to when she was simply 'Aunty Clarabelle,' his best friend and not, 'The Queen,' wearing 'his crown.' He remembered how he used to curl up on her lap when she was with 'Uncle Micky' and Fred melted, surrendering completely to her touch. He felt his fur regrowing, his lip healing and his eye coming back to life from its swelling (as it reduced). He felt the blackness fade, and he felt his sore and painful tail repair. Fred let go some more and eased away into a lovely floaty space of love and tranquillity, then fell into a deep and peaceful sleep.

Metatron watched silently from above. Neither Clarabelle nor Nathaniel were aware of his presence - he didn't want them to see him. There'd be too many questions if they did! He'd been watching periodically over the years, monitoring Fred's progress. He, and 'The All That Is' had been pleased - until recently! He sighed. It's my fault, this 'crown business,' and its resulting gulf between Fred and Clarabelle. Metatron thought back to the afternoon, a few months ago, when Fred was sleeping and he'd used the dog's dream-time as an opportunity to call Fred to a progress review upstairs with the Boss. The Grim Reaper was half way through his lifetime down on earth as a dog, and they wanted him to know that he'd passed all the tests that they had set; that he'd won his promotion out of the Transport Department and would be coming back as a Guardian Angel! They'd even shown Fred the golden halo that was waiting for him, when it was his time to go 'back upstairs.' It had been placed on a soft golden cushion in the Boss's office - all glowing and shining, on a tall stand with Fred's name engraved on it. Fred had been, of course, completely blown away - shaking, overwhelmed, in shock! To be fair, no Grim Reaper had ever been promoted out of transport and up to The Higher Realms before, and it was a huge achievement! I thought it would encourage him to keep going as he'd been going these last five years, if he knew that he'd passed! But it hadn't! It had backfired, and backfired badly! Despite wiping Fred's memory of the meeting when he had left the Boss's office, Fred had held the image and the pleasure of the halo and the promised promotion from Grim Reaper to Trainee Guardian Angel so strongly, that he'd felt it in his being on every level, wanting that halo now! Only he'd interpreted it wrongly, thinking like a dog, not an angel, as soon as he was back on earth. He believed that the halo was like a crown: symbolising power and control, being in charge, and seeing Clarabelle as the one blocking his way. Metatron smiled, knowing that in the doggie world of the alpha/beta pack order, the dog that wore the alpha crown was in charge of the whole pack. At the end of the day, Fred may be a Grim Reaper inside, but for now, he was currently living the existence of a dog on earth, so it wasn't surprising that he was interpreting the halo like a dog would - top dog in charge of the pack. The war with Clarabelle was the fight for the top position, as any dog worth its salt would do on earth - fight the alpha dog for control of the pack. If he won, he was the new leader - if he lost, he had to leave the pack. "Oh dear!" Metatron muttered quietly. "Must fix this, and quickly!" He hoped that his presence at the face-off with the cat just now had helped to repair some of the damage done. He'd overseen the fight, holding Clarabelle back from helping (although she didn't know it, of course!), allowing Fred to get really quite badly injured, temporarily, so that he would have to allow Clarabelle to heal him, and thereby building the bridges across the divide between them a little. He watched them now, rebonding as she healed him - both parties remembering their friendship through the healing energy, and Metatron sent a little more peace and love into the mix. It was important that this was fixed if these two were ever to work together. Clarabelle had already been chosen to be Fred's trainer and mentor, in his new role as Trainee GA when the time came, so they just had to get on and be friends like they used to, or he'd have Hell up back upstairs!

Sarah woke from her nap, gently moving Simon's head away from her arm. Blimey the house is quiet, she thought! So peaceful with the twins at school. She looked at the bedside clock - two o'clock. Time for lunch, let Fred out, see to the washing, then off to the school, she thought, wondering how Fred and Cassie were getting on downstairs.

Fred and Cassie were ignoring each other, again! Cassie lay on the sofa, watching him from her place on the sofa through one, half-shut green eye, as he lay on the floor by the fire. Bless him, she thought. He really was a stubborn old goat! He'll learn, but he has a long way to go!

Stuff her! Fred was thinking, watching Cassie

discretely through one, half-shut brown eye. She may have won the battle but she hasn't won the war! No Sir, not by a long chalk! And he fell back into an exhausted sleep.

Chapter 5

The late summer September sun had faded into the hues of autumn golds when the Brown household finally regained its peace, and the war of the pets was, at last, over. The half-term school holiday, six weeks after the start of school, and of Cassie's arrival, had seen the turn in the war and its subsequent surrender; a mutual surrender - for the sake of the children. There had been plenty more battles since that first fight in early September between Fred and Cassie, generally during the day whilst the children were at school and when Sarah was out. Each time Cassie had won, each time Clarabelle had healed Fred, and each time the dog and the angel had become closer as a result. But the final turning point in the war came just at the end of the half-term school holiday week, when both children were home from school and unwilling witnesses to the fighting - Angelica crying and upset over Cassie, and David crying and upset because Fred was hurt. There was something about witnessing the crying children that melted both pets' hearts simultaneously, dissolving their determination to outwit and/or kill each other. For the sake of the children a compromise had to be reached, and reached it was. Fred magnanimously agreed that Cassie was supreme in the fighting stakes; with a new, deservedly earned title of 'Ninja Warrior Cat' being given. Cassie in return, agreed that Fred was a battler, with 'dogged determination,' and, therefore, deserved respect. As the peace terms were drawn up, with Clarabelle and Nat overseeing the proceedings, both pets agreed to share seventh place in the pack order, to learn to get on and, most importantly, to accept each other as valued members of the household.

Fred had to admit, Cassie has done wonders with Angelica. The miniature diva has thawed hugely, and she was even considerate now - sometimes!

"Shake paws!" demanded Clarabelle, heaving a huge sigh of relief as she put the final touches to the peace agreement. David and Angelica sat on the sofa watching, wet tissues scrunched up in their little hands from their earlier crying. Fred and Cassie looked at the children; they saw the red eyes, their wet tissues and both obeyed without hesitation.

"Yes, Aunty Clarabelle," they said together, lifting front paws and tapping each other with them in a show of 'shaking hands.'

"Kiss and make up!" demanded Angelica, as another tear slid down her pale face.

"Umm, okay then," Fred grumbled, "But only a little one, okay?"

"K," grinned Angelica, wiping the tear away.

Fred took a breath, held it and licked Cassie's ear.

Doesn't taste too bad, for a cat, he thought with surprise! Cassie in return licked his swollen ear - Gosh there was a huge lump! I really don't know my own strength! she thought with alarm. Then both pets lay down for the obligatory healing from 'Aunty Clarabelle' - finally now reaccepted as 'Pack Leader' by all.

Feeling the shift in energy and knowing that peace was back in the Brown house, Clarabelle was delighted! "Smashing!" she declared emphatically. "Now, perhaps we can get on and do what we need to do! I have work to do with Sarah, and Cassie is going to help me, aren't you, dear?" She smiled at the black cat, who grinned back, as she thought of the teaching that she could share with her new Ma over the coming weeks. "Now then, Fred, let's sort that ear out, my dear?" And she went to work on healing both animals.

***

The low, soft light of an early November morning poured through their bedroom window the following week as Sarah awoke with new energy. She felt an excitement, anticipation and nervousness of what was to come.

Clarabelle had filled her in the night before of her plans. She would be teaching Sarah how to use divination cards and implied that, somehow, Sarah would be able to use her new knowledge to help people. She had no idea how or why! She didn't believe in fortune telling, and had told Clarabelle so. They'd had a long discussion about fate versus free will and she was still rather confused. That being said, she was eager to understand and know more. It had been years since she'd done any new learning - there simply hadn't been time with two young twins and a mad dog to sort, as well as working periodically at her store.

Since Tim had taken over as manager, all was right and well at her store, and, whilst he had a very capable deputy manager to cover him when he was away, there were still things that only Sarah could do. Organising renewals on insurances, dealing with the buying of new lines and the negotiations on price and quantities, had always been Sarah's responsibility, filling what little time she had completely. There'd been no new learning of anything to do with the universe or metaphysical matters since Simon's accident five years before, and whilst Sarah meditated, when she could, that had been the limit - until now!

She stretched happily, enjoying the warmth and cosiness of the wonderful king-size bed, contemplating whether she could squeeze another few minutes to sprawl out across it and enjoy the moment of having it all to herself. Simon had taken to going into work early these days, leaving the bed before Sarah had awoken most mornings, meaning that she had the luxury of the whole bed to herself; just for those few minutes before the children got up. Just as she was contemplating sprawling sideways across the bed, Simon walked into the darkened room quietly, putting the mug of steaming coffee on the bedside table next to her.

He bent to kiss her awake, as he often did before he left for work, but she beat him to it; sliding her arms up silently, she grabbed him and yanked him full force, down and over her in one swoop. He collapsed onto her laughing. "Get off, get off, woman! I have work to go to!" he smiled, moving a stray curl away from her face with his finger tenderly. "Don't start me off," he begged, as Sarah kissed him passionately, hearing his deep groan as she did. "Damn you, woman," he laughed. "I can't go to work with a boner!"

"Go on then, get off, be gone!" she giggled, "before I change my mind and drag you into this bed."

"Later ..." his tone promised, the twinkle in his eye betraying his body, not to mention the bulge in his suit trousers, visible as he stood up! He readjusted his clothes, turned and kissed her nose, and ran from the room laughing. "Later, you gorgeous woman, I won't be late!" he yelled, as he ran down the stairs, two at a time, with his long legs.

Sarah heard the front door bang as he rushed off for his day at the bank. He had recently been promoted to Branch Manager, taking over from Mr. Godwin, and was taking his new role very seriously. He'd been going in around 7 a.m. for the last two months, wanting to be ahead of the game, not to mention setting a good example for the staff. She was incredibly proud of him! He'd worked so hard and she knew that he had been delighted when Mr. Godwin had called him into the office one day to inform him that he was retiring early, following a recent health scare, and that he was recommending Simon for his position. Initially, Simon had been concerned that Ben would be hurt at being passed over; he didn't want anything to come between them and spoil their friendship. Aside from being his colleague and friend in the bank, Ben was also Sarah's brother. He both admired and respected Ben, and was aware that Ben had been at the bank since he left school at eighteen, straight after his 'A' levels. Surely the promotion should be his, he had wondered, but Mr. Godwin had explained that whilst Ben's service record was immaculate, he had neither the qualifications nor the experience that Simon had, and Ben was unable, therefore, to be considered for the position of Branch Manager. Simon, in contrast, had begun his financial career in the city at the age of twenty-one, following a first level honours degree in Economics at a prestigious university. He had moved into banking in the city, starting in commercial banking, then moving into investment banking, and finally into corporate banking and account management, and was, therefore, far more experienced than Ben. Ben had done well, but he had never gone to university, nor had he worked in a large bank with the opportunities they presented, unlike Simon. No, Mr. Godwin had assured, Simon was the only internal candidate that would be considered; and with his recommendation, it was a given that the job was his, should he want it.

Oh yes indeed, Simon wanted it and had thanked Mr. Godwin profusely for the opportunity. Ben had been delighted for Simon when he'd been told, understanding completely the bank's choice of candidate, and they had gone out celebrating until the wee small hours, following the announcement. Sarah had been thrilled, and the two families had celebrated several times over the following week; with many hangovers and blurry eyes to show for it!

The interview that followed had been a formality, and Simon had moved into Mr. Godwin's office just after, taking over as Branch Manager. That was now two months ago. He'd worked long hours for the first month, just as the twins were starting school, and had been sad not to be there for them on their first day. Over the weeks that followed, the late nights had stopped, thank goodness, thought Sarah, and it wouldn't be much longer before the very early starts calmed down too. Woohoo!

Sarah thought about her husband again. God, I was tempted to drag him back to bed just then! But she knew her husband, and had controlled herself, and her desires, to support him in his new role and let him go off to work early, as he wanted. "I'll shag his brains out later!" she grinned to herself, pulling herself out of bed to start the day.

"Shag? Lovely turn of phrase, Sarah! I do think you really should have more respect for the 'love making' that you and Simon have! Shag indeed!" admonished Clarabelle, sitting on top of the clock by Sarah's bed tutting.

"Yes, Mum," laughed Sarah. "Stop nagging woman!"

"I am neither nagging, nor I am a woman, Sarah, as you well know! And as for being your mother, well - I don't need to comment on that one! I am an angel: I repeat, an angel - A.N.G.E.L., Class 2 in fact! And I am not nagging - I am merely trying to help you to see the wonder that is, you and Simon, and to help you to give your beautiful relationship the respect that it deserves. So there!"

"Yes, dear, I know." Sarah smiled. "So what time do you want me? For the lesson I mean?" She deflected

Clarabelle's sermon wonderfully, moving the attention away from her and Simon's sex life, to Clarabelle's teaching. It worked!

"Oh, I think nine-thirty shall we say, dear? I shall get the room ready - you go and see to the twins and get them off to school. I must prepare!" and she was gone! Poof - just like that!

***

"So, Clarence, I thought we'd start with the Angel cards, then when she's got the hang of them, we can move onto the Universal Tarot deck; what do you think?" Clarabelle enquired, excitedly.

"Oh, yes, I agree!" he smiled, thinking that Sarah really shouldn't have too much trouble getting the hang of the Angel cards after all these years of having Clarabelle.

"Smashing!" she beamed. "I've already ordered them in readiness; they'll be waiting for her in the morning post when she gets back from school. I will have to teach her everything, right from the beginning, but it shouldn't take long. She already knows about cleansing her home and energy, so explaining how she must cleanse and charge the cards will be a synch!"

"Yes, and, of course, the trust issue isn't there, so that makes it quicker too, don't you think?" he nodded, smiling his approval. "It's when they question everything that it takes so long, but with your Sarah, she already knows to trust you, so moving that trust onto the cards should be simple."

"And with Cassie to help as well, we should have this sorted in a few weeks, don't you think, Clarence? Time for

Sarah to be able to help Frieda before it's too late?"

"Depends on Frieda, of course, my dear; her progress very much depends on her own willingness to want to heal." Clarence's eyes were sad, thinking of poor Frieda. That girl has had such a rough ride, poor thing. Been stuck forever! Stuck in her rut of mistrust and pain, so much so that she couldn't love, or live, fully. She is missing out on so much - so much! Her pain was palpable at times. They often felt it upstairs in The Realms; waves of sadness, hurt and despair emanated from that poor woman. It was time for it to stop, and the only one that could possibly get this ball rolling was Sarah; she was the only person that Frieda trusted enough to begin to start this journey out of pain. She had been her best friend since she was five years old; their friendship had endured forty years now. Yes, if Sarah couldn't sort Frieda out, no one could. Not on her own, of course - the Angelic Realm would be involved, hugely involved - but Sarah's task was to start the ball off.

"Have you squared it all with Miya then, Frieda's angel? Got her ready, Clar?" Clarabelle was asking - again! She assumed her brother had, of course, sorted it, but couldn't help herself. "And the AA's, of course - we shall need Uriel to be ready to help heal her emotions, and Michael to give her the strength to face her demons, and a whole host of angelic energy to get her through the next year, whilst she faces her past and lets it all go - don't you think, Clar? I mean, her Andrew is waiting, and if we don't get her sorted soon, she's going to miss out, again!"

"Yes, of course, it's all in hand! As if!" he declared. "Of course, it is! Everyone is ready - has been for years! We just couldn't get it started - she's just too closed off and closed down for us to be able to help; but once she is open, once Sarah's done her bit, well then the ball will be rolling, and everyone up here is ready to roll with it, trust me on that one, Clarabelle!"

"Smashing!" she beamed. "I do just love a happy ending, don't you, dear? It's time that Frieda had hers - more than time!"

Both angels gazed down from their cloud towards Redville, staring sadly at Frieda's house in the centre of the large town eight miles away. As usual the red brick house was surrounded with a big, dark cloud of sadness - Frieda's sadness - sadness mixed up with fear, shame, blame and a whole load of other nasty stuff! Not noticeable to the humans down there, of course, but from high up on Cloud 322, it was completely visible. Sarah's house, directly below them in the little town of Redfields, on the other hand, stood beaming beautiful white light all around it, high up into the atmosphere - the light of love, joy, peace and harmony shining from every window.

Smashing, thought Clarabelle, delighted with Sarah's energy and that of her home. Just perfect!

"And don't forget, Clarabelle; your Sarah is going to go through that hurt with her, and she's going to be shocked when she finds out, as you know. She doesn't have a clue! She always sees Frieda as a little ball of fun and fire, always has. She's going to be so hurt for her friend when it all comes out, you do know that don't you, Clar? It's not just those with the pain that feel it, my dear - it's everyone around them too!"

"Yes, dear, I know; of course, I know! I'm ready - aren't I always?" She pondered Sarah's reaction for a moment -

she knew her well enough to know that she would cope. In fact, it would just increase her determination to learn more and be able to do more to help! "Right oh, Clarence, off I go to work. Wish me luck, dear!" she beamed happily at her smiling brother.

"Always!" Clarence grinned, and then they were gone.

Chapter 6

Sarah stared at the cards with anticipation, and a bit of trepidation!

Clarabelle grinned, looking at Sarah and feeling her nervousness. "Nothing to fear, child, nothing!" she promised. "Now, shall we begin?"

Sarah unwrapped the small box, staring at the front cover. A beautiful angel, wings outstretched, looked up at her from the top of the box. She took the cards out slowly, and turning them over to the face-side up, she started sliding the cards one under the other to examine them. They were beautiful! The smooth cards glided easily through her fingers; she slid each under the other to examine the next, then the next, working her way through the entire pack.

Clarabelle watched her delightedly. "You will see, Sarah dear, that there are angels of different looks, colours, names, and each, of course, has its own energy and focus. In addition to the Angel cards, in this pack, there are also four Archangel cards within the deck: these are the power cards in the pack and bring in additional energy. You will see that Archangel Michael is the angel of strength and courage, Uriel is emotional healing, Raphael, physical healing, and Gabriel, of course, is communication." Sarah nodded, pouring over the cards more slowly, taking it all in. "There are literally thousands of different packs of divination cards, Sarah, all sorts! Hundreds of different types of Angel cards alone, thousands of different Tarot cards, not to mention Wiccan, shamanic, fairy and planetary cards. Many, many different ones! Each pack has its own energy, its own vibration; it is most important that you use the pack that resonates with your own energy, or you simply will not connect, not at all, and then it won't work. This is why many people give up with cards, you know, dear; they try to use a pack they have picked up somewhere, and they simply do not connect with them on the right vibration because it doesn't match their own. These, of course, are perfect for you! Now then, before we begin anything, there are certain things you must first do, Sarah," declared Clarabelle, focusing on Sarah intently. "Most important, most important!" she chirped. "First you must 'tune in'; that is tuning in to your own soul energy and being. Then you connect your soul energy to your Higher Self, and through your Higher Self to Source; the 'All That Is.' Your intention is quite sufficient, quite sufficient!" she beamed.

Clarabelle always repeated herself when she was excited, and excited she clearly was! Her eyes sparkled, her halo glowed and the white light around her was definitely whiter than usual, Sarah noted!

"Next you must ask for divine light to enter your being

and fill you with love and protection."

Sarah followed instructions and did as she was told. "I know this bit, Clar," she said. "It's the same as when I meditate."

"Precisely, child, precisely!" Clarabelle smiled happily. "It is indeed the same. Now then, you, of course, ask your angels to come in and help you - but as I am already here, you can skip that bit." She winked at Sarah, focusing again on the cards. "Next you must cleanse them. Before and after working with any divination cards, they *must* be cleansed. Most important, most important!"

Sarah focused on the cards in her hands, imagining the divine white light of love and protection that was now within her, pouring into the cards, lifting away any negativity, any anything!

"And don't forget to ground! Most important, definitely important!"

Sarah nodded, visualising little invisible zips on the sole of each of her feet opening up, and long strong roots growing out of her, stretching deep into the ground below her. *I am connecting to mother earth, whose permission I have to do this,* she silently mouthed. *The Divine light within me is spreading down through my roots, connecting me with Mother Earth below, and the Divine above,* she said in her mind. *I am protected from all harm. I am connected above and below, within and without, on every level - mind, body and spirit,* she chanted quietly.

"Perfect!" grinned Clarabelle happily, watching Sarah concentrate intently. She felt Sarah's energy, and was satisfied. "Excellent! Now, next step is to 'charge' the cards."

"Charge? What's that?" Sarah looked confused.

"Charge it with whatever you want to use them for, my dear. Easy really! If you are going to use the cards to perhaps find out something, you would charge the cards with 'information and knowledge,' or if maybe you were using them for healing, or for inspiration, or for advice, you would ask for that. Lots of things! Generally, my advice would be to charge them with them all; that way you have it covered." She grinned at Sarah, loving teaching her. *So exciting,* she thought happily!

Cassie watched quietly from the top of the sofa. *Wonder if this was how Ma started?*

"Now, you may want to think about who else you could call on to help you, to increase the power and information, as it were," Clarabelle added thoughtfully. "For example, if you were to trying to gain information about family, you may ask for loved ones, previously passed to spirit, to come in, as they may be the best people to ask. And if you were doing a reading for someone else, say a friend, you may ask for their Guardian Angel to be present and help, and their loved ones - that sort of thing. Do you understand, dear?"

Sarah nodded. "I think so," she smiled. "But like I said to you the other day, I don't know if I agree with 'fortune telling,' Clar."

"Fortune telling? Hocus pocus nonsense, my dear! No such thing! No one can predict anyone's future, Sarah, for that can change from hour to hour, from day to day. The future depends on actions, and as actions change, depending on the person, you can never predict the future. What you can do..." she paused dramatically for effect, "is to see and say what is *likely* to happen, if they stay on their current path, and what is *likely* to happen if they take another path, make a different choice. See?"

"Umm, I think so." Sarah didn't really see.

"Alright, how about if I give you an example?" Clarabelle smiled gently, searching for a way to help Sarah understand how the cards work. "Let's say, you could see a romance for someone in the future, yes? Daniel, the angel card of marriage came up - the cards would be showing you that there is someone there for that person, and in time, you will even be able to pick up *when* that romance or thing is likely to happen, timescale and that sort of thing. Anyway where was I? Oh yes, romance. Let us say that there is a romance for someone, and it shows on the cards - the cards are saying that it is a possibility. However, if that person (let's say it's a heterosexual lady), chooses to avoid men, avoid going out and any men that come anywhere near her she runs a mile from, then she is choosing not to go down that road, and that is her prerogative, of course, under the rules of free will, so no romance will happen. Sometimes she may be consciously aware of this choice, other times it will be subconscious - automatic avoidance. In other words, she may not know that she is blocking it, or she may. Does that make sense, Sarah?"

"Yes, thank you, it does." Sarah grinned happily.

"So it is not really 'fortune telling,' Sarah - it is simply showing someone their path, what lies before them, but it is always their choice. That choice gives them power - it empowers! It can be, and often is, very healing, encouraging, supportive and lifting. The cards can give hope, where there was none; inspiration where there was despair; support when there was aloneness; understanding where there was confusion. Do you see? Anyway, nothing in the future is guaranteed; but what the cards are good for, very good in fact, is seeing the past, and seeing the past can help you see what is coming in the future, based on the past experiences. Do you see, dear?"

"Umm, yes, I think so." Sarah felt the cards in her hands a little more. They felt nice in her fingers; sort of comforting, warm even.

"And don't forget to tell her about reading the person's energy field, Clarabelle," Cassie called, watching intently. "She needs to read their heart energy too, and their emotional energy, auric field and soul light. And if she gets really good, she can talk with the person's Higher Self too, just like Ma did."

"Yes, dear, I will. Leave it to me," beamed Clarabelle, grateful for the extra help from Cassie.

Fred watched silently from the door. He felt rather left out! *Maybe I could help?* he wondered. *Join in a bit?* He looked at the small, round table where Mum and Aunty Clarabelle were sitting in the corner of the room, and could just see the cards on the top, but with difficulty. "It's alright for her, sitting on the top of the bloody sofa," he grumbled. "She can see fine from up there!"

"Yes, Fred, I can! And you are too short down there on the ground to be of any help whatsoever, so go and play with a bone!" Cassie hissed, wanting him out of the way so that she could concentrate.

"Fine! I will!" he moaned, grabbing a stray bone that

had somehow been forgotten from the doorway, and plodding back out of the lounge to his bed.

"Higher Self! Don't forget the Higher Self!" Cassie nagged. *So important that she learn about the Higher Self!*

"Yes, yes - Higher Self!" Clarabelle grinned to the smiling cat. "Now then, Sarah, you have heard me mention Higher Self before, yes?" Sarah nodded.

"Yes, it's like all the soul lives rolled into one, isn't it?" she asked.

"Quite right yes, my dear, well done! It is indeed. So the soul energy in you now, is the soul for this lifetime. It knows all that has gone on so far in this lifetime, so it is the soul that you need to connect with, in order to know about the person's past experiences so far. Yes?" Sarah nodded. "And then when you die, the soul passes back to spirit - it is the body that is dead, not the soul, Sarah - the soul is infinite! And then the soul comes back again, and again, and again, into different bodies, learning and growing all the time. Well, the Higher Self, which is located approximately eighteen inches above the crown, and with which you have just connected, has all the knowledge from all the past lives that have been lived - but also has knowledge of the future in this life, and of future lives in other bodies - that which is planned and probable, of course, but not guaranteed. As we have discussed, free will can, and often does, change things in the plan. So when you are doing a reading, most of the past information comes through from the soul, and most of the future information comes through from the Higher Self. What is most important though, Sarah, is that you ask permission from the Higher Self, to ascertain that which is right and correct for the person to know - this is called 'within your highest good.' Sometimes it is not good for the person to know what is in store for them, for it would cause fear or worry, and would be of no purpose. Other times, it can be helpful for them to know; to give hope and direction, an action plan, an understanding, and a purpose. You don't know which is which - if it helps or hinders - but the soul does, and the Higher Self does; so always ask, 'if it's within my highest good,' or 'their highest good.' That gives them permission to block that information which isn't good for you to see or know. Do you see?"

"Yes, I think so," she said, raising her eyebrows. *So much to take in! So complicated! Blimey!* "So, basically I need to connect with the world and his wife!" she grinned, "... God, the universe, the angels, the soul, the Higher Self, Mother Earth; and that's just me! Then there's the person I'm doing the reading for and their Higher Self, their soul, their angels and all the rest?"

"Precisely, indeed!" Clarabelle affirmed.

"And cleanse the cards and charge them?"

"Yes."

"And ground, connect, protect."

"Exactly."

"And to remember the 'within my/their highest good' thingy - blimey! There's a lot to it, isn't there?"

"Oh, you'll soon get the hang of it, and it will come automatically, promise!" Clarabelle reassured.

"And all that's before I've learned the cards, what they mean and how to work with them?" Sarah quietly blurted the slightly panicked statement of fact.

"Indeed. And then there's where the cards lay in relation to each other which also needs to be taken into account, and whether they are inverted or..."

"What?" squealed Sarah, very panicked now. "What's inverted?"

"Whether the cards are upside down to you, or facing you, my dear. Makes a difference as to what they are saying, depending which way they are facing. Now then, shall we discuss the other bits - energy! The cards are just the starting point of the reading, my dear. They get the energy flowing, but are less than half of the story. Other information, the meat on the bones so to speak, comes from the heart centre, the solar plexus - that's where the emotional baggage will be, Sarah - then there's the mental blocks in the mind, the auric field and any damage there - lots of information all over. ..."

But before she had time to continue, Sarah had removed herself from the table, heading quickly to the kitchen as she muttered, "Coffee! I'm going to need a shed load of coffee for this! Jesus!"

"Yes, and Him too," Clarabelle called, "You can call him too - He's very helpful, most helpful indeed!"

***

"So it's a minefield, Frie," Sarah moaned despondently. "A bloody minefield, or mind-field! Explosive; mentally, unbelievable! She's had me learning these cards for weeks and I still haven't got it! Weeks - and that's just the Angel cards! She wants me onto the Tarot soon and it's a nightmare! I'm never gonna get it!"

Frieda was rather blown away with it all too! She'd had no idea there was quite so much involved in this 'reading cards business'! Her friend looked panicked. *I'm not surprised*, thought Frieda! *I would be too!* "So what's the plan, mate?" she asked, not really quite sure what to suggest.

"Apparently I need to practice! I need guinea pigs. What do you think, Frie; you up for it?"

"No bloody way, matey!" Frieda grimaced, shuddering at the very thought. "Not until Hell freezes over anyway!" she declared emphatically.

"Oh, come on, mate, pleeeeeezzzzzzz!" Sarah begged, grinning cheekily. "It'll be fun - well, maybe fun. Give it a go, let me practice on you, go on?"

"Na, mate, sorry. No way in Hell! Get Angie! She'll do it!"

"But you're the one up for anything, Frie! You always have been - nothing scares you - you'll try anything, once!"

"Tell you what, hun, I'll have a think about it, okay? That's the best I can do." *Yeah right, for about a millisecond! ... Thought about it ... Still no!* She looked at Sarah warily. "This is all new for me, this 'psychic' stuff that you're into, don't forget. I only found out about your Clarabelle thingy last year, and I'm still getting my head around that - you talking to angels and stuff - it's freaky! Now this 'psychic readings' stuff as well; it's so weird!"

"But you like weird! You've always liked weird, Frie! You're the adventurous one! You're the dangerous one! Always have been. I thought you'd be fine with this, really I did - but if you're freaked, then yes, of course, we can leave it." Sarah's face fell, realising she'd pushed her friend too far. Frieda really did look scared to death! She'd had no idea that Frieda would have a problem with this, none whatsoever! "I'm sorry, mate, forget I mentioned it. I'll ask Angie instead," she promised. Angie was their mutual friend, and *probably up for it,* Sarah thought. All three were close, had been since they'd met at school years ago, and she was sure that Angie would be happy to oblige. *Mind you, I thought Frie would, and look at her reaction!*

Frieda looked at the floor, embarrassed to have made such a fuss about a few silly cards. She really didn't know why she was so resistant to this. Sarah was right - she was the adventurous one - usually! Why then, did this scare her so much? All she knew was that at the mere mention of having her cards read, her heart had started pounding, her stomach clenching, her palms sweating; she was on the verge of a full blown panic attack, and right in front of her friend - God, how awful! She'd suffered with panic attacks for years, but no one knew, absolutely no one, not even Sarah! They all saw her as 'Frieda the Invincible,' Frieda the strong, courageous one, the funny one, the 'have a go one,' - 'Frieda the Formidable'! No one saw her, ever, as the scared one, the terrified one, the one doubled-up in pain, sometimes on the floor, collapsed, in agony from the panic attacks that came and went with such force, as they had done for as far back as she could remember. She hid them well, keeping a pack of anti-anxiety pills in her pocket at all times; slipping one discretely into her mouth whenever she felt that first tightening in her chest coming on. She looked at the cards on the table once again; just innocent pieces of plastic coated cardboard, but it was like looking into the gates of Hell! She had no idea why! All she knew was that she did not want - totally did not want - a bloody reading!

She excused herself for a pee, slipping a double dose of the tiny red pills into her mouth quickly as soon as she was out of Sarah's sight, and began the countdown as she stared into the bathroom mirror - slowing her increasingly fast breathing down with determination, and practice. "You are safe," she mouthed silently to the image before her. "You are in control," she chanted. "This too will pass," she affirmed. Gradually the rapid breathing slowed, the pulse returned to normal, the clamminess dried up in her palms, and finally, her chest released its tightened grip, enabling her to lose the feeling of suffocation. "All is well," she smiled at her reflection, wiping her wet brow with the damp tissue that she held in her hand as she waited for the last of the attack to pass, and eventually, it did.

Frieda returned to the lounge with a huge smile, patting Sarah on the back as she sat down. "So what's for dinner then, mate, I'm starving!" she grinned. "And where's the wine? Let's open a bottle – it's wine o'clock!"

Sarah was relieved to see Frieda back to her old self. She really couldn't get over her friend's reaction to her request for her to be a guinea pig. Frieda was always so 'up for anything,' but at the mention of the cards, all colour had drained from her face and she'd looked seriously like she was about to pass out! Sarah was bemused. Whatever the reason was, she was wise enough to know now to stay away from the subject of a reading with Frieda, and stay away for good!

Clarabelle looked at Miya and sighed. "Oh dear," she said sadly, noting that Frieda's angel looked as worried as she was. "This is going to take a bit of doing to sort this out, Miya! We must go and see Clarence, see what we can do! We need a plan - reinforcements! Lots to do, lots to do!"

And the two angels were gone. ...

Chapter 7

Clarabelle stared at Clarence in amazement! "You have got to be kidding me!" she cried. "We can't do that! What if she isn't ready?"

"Clar, she'll never be ready! We are just going to have to push this, and deal with the consequences ... that's our only option I promise you! I've spoken with the Bosses, and they agree - we need to force her hand."

"But ..." Miya's voice trailed off. She had asked Clarabelle and Clarence for advice, for help, and she wasn't liking what she was hearing; not one bit! *But what? What other options did they have?* No matter which way she looked at it, she knew that Clarence was right. *They were going to have to force it.* "Dear, dear! Oh me, oh my," she fretted. Her eyebrows furrowed as she considered what her ward had in store. "She's already been through so much!" she cried. "Does she really have to go through this as well?" she implored.

Clarence nodded his head sadly.

Miya turned to Clarabelle, wringing her hands with

anxiety. "Isn't there another way?" she asked her friend, desperate to avoid any more pain for her poor Frieda. "There simply *must* be another way!"

"Sadly not, my dear Miya, sadly not!" Clarabelle shook her head slowly. She smiled softly at the angel, trying to show support and solidarity. "I'm afraid Clarence is right, my dear. There simply is no other way."

"We hoped, as you know," Clarence explained, "we hoped so very much, that she would take the opportunity that Sarah presented, but she is too full of fear, my dear. She simply cannot do it. We must force it; we simply must!"

"Yes, I know," Miya concurred regretfully. She sighed heavily, knowing they were right. She thought about Frieda's resistance and sighed yet again. "Her soul knows that it's time to release this and let it go, to begin to heal the scars that are still so raw, and yet her humanity resists, and resists so very strongly! But ..." she trailed off, "you are right; the only option is to force this." She shook her head sadly, knowing what was in store for her Frieda, and could have cried for her, *poor lamb*.

"Miya," Clarabelle quietly said, "it will be alright, my dear, in the end - it will be alright, I promise you. We will help you - we will all help you - of that you can be assured."

Miya's head hung. Her brown eyes were sad, cast down to the bottom of the cloud they all sat on now - Cloud 326. Her dark hair hung heavily on her shoulders as she contemplated the coming days and weeks for her Frieda. "God, bless her," she implored, to an unseen force. "Send her healing, strength and love; healing to overcome that which MUST be overcome!"

The three angels stared down at Redville, far below them, and at the black shadow that hung over Frieda's house, palpitating menace and foreboding. A dark storm of pain and fear had been building, and building for nearly forty years; fear that would either make or break the lovely Frieda - who, far below, had no clue as to this conversation, or the very high level of concern for her wellbeing that was going on in the stratosphere high above her.

"Dreams then, to begin with?" Miya asked, resigned to the inevitable.

"Dreams. ..." Clarence and Clarabelle quietly said together.

"Nightmares. ...!" Miya cried, as a silent tear fell from her anxious eyes.

And so it began. ...

***

Frieda really didn't understand what the fuss had been about at Sarah's house earlier.

She considered her reaction carefully as she lay in the hot, deep bath, the winter's eve closing around her home. Darkness came quickly, on this mid-November day, the daylight ever shorter, the night time taking its victory, even at a mere five o'clock. It was now nearly nine, and candles flickered around her, the scents of the bath bomb filling the room with lavender and juniper. *Why had she reacted so?* she asked herself. *What was that all about?* They were only cards, and Sarah was her friend - her very best friend - and she needed some support! Really, she needed to get a grip! The hot, soapy water washed over her soothingly as she pondered her reaction. She knew Sarah's opinion of her - Frieda, the wild one; always in trouble, always taking risks, always having a go at anything, whether she could do it or not! They had been friends, the three of them, Sarah, Angela (or Angie, as they all called her) and Frieda, since they had all begun in infant's school together, nearly forty years ago now. In Sarah's eyes, Frieda, with her wild, bright red curly hair had had the personality to match. She always seemed to run everywhere, have boundless energy and a happy disposition that never seemed to be serious - Frieda, the wild one of the three, the adventurous, brave, 'have a go hero' of the three. *God, Sarah would have a fit if she saw this side of me - the panicked, shaking, afraid side of me! She only knows me as the fun one, the humorous one, the one that laughs at everything! She has no idea how I use that humour to hide behind - to mask, to conceal, to protect! She must never know, never see, this real me, never! I'm going to have to do the bloody reading! Shit!*

Frieda considered it again - *let her do a reading with the silly cards then - so what!* But as soon as she thought that thought, a wave of pure terror ran through her body. From her toes to the top of her head, all Frieda could feel was panic. She had no idea why! She clocked the tight ball in her tummy - deep, deep in her belly - a ball that screamed, 'run, run!' She felt the corresponding, and correlating tightening in her chest, the tightness that signalled another panic attack, and she forgot all about Sarah and her silly cards as she fought to retain and regain control of her panicked body. "I am safe," she chanted.

"All is well, this too shall pass," she firmly said, focusing on her breathing and counting to eight. Eight breaths in, hold for eight - eight breaths out, and hold for eight. *One, two, three ...* she counted, and counted, focusing on her breathing for what seemed an eternity, until finally her breathing returned to normal. *Really, two panic attacks in one day - what on earth is going on? It must be that reading!* Frieda considered the panic attack that was now passing, coming to the conclusion that it was, indeed, the thought of having a reading with Sarah that had created such a storm within her. *I can't do it, I just can't do it! God, give me bloody strength!*

Miya stood over her, sending her healing, love and strength. "You're going to need it, my love, and you're going to need a lot of it!"

***

"So what's next?" an excited and euphoric Sarah asked a very happy Clarabelle. "Am I ready now, ready for the tarot?" she grinned.

Clarabelle beamed. "Oh yes indeed!" she exclaimed. "Oh yes indeed!"

Sarah had worked hard, practicing every day, and now had the Angel cards down to a tee! She knew every single one, including how to interpret the meaning of the inverted cards and how the surrounding cards impacted on the layout, and, therefore, the impact upon the outcome. All she needed now were people to practice on! She had 'done' Simon, of course, and Fred, and even Cassie! *That had been weird! The cards for the cat showed familiarity, family, a coming home ... most strange,* Sarah thought, *especially as Cassie is so new to this house ... and yet there had been cards for beginnings too - but there you go - stranger things in Heaven and Earth,* as Clarabelle liked to say! She had also 'done' Ben, and Gina, his wife, and a couple of Gina's friend's - that had been great! She'd loved that! They'd all been happy with their free, 'Angel Reading,' and Sarah's confidence with the cards had grown as a result of their 'ooh's' and 'ahh's,' but it wasn't enough! For some reason, Sarah felt that she hadn't got to the crux of the matter - the reason that she was doing this. There felt a ... she wasn't sure, but it felt like there was something more; some other purpose to this than just doing card readings for family. She hadn't, of course, approached her mother – God, no! Margaret Smith would have a fit! And anyway, it wasn't like she didn't already know what was going on, or had gone on, for her mother ... Clarabelle had made sure of that, years ago! "Something else I'm meant to do with this," she said thoughtfully to herself. "And it's important! Very important!"

***

Frieda was deep in sleep, and she was dreaming. ...

The man stood over her, beckoning her to come closer. He smelled funny - nice funny! She knew that she knew this man, and yet, she couldn't see his face. He was beckoning her to climb up onto his lap, and she did so willingly. Like every small child, always up for a cuddle! The man cuddled her tightly, and it was nice ... but it was rough too. She could feel his corduroy trousers underneath her as she sat; her summer, cotton dress, flimsy beneath her; no barrier to the rough cloth beneath. They felt rough, the trousers; rough against the softness of her thighs as she curled into him - cheap, harsh trousers that scraped her tender skin. But she felt the arms around her; protective, loving, nurturing, and she snuggled in for more cuddles, despite the roughness. The man stroked her back gently, reassuringly, wondering at the softness of her young, fresh skin. He held her tighter. "I will never, ever, let anyone harm you, Princess," he softly said, stroking her back, drawing her into his embrace with his gentle words. "You are my Princess, you are my special and wonderful girl, and I love you very much," he smiled, deep into her arms.

And she felt his love, and she felt his protection, and she knew that she was safe. ...

Frieda watched the scene from the back of the small room; the small girl, cuddling up with the man, and she was afraid. She was very afraid. She did not know why she was afraid, but she was. "Wake up, wake up now!" she commanded herself. "This is a dream - wake up now!" And Frieda awoke. She awoke trembling - she did not know why ... and she cried.

***

"So there we are, Clarence, she has it! She has the Tarot cards! It's taken an age mind you, an absolute age to get her there, but she knows them all, at last!" Clarabelle was beaming, from halo to dainty foot, totally beaming! A huge grin plastered on her face, she sat perched on top of the sofa in Sarah's lounge grinning at Clarence.

"Fantastic, Clar! That's great news, really great!" Clarence replied cautiously, wondering quite what had taken Clarabelle's Sarah so long! *Really, with Clarabelle's teaching and what she already knew, I'd have thought it would be a few days, not a few months!* he thought. *She started them in November, and now here we are in February, months later!* "Yes, dear, wonderful!" he smiled, adding in, "She's learned them really quickly!" His fingers were crossed behind his back (to cancel out the tiny lie, nay, minute lie), that he was now spouting. *How many is that now?* he wondered. *There are only so many porkies we can get away with before we're in trouble with the Bosses for 'un-angelic behaviour'! 'Conduct unbecoming,' they call it upstairs. Oh dear!* This additional 'untruth' would be added to his record - he couldn't get away with it - they knew everything upstairs; well, nearly everything! Clarence did a quick double count of the many 'porkies' he had told over the years, and yep, sure enough, he was pretty close to the limit now, he knew.

"Oh, don't shit yourself, Gramps!" spouted Fred from the fireplace, as he licked the bone jammed between his sticky paws noisily. He'd grown quite fond of 'Old Clarence,' since his first hatred of 'The Spy' all those years ago. "Just keep your mouth shut and they'll never know!" he grinned, and as he did, revealed bits of meat stuck between his teeth as he gnashed away.

"Fred! Don't speak with your mouth full!" scolded Clarabelle. "And don't forget to floss after you've finished with that bone!" she ordered.

"Yeah, yeah, nag, nag," he mouthed, although he couldn't actually get the words out, due to the chunks of tender meat that were now being swallowed; torn expertly from the old leg of lamb left over from Sunday lunch. *Just as well they can read my thoughts,* he thought happily; *saves me from having to pause from my bone to speak!*

"And Sarah is going to murder you if she sees that greasy bone in here!" Clarence spouted. "I really do think it's best if you take it outside, Frederick, don't you? Save a lot of trouble all round!"

"You keep your mouth shut, Gramps, and I'll keep mine shut!" Fred grinned, showing lamb debris between his teeth as he spoke; bits poking out, firmly jammed between each canine as he chomped.

"Tsk!" muttered Clarence, knowing not to argue with Fred, especially when he had a bone!

"Tsk what?" enquired Clarabelle, having been left out of this particular conversation, due to Clarence's quick placement of a sound barrier between her and Fred.

"Nothing, my dear," he lied again. *Gosh that's two now - oh dear!* he thought. "So what's the plan with your Sarah then, Clar, now that she has the tarot sorted?" he asked, swiftly changing the subject from his ever increasing amount of untruths.

"Oh, you know, get her to practice every day - on herself first, then on others. Don't forget, my dear, it took her a whole month to understand the Angel cards, and the whole concept of them, so another two months for the tarot is really very good. Don't you think, Clarence?" she beamed, adding in, "I do!"

"Yes, dear," he smiled. "Very good."

"And how is Frieda coming along with her dreams, do you know?" she enquired. It was most important that Frieda's progress mirrored Sarah's own, and that she was facing her demons, albeit through her sleep! "Had an update from Miya yet?" she asked.

"Well yes ... Miya has already called in AA's Michael, Uriel and Raphael as reinforcements, not to mention Saint Germaine, you know the one? The chap with the 'Violet Flame'?" he asked questioningly.

"Oh yes, I know! He's very good, isn't he? Smashing!" she grinned. Saint Germaine had been put in charge of 'The Violet Flame' some time ago, and was doing a smashing job, in her opinion! He wrapped the violet light around negativity and the violet flame inside it just burned it all away; transmuting it and neutralising it beautifully! She was pleased that he'd been there to help poor Frieda. *Most kind, most kind!* she thought. "So, how's she getting on? Working is it? Coming to terms with it all, is she?"

"Hardly! Apparently, every time she gets to the dreams, she wakes herself up! We've been pushing, of course, pushing to keep her there, and each time we get a little further, but it's slow progress, Clar, very slow!"

"Well push harder!" she said firmly, her voice rising in volume and pitch with her passion, her zeal to see results. "Push as hard as you can, Clarence! Time is of the essence! She's not getting any younger you know, and if we've any hope of getting her to a happy ending sometime this century, we need to speed up. Quick smart!"

"Could try some memory joggers maybe? How about a film? They're always useful to trigger stuff. I shall have a think - yes, leave it with me, I shall come up with something!" he said firmly, then 'poof,' he was gone.

Chapter 8

She watched the end of the film with tears streaming down her face, understanding the message. Oh yes, she understood the message all too well! She was aware that most would not, and was glad for their ignorance.

She knew that the majority of the film's message would have passed them by, and she celebrated that they would not know what she knew. Most of those watching would never understand the beauty, or the accuracy in the script - they would not truly comprehend the story of 'The Butterfly Effect' - the hope or the damage, the irreparable damage that happened to those who had experienced *that* pain, *that* betrayal, that *immense* loss of innocence. How could she ever try to explain this kind of horror to those who had only ever known safety; the innocents who had never had these secrets thrust upon them at such an early age - an age so young, that they could not understand it themselves, let alone try to analyse or comprehend it; blanking out the unspeakable, the memory repressed, suppressed and hidden behind a wall so high that it was lost. But deep in the subconscious the mind knew better, the memory was not lost - it was hidden behind a wall of protection - as best it could; the mind holding back that wall in abeyance for another day, a day when the mind was older, more mature, could cope, would be stronger, could begin to deal with it and understand it. That day had come for Frieda when she was just fifteen years old ... the age when she had first become aware of sexuality, desire, sensuality, and how it *should* be ... the day she first, fully understood the horror of what *had* been ... the day the nightmares had started ... the flashbacks, the horror, the sickness ... the day the damage had really begun ... taking hold, and growing. ...

She had watched the film to its end. She'd watched its conclusion, and whilst knowing and seeing where it was heading, ever the optimist, she had hoped for a different outcome. *He had tried, the hero, tried so very hard in the film, with his ability to time travel, to change the shape of the future, and he had failed.* The film had started with four children being betrayed; betrayed in the most heinous way imaginable. Four children and their lost innocence, and he, the hero, the one with the blackouts, with no memory; he, the least damaged, on the surface, as he could not recall the horror of those memories. But the other three could, and they did. They recalled through their nightmares and their flashbacks - but not being able to tell, to share, to speak of such unspeakable horrors. But he was safe; safe within his walls of forgetfulness, of a memory repressed, of blankness. And the others? They envied him his lack of awareness, his lack of fear, his lack of knowledge; knowledge that children of seven and eight years old should not know, should not be aware of. But they did know. They knew, at such a tender age, the understanding of secrecy, of subversion, of perversion, and it was sad, it was a tragedy. It was mercifully a tragedy he knew nothing of, within the confines of his memory loss. The trauma so deep, so shocking, his mind could not comprehend, so chose not to; chose to close down, chose to forget, totally and absolutely, that which it should not know. ...

Frieda processed the film and its message. She couldn't possibly go to bed until she had got it out of her system, she would never sleep - well, not any kind of restful sleep that was sure! She considered the hero in the film and his lack of peace, or of any kind of solid relationship for him; no loving, lasting relationships whatsoever. He'd spent the entire film trying to find love, and failed. She shook her head sadly. It reflected the mirror of her own life so much so, that it was painful. The hero had been single, permanently single, for all of his adult life. He had wondered why everyone else around him came to settle down; to marry, to make a life, and yet he could not. He wanted to, oh, he wanted to so desperately, *that was very clear in the film,* and he could not understand why he was still unattached. The wrong girl perhaps? The wrong time perhaps? And as the years had gone by, he had begun to stop wondering why, and just accepted his aloneness. It was an aloneness that he wanted to change; he wanted to be part of something more, but did not know how.

As Frieda processed the film that she had just watched, the film and the lives of the characters in it, her life became so intertwined with theirs that she began to get confused where they ended and she began. Like the hero in the film, she knew that blankness, that void. She too had experienced the horror depicted in the film, and more; she too had kept the secrets buried far below, hiding them from everyone she knew or had ever known. And it hurt! God, how it hurt - even now, all these years later! Like the characters in the film, she too, had experienced those flashbacks; each and every one of all those sick memories rising to the surface, to torment, torture, enslave; and regularly so. Yes, she understood this film; she understood it all too well.

As she had watched the film, wanting so much to turn it off, but somehow unable to, it triggered something deep, deep inside her. Somehow, somewhere, something changed inside Frieda. This film, it touched her, and within that touch she began to see how she had grown to be who she had become, and with that growing awareness came the desire for change. She had read once, 'where there was life, there was hope.' For her, hope was to love and be loved ... to trust and to be trusted ... to be part and part of ... and to belong ... and that was the hardest ... to belong - for that was something she had never known, or understood, or even explored. How to belong?

Frieda processed some more as she made her way to bed. She reflected back on her aloneness, her distance from others, and her past. She had been married three times; each one ending in divorce - each time the marriages lasting just a few years. She had also been engaged three times, and each time it had been broken off. There had been countless lovers, countless attempts at love, and each one had failed, and failed miserably. Frieda felt the aloneness around her, wrapping around her like a blanket - a blanket of protection; protection that kept the world out, protection that said, 'stay away.' That blanket, she knew, had started out trying to keep her safe; safe from the pain of betrayal; keeping others out, and away - but now, now that blanket was just a prison - a prison that kept others out and her locked inside; locked deep inside with her aloneness.

She had never felt more alone than she did right now, in this moment of awakened awareness, awareness that watching this film had triggered. Awareness that screamed, 'change.' She was, she knew, just like the hero in the film, and always had been; locked away from love, and from the ability to build a trusting, loving relationship. It was beyond the high walls that she had built, and built well. The other side of an impenetrable wall of defence, the other side of a solid wall of mistrust, the other side of her deep and dark fear of betrayal. On this other side - this other side that she knew was there, that she could often see, but never hold, *well never hold properly, never hold tightly* - was 'belonging.' It slipped through her fingers, this 'belonging,' as if each and every finger on her hand had been greased with the strongest, purest lubricant possibly ever made. Her fingers had reached out to this deep intimacy of togetherness, oneness, closeness, many times, and yet each time she had managed to even touch it, before she could grasp it tightly, it had slipped away; far, far away from her reach - this elusive togetherness, yet again, denied.

She had never truly belonged, or really been part of anything! Nothing real, that was sure. *Is it possible that I can find this belonging?* she wondered. She knew that it was due to her mistrust, this deep inability to trust, that had caused so many relationships to fail. Could she find this part of her that was excluded - excluded from that belonging? Could she repair it, and her trust, and be able at last to connect fully with someone? She didn't know where it would reconnect, or to whom, but wouldn't it be wonderful? Frieda smiled quietly. *Maybe it's time?* she thought. Maybe she could finally let go and find a peace inside her, and maybe through that peace she could finally find that missing togetherness, that missing belonging.

Frieda made a decision there and then that it *was* time! "Tomorrow," she thought, as she fell asleep, tears still wet on her cheeks. And she fell into a void; a void full of dreams of tomorrow, of brighter days, of summer suns, of closeness and belonging all around her, and she reached out to it in her hope, for hope was all she had.

"I think not!" smiled Miya, watching her thoughtfully as she slept. "Only hope? You have me, my dear! And you have Sarah, your oldest friend, who is willing, ready and able, to show you the way to that belonging - with our help."

***

"So there we are, Clarence, it worked! It worked a treat!" Miya beamed at Clarence, happiness sparkling in her soft brown eyes. "Wonderful, just wonderful!" Miya was delighted. She really hadn't been at all sure this would work, no, not at all!

They were having another 'inter-angel-cy' meeting, high on Cloud 326 above Redville. Miya smiled at the gathered angels, thankful for their help. It had been a risk, she knew, but a risk that had paid off!

"Indeed," nodded Clarence. He was chuffed to bits that his plan had worked. He'd spent an age, an absolute age, deciding which film would be the best to trigger Frieda's desire for change. 'The Butterfly Effect' had been a massive success!

Clarabelle nodded happily too, grinning at Miya. She was so pleased for her friend, relieved that things were finally moving forward for them. She looked around her at the contented band of angels, sitting relaxing on Cloud 326. Several angels had gathered for the progress meeting, including some of the AA's - the Archangels. Uriel looked quite happy with himself, she noted, as did Michael. Both had been present throughout the 'watching of the film,' helping Frieda open up to the similarities and possibilities that it presented. She had watched Michael pouring courage, strength and love into Frieda as she'd watched the film; box of tissues on hand; whilst Uriel had been helping her to open up her emotions, and begin the task of bringing down her protective walls - another box of tissues!

"So she finally sees her defences," Michael grinned. "Finally sees the damage they are doing!"

"Yes," agreed Uriel, "and how they've been holding her back! Now she can begin to dismantle them."

"And, oh my, the fear coming off that girl all evening was intense, was it not?" Clarabelle exclaimed. "It pulsated all around her, in to the room and right up into the rafters in the roof! I had to go and call Saint Germaine to come in quick, to invoke the Violet Flame and neutralise it, before it spread out and contaminated half the county!"

"Yes, good job, Clar, good job," Clarence smiled. He'd watched it too, the dark cloud of fear emanating out of Frieda as she'd watched the film. "Better out than in, though, aye, Clar?" he grinned. "And about time too!"

All the angels laughed happily, congratulating themselves on a job well done.

"Now hang on a minute," Daniel, just arrived from 'upstairs,' dove in without hesitation. "What's with the celebrations? You've missed a bit, a rather large bit too! We haven't dealt with the other thing yet - the guilt thing! That's huge! You can't go celebrating when you've only done half a job!"

Silence fell over the group. They looked at each other, and then down to Redville, and Frieda's house. Sure enough, Daniel was right! Reluctantly, they could all see it. There it was, hiding in the basement of Frieda's house - another huge cloud of blackness; a cloud created from shame, blame, guilt and remorse, not to mention self-loathing, pulsating menacingly out of the dark shadow of negativity that hung heavily.

"Oh dear!" cried Clarabelle. "So we have! Oh me, oh my!"

"And if you guys want me to do my job - to sort out her love life and get her that 'belonging,' that she wants so badly, then *that*," - he pointed at the black shadow - "needs to go!" Blimey, did they think he was a miracle worker? Well yes, he was good, and yes, he could do the odd miracle here and there, but really? *I can't possibly sort out any romance for her with THAT hanging around,* he thought to himself. *Impossible, just impossible! I may be the angel of love and marriage for that lot downstairs, but even I'm not that good!*

"Perhaps Sarah could help with that one?" Clarabelle suggested, wondering if 'her Sarah' had the know-how to do the job.

"Yes, that could work!" Miya agreed. "Use the cards? Show her what she needs to see through the cards?"

"Maybe a few more dreams?"

"Yes!" they all said at once. "Yes!"

"Work to do!" Clarabelle chirped, and rushed downstairs to Sarah and 'The Cards'!

Chapter 9

Fred glared at Cassie with pure hatred. The cheek of her! He just couldn't get over it! *Who the bloody hell does she think she is? Not okay! Not okay at pigging all!*

"Oh, Fred, don't sulk!" she proclaimed happily, grinning a huge, wide grin, doing her best impression of the 'Cheshire Cat' from Alice in Wonderland; her totally favourite book! "We are the superior race, as well you know, and it is my job to work with Sarah and show her what's what; to use my expertise, my know-how, my knowledge, and my training skills - not yours!" Cassie purred loudly, revelling in her superiority. *Fred, help Sarah?* The very thought was enough to make her laugh out loud!

"But I can do it! I've been watching; I have, I have!" he barked. "And I've been here the longest!" Dog, he was so annoyed! "You've been here five minutes, five bloody minutes, and you're taking over the bloody world!" *Dog, I hate her sooo much! Aunty Clarabelle has always been the one to show Mum what's what, and now SHE's here, taking bloody over! Dog, it isn't right!* he declared to himself in disgust.

"And what, precisely, Fred, do you have, in the 'experience' stakes?" she asked, knowing the answer perfectly well.

"I can, umm ..."

"Yes?" she asked, practicing her 'claw showing clench' in full display of the stumbling Fred. "You can, umm ... what?"

Fred looked at the floor. *Dog, she was so annoying!* So okay, he couldn't read, not like she could, but he could look at pictures, and he could see the pictures on the Tarot cards. *I know what they say*, he thought, *but ... okay ... I don't actually understand them! Bollocks! Well, bollocks if I had any!* Dog, was he going to have to admit she could do something that he couldn't? *Dog, no! Never!*

Cassie looked at the bemused Fred with a smile. *Bless him!* she thought. *He's doing his best, but he hasn't lived six lifetimes like me;* six opportunities to learn, study, grow and gain knowledge. "Fred," she smiled, taking pity on the fumbling Fred, "you've had just the one lifetime, Flopsy, whilst I myself, have had six. And I *am* a black cat, which, of course, are simply *the* most aware, *the* most psychic, and *the* most amazingly magical, metaphysical cats on this planet! I know tarot, I know spirits, I know angels, and I know people," she declared triumphantly. "And ... I can read!" Fred looked at the floor, his bottom lip just beginning its tingle ready for the coming pout. Just to rub salt in the wound, she added, "and, I can read words, auras, chakras, energy, blocks, barriers, fears, hopes ... shall I go on?"

"I can read pictures!" he grumbled, seeing defeat looming. "And I know angels! I know lots of angels! And I can speak three languages; dog, human and angel, so there!" Fred's lower lip pouted fully now, as he pondered Cassie taking over as teacher to help Mum. "And what the hell is this 'Flopsy' business?" he growled. He was getting really, really annoyed now!

"Oh, Flopsy? You have floppy ears, my dear Fred, so I have decided that it's your new nickname. Now then, where was I, oh yes, showing you quite why there is no contest! I can speak eighteen languages you know, to your three, and that's just on this planet! And that doesn't include being able to converse, quite extraordinarily, with seventeen dimensions, and twenty other planets and their respective inhabitants, and that's just in this lifetime! I have lived across more than one hundred years. Still think you're the best person to help Ma, I mean Sarah?" She corrected herself quickly, wondering why she had even considered such a thing. To compare Sarah to Ma? Ridiculous!

"Flopsy? Bloody Flopsy! I don't think so, madam!" he barked in fury. *She's taking the bloody piss now! Flopsy indeed!* "I, I will have you know, am, 'Fred the Fantastic!' 'Fred the Magnificent!' Bloody 'Flopsy' indeed! And anyway, how do you know you've had six lifetimes and I've only had one? I may be on my one-hundredth for all you know!" But as he said it, he knew, somehow, that it wasn't true. She was right - this was his first lifetime, his *only* lifetime - but he had no idea why or how he knew that! *How strange! Dog, she's right! Bugger, she IS better than me! Dog-damn-it!*

Seraphina watched the two squabbling and sighed. Really, this was getting a bit much! *I thought they'd accepted each other now, made friends even?* But this thing with Cassie helping Sarah had made Fred jealous. She could feel the energy of inferiority and inadequacy within him, created by Cassie; his poor little ego severely dented. She honed in on Cassie, feeling for her energy. *Oh yes, far too superior that one,* she decided. *This relationship is way too unequal! Now then, what can I do to equalise things between these two?* she wondered. *Ah-ha! I have it!* And she popped upstairs to the first floor to have a little word in her ward's tiny ear. "Angelica, my dear, are you there?" she called. "Shall we play?" she grinned, a naughty twinkle sparking in her eye.

***

Angelica was busy. She didn't have time for Sephi right now! She loved her angel to bits but she was far too involved with playing 'dolls.'

"Sit still, Molly!" she commanded, her tone bossy and authoritarian. "No sliding down in the pram now, do you hear? Now, don't be naughty, Molly!" she scolded, chatting away to the plastic doll, totally absorbed in her imaginary world, as only a six year old can be. It had been her and David's birthday last week and she had been given the most exquisite doll that she had ever, in her whole, entire life, seen! Molly was a full size baby doll, dressed in a beautiful pink satin dress, with bows and little ribbons sewed into it. She also came with a tiny baby-grow-romper-suit in the most beautiful cerise; her bedtime outfit. It even had a little hood so that the doll's head didn't get cold! The doll's tiny mouth smiled, her eyes watered when she cried, and if she pressed her belly, Molly chortled. Little blonde curls spouted from her head and her little hands clenched a feeding bottle. Angelica was smitten! "Now what have I told you, Molly? No sliding!" she glared, stopping the pram abruptly, forgetting all about her 'smitten-ness' of her wonderful doll in her annoyance!

Seraphina smiled, watching the child play. Children's imaginations were just so beautiful!

"Right oh, madam," Angelica firmly said, mimicking Sarah perfectly, "off to bed for you!" The doll had slid half-way down the pram as she'd been pushed, due to Angelica wheeling her around the bedroom so enthusiastically. "No more play for you, you little minx," she declared. "You've been naughty! Again! Off to bed!" She pulled Molly from the pram by the doll's elbow, and carried her to the toy cot that lay beside her own bed. "Bed!" she said firmly. The doll was plonked, unceremoniously into the cot, and Angie sat down on her own bed with a loud, "humph." She folded her arms crossly, stamping her feet on the soft carpet beneath her in frustration.

"I do hope you can learn a little patience before you have your own children," Sephi grinned, tickling her playfully.

Angelica smiled at Sephi, immediately calming down. "Wanna play, Sephi?" she asked hopefully. She loved playing with her angel, just loved it! She mainly loved the way Sephi's long auburn hair fell right down to her waist, covering half of her small, dainty frame. Sometimes, she'd let her play with it, plaiting it and making it pretty. Seraphina's halo always shone brightly around her sweet face; and her eyes, the deepest blue of the ocean, always sparkled. They were sparkling now, with anticipation, and a hint of naughtiness!

"Aren't you going to tuck her in?" Sephi enquired. "She doesn't look very comfy there, hun?"

Angelica jumped up immediately, tucking the doll under the soft sheet with a, "There! She's asleep now; look, Sephi, her eyes are tight shut!"

The dolls eyes were indeed 'tight shut,' as they always were whenever the doll was placed horizontally, but Sephi knew that Angelica didn't know that. "Yes," she agreed, "she's fast asleep. Well done, Angelica, great job!"

"So, you wanna play then?" the child asked sweetly.

"Why don't you play with Cassie, hun? You haven't played with her for an age. That would be nice, don't you think?" Sephi grinned at the child, trying not to giggle. She had a plan and was quite sure that it was very naughty - but necessary!

"Cassieeeeeeeeeeeeeee!" Angelica immediately yelled. "Oh, Cassieeeeeee, come and play!"

Dutifully, Cassie ran up the stairs to Angelica's room in response to the screeched call to play. "Yes, dear, you called?" she smiled. Really, it was such a relief to remove herself from Fred's presence - he was just such a grump!

Angelica looked at the empty pram, and then at the 'naughty Molly,' tucked up in bed. She wanted to play 'prams'! She looked at Cassie and suddenly a new thought occurred (with a bit of help from Sephi!) - it would be a wonderful idea to use the cat, instead of the doll, so that she could resume playing 'prams'! "Cassie, come to Mummy, Cassie!" she squealed, delighted with her new idea.

Cassie looked at Angelica in horror. "You have got to be kidding me!" she screeched, or tried to, but for some strange reason, she couldn't speak, and neither could she move! She was paralysed! Again!

Sephi smiled happily, watching Angelica with delight as she picked up the cat and plonked her into the pram. She sped around the room with her, doing wheel spins for effect. Only the cat's eyes spoke her disgust - the rest of her could not move, not a single muscle!

And then (with another bit of help from Sephi,) Angelica had a second idea. "Now, where does Mummy put her scissors?" Angelica sped off to her mother's room and the 'banned nail scissors.' She wasn't allowed in her mummy's room, and she certainly wasn't allowed near nail scissors, but she had had an idea, and it was perfect! *Mummy's downstairs looking at her silly cards again, she'll never know!* Ten minutes later, the doll's bright cerise baby-grow-romper-suit had two new holes cut expertly into its hood and another one cut into its backside - it was ready!

Cassie was dressed carefully; her two front legs were pulled through the arms of the brightly coloured baby-grow, her back legs shoved into the legs, then her tail was shoved through the hole in the bum! The buttons were done up carefully, and then, the 'piece de resistance,' the hood was pulled up and over the cat's head. Angelica surveyed her masterpiece. "Oops!" she declared, "I forgot the ears!" She reached her tiny fingers into the hood, pulling out Cassie's black ears one by one through the holes that she had cut out. One black furry, angry ear, now poked out through each hole, setting off the brightness of the pink just perfectly! Angelica stood back to admire her handiwork. "Perfect!" she announced, and proceeded to go back to her 'Brands Hatch' race track with the cat and the pram.

Just then, she had another brainwave! "Oh, Freddieeeeeeeeeeeeeeee!" she called. "Come to Mama, Freddieeeeeeeeeeeeeeeee!" she yelled. Fred came lolloping up the stairs to see what 'Madam' wanted, and just could not believe his eyes when he plodded into the room!

"Oh, my Dog!" he screeched, falling over in hysterics. "Oh, my bloody Dog!" Fred fell about laughing hysterically for at least ten minutes. Cassie looked beyond ridiculous, sitting in the pram in the bright pink romper-suit!

She scowled at him in disgust. "Do ... not ... say ... a ... single ... word!" she growled menacingly. "Not ... one ... single ... word!" Cassie's voice had come back, although she noted with disgust that she was still unable to move and, therefore, unable to save herself from this humiliation! "Argh!" she cried, pitifully. "Just ... argh!"

"Oh, my Dog! I gotta get me a photo of this!" he yelled, delightedly. "This is bloody classic! Just classic!" and he ran down the stairs to the kitchen table. Grabbing Mum's mobile phone from the top of it, he held it in his jaws carefully as he ran back upstairs as fast as his legs could carry him. "Quick, Anj, take a pic!" he grinned, pushing the phone at her. "She looks ... lovely!" and burst into more hysterical laughter. Seeing Angelica click photo after photo, he was crying now, he was laughing so much. "Stop it, stop it, I'm gonna pee myself," he howled. "This is *the* best; the totally *bestest* photo, in the whole, wide, world! Ever!"

Cassie's lamented cries of humiliation went completely unnoticed, by either Angelica or the hysterical Fred!

Angelica suddenly (with yet another bit of help from Sephi!), had another idea! "Yes, perfect!" she grinned, running back to Mummy's room at speed. Two minutes later she returned with Sarah's make-up bag clutched in her excited hands. "Sit!" she commanded, looking at Fred expectantly. "Sit, Freddie!" And Fred sat! Unbelievably, he sat! For some strange reason, he was unable to disobey, ignore her, or to run!

Sephi smiled happily. "Strike two!" she grinned.

Fred could not believe what was happening to him. As Cassie looked on, at first suspiciously, and then delightedly, a disgusted Fred was 'made-up' in full make-up. Bright red lipstick was applied to his mouth, blue sparkly eyeshadow gleamed above his eyes (right up to his eyebrows), pink blusher was applied to his cheeks (by the shovel load), and then, the humiliation of humiliations - his ears were tied up high above his head with a pink scrunchy! "OH, MY DOG!" he howled. "OH, MY BLOODY DOG!"

Now it was Cassie's turn to fall about in hysterical laughter. For some strange reason, movement had come back to her limbs (with a bit of help from Sephi), and she fell about in the pram, screaming with laughter at the disgruntled Fred. Paws in the air, she was on her back laughing, tears streaming down her furry cheeks, as she looked with delight at the disgusted Fred.

"Yeah, babe, don't shit it!" Fred barked. "You ain't in no position to be laughing at me, babe, not with that pink suit on!" And then it came - the photograph! "Oh, my Dog, oh, my bloody dog!" he screamed, "No, no photo, no evidence, noooooooooooooooo!"

But it was done ... despite the protestations; the camera lens clicked, and clicked, and clicked. Photo after photo was taken, and more, and more, and more! Angelica studied the photos in delight, extremely happy with her handiwork, as both pets sat, still unable to escape. "No, not quite done!" she announced firmly. Picking Cassie up from out of the pram, she placed her next to Fred on the floor. "Smile for the camera, Cassie," she grinned, "and you, Fred," and proceeded to take more photos of the two pets together, side-by-side; gathering even more evidence of their joint, total humiliation, evidence that would stay engrained in the Brown household - to be printed off and placed forever on the fridge door, for all to see!

Sephi was laughing, watching the scene, waiting for Angelica to finish. Finally the six year old was done.

"Now then, you two," Sephi grinned, directing her lecture at the two warring pets, "Now, who is the most important, mmm?" She watched them hang their heads in shame. "Yes, precisely, I think not! Now, you are both as bad as each other, and both as good as each other, yes?" She turned the large mirror on the wall to face the pets, so that they could get a good look at their mutual humiliation, and sure enough, as they glared into it, they both knew that they looked as ridiculous as each other. "Quits?" she asked, a huge smile on her face.

"Quits!" they both agreed sullenly.

"Perfect!" Sephi grinned. "Perfect!" She smiled at Angelica, placing a thought into her little mind. Seconds later, it had the desired result. (Well, she couldn't leave them looking like that for too long, someone had to rescue them!).

"Mum... come and see what I done!" Angie yelled, "Come an' see Freddie and Cassie, Mum! Mummmmmmmm. ..."

"Oh, Dog!" mumbled Fred.

"Indeed!" agreed Cassie.

Chapter 10

Simon sat at the kitchen table grinning. Every time he looked over to the fridge, and *that* photo, he just couldn't help himself. Fred looked ridiculous; it was the look on his face that was even funnier than the hair/ears and make-up! Priceless! He ruffled Fred's fur playfully. "Never mind, Fred, aye?" he grinned. "The little minx did it to me once, when I was sleeping - woke up to a full-face make-up job, mate, wasn't pretty I can tell you!"

Fred smiled. He remembered! It was the Christmas before last, when Dad had been home from work for a few days.

"What happened?" Cassie asked, curious to know. She hadn't been here for that Christmas and hated to be kept out of the loop.

"Oh, you know, the usual at Christmas time. He'd had a bit too much of the sparkly fizzy stuff and had dozed off in the chair. Mum said he was pissed, whatever that is! Anyway, where was I? Oh yes, well anyway, she was busy in the kitchen, and Angelica had had some play make-up for a Christmas present. While everyone was snoring, she used the peace and quiet to learn and perfect her make-up technique, on Dad! Dog, that was funny!" Fred was giggling away to himself quite happily, until he remembered, and saw the photo of himself on the fridge door. His giggles stopped abruptly!

"Don't worry about it, Fred," Simon grinned, "It happens to us all, mate," and ruffled his head some more.

Fred always thought Dad was really soft with him when he petted him, despite his large 6'4" frame. His hands were like shovels, but they were always gentle. He had blonde, floppy hair that Mum was always stroking, for some strange reason. He'd often see her pushing it gently away from his blue eyes, and then she'd kiss him, again!

He turned to Cassie, chatting away, now that they were friends. "They're always kissing, those two - no idea why, mind you, but they seem to like it," he said to his new pal, authority that he was, on the subject of 'Mum and Dad.' Mum was smaller than Dad, a lot smaller! She was only 5'4", so a foot shorter! She'd reach up on her tippy toes and kiss Dad, craning her neck to be able to reach. He'd help, mind you - bend down to help, cos he's like that, is Dad, helpful you know!

Cassie nodded her head thoughtfully. Yes, she'd seen it too. Always kissing they were! A nice couple. She liked Sarah, she liked her a lot! Simon was alright too, for a bloke!

"And Dad strokes her hair too," Fred was saying, curling up against Cassie as they sat on the floor of the kitchen together, the new comradery between them building nicely. "Look, he's doing it again!"

Dad was indeed, stroking Mum's hair, again!

"They seem to like hair, these humans, don't you think, Fred?" she asked, rubbing up against him. "They're either stroking each other's hair, or they're stroking us!" She studied Sarah a bit closer, noting that she was a dress size eleven (although she may be pushing a twelve). She had soft turquoise eyes, chestnut hair that fell to just below her chest and she was really, very pretty. "Yes, I like it here, Fred, you're right, they are a happy couple aren't they? And the stroking is good too, very good!"

And both pets dozed off, content in their new friendship, and in their home.

***

Sarah studied the cards again. She was ready. It was time! She had no idea what that meant, but she had a strong feeling that something important was about to go down. "Ah well, enough for now," she sighed, putting the cards back in their pack. "Frieda will be here soon, so best put kettle on. And it's not like I'm going to need them for her!"

Her friend was coming over for dinner and she was looking forward to the evening. It had been an age since they'd spent a whole evening together. *Bit of 'girlie' time will be good,* Sarah thought. Simon was away on business overnight; a conference to do with the banking world, so she had the house to herself. She wasn't sure if Frieda was staying over, but had bought a few bottles of wine in, just in case. If she wanted to stay, Frieda's children were old enough now to be left, without the need of calling in babysitters, so they could play it by ear. Her eldest was twenty-five, the others, twenty and eighteen; adults now. Frieda had a new independence that she'd never known before; unlike Sarah, whose twins had just turned six. Sarah felt for her friend; she knew that she was lonely, especially now that her children were grown. Her eldest was preparing to move out, getting ready to go and live with her boyfriend, and Sarah was sure that the other two wouldn't be far behind her. Frieda had had all her children young; the results of a series of failed marriages - three divorces before she was thirty, with a child from each short marriage. After that, there had been a series of boyfriends through her thirties, three of whom she had even got engaged to, but all three relationships had failed, long before any altars were walked down. Now, since she'd turned forty, Frieda seemed to have given up on men. *Too many dents to her heart, maybe?* Sarah wondered, but thought, *probably not, Frieda's made of rubber - she always bounces back!* It was still sad that she was single, though, and a little surprising. Frieda was so loving, bubbly and warm; and she was so incredibly sexy! She loved men, and it was just a shock that she was still single at forty-six! *That's nine years now, since she's had a boyfriend! Wow!* Sarah was bemused. With that, the doorbell rang and Sarah went to open it.

"Hi, hun, I'm here, where do you want me?" Frieda grinned. "Kitchen or lounge, story-time or wine-time?"

"Oh, wine-time, if you're staying," Sarah laughed. "The kids are asleep, so no story-time tonight; I put them to bed early so that we can relax. Dinners on, come on in. White or red?" And the friends settled down for their 'girlie' night.

Dinner had been lovely. The steak was perfect, the dessert a delight, and the wine had flowed, straight down their necks! Both girls were a little drunk as the evening went on, and just as Sarah was deciding that she'd had enough, Frieda produced a bottle of brandy from her bag. "Ta-da!" she giggled, holding the bottle up triumphantly. "Glasses, madam, if you please!" she laughed.

"Oh God, not for me, hun," Sarah said, shaking her head. "I've had enough. I'm gonna get myself some water; I got to be up at stupid-o'clock in the morning with the twins, mate. You go ahead though, Frie; I'll get you a glass. Do you want coke or something to go in it?"

"Nope, just neat, ta!" she beamed.

This isn't like her, Sarah thought. *Hardly ever see Frie drinking the hard stuff! Hope she's okay?*

But Frieda wasn't okay. She was far from okay! She'd had horrific dreams again last night - *that's three this week,* she thought to herself. *Ridiculous!* Maybe a reading could help her figure out how to get rid of them and get some bloody sleep! She'd come to the conclusion that all these dreams were somehow related to 'the stupid cards' and had made the decision earlier in the day to let Sarah do 'the stupid reading' (anything was worth a go), and she was shitting herself! The brandy was for 'Dutch Courage' to get her through 'the silly thing,' as she saw it.

Clarabelle and Miya squealed with delight, sitting on top of the mantelpiece watching the girls.

"She's going for it! Oh, how wonderful, she's actually going for it!" they exclaimed.

"She said she would, after the last dream I gave her last night, but I didn't think she'd go through with it!" Miya said happily.

"Ooh, better get Sarah to sober up quick!" Clarabelle declared, flying into the kitchen in haste.

Sarah was standing by the kitchen sink drinking a large glass of water when Clarabelle appeared, perched on top of the kettle. "More water, Sarah," she declared excitedly. "Much more water! You've got work to do!"

"Aye?" Sarah looked bemused. "Work?"

"Oh yes indeed, work!" the angel beamed. "Frieda is going to ask for a reading, my dear, and you'd better be ready! Quick smart, ready!"

Over the next hour, as the girls chatted, Sarah managed to drink several large glasses of water, one for each of the very large brandies that Frieda was necking down, doing her best to sober up, just in case Clarabelle was right.

Frieda felt the anaesthetising calmness of the brandy within her and eyed the small, round table in the corner of the lounge with less trepidation. She could see the Tarot cards sitting in its centre and felt for the knot in her stomach; it had gone! Or if it hadn't gone, she certainly couldn't feel it! She couldn't feel anything - thank God, for brandy! "So when did the table appear then, hun?" she asked, nodding towards the new table in the corner of the room.

"Oh, that! Yes, Simon got it for me last week. I was doing the cards in the kitchen, but with the noise from the dishwasher, and with the pets in there, the noise of the kettle boiling, all that, you know - it just wasn't working very well. I thought it might be better to do it in here; bit quieter, so Si got me that table. Looks nice doesn't it?" she grinned. "I love it!"

The new table stood proudly, its wood gleaming, the candle light flickering from the room bouncing off its shiny surface. Frieda had to admit, it was a lovely piece of furniture. "So how are you getting on with these cards then, hun? Any good?" she asked nervously.

Sarah eyed her friend carefully. *Is she interested now?* she wondered. "Yes, great," she replied, adding in cautiously, "why, do you want a go?"

Frieda laughed nervously; trying her best to hide it, she sucked her teeth and grinned, "Oh, go on then, why not! It'll be a giggle!"

Sarah looked at Clarabelle in surprise, although she didn't know why! Her angel was never wrong; she had said earlier that Frieda would want a reading but as the evening had gone on, and Frieda had got more pissed, she herself had doubted it. But seems not, seems Clarabelle was right, again! "Come on then, girlie, let's do it!" she smiled, feeling somewhere, deep inside, that this reading was going to be very, very important!

Miya stood nervously, Clarabelle too, both watching Sarah take her place at the table, and a half-drunk Frieda join her on the other side, sitting down on the small chairs that were placed either side of it.

Cassie had been called, and was ready. She watched

Frieda carefully, noting the darkness around her stomach and chest. *Oh yes indeed, those chakras are well and truly blocked, and the negative emotional energy trapped in her belly is just unbelievable!* she thought to herself.

Sarah shuffled the cards; closing her eyes, she connected as Clarabelle had taught her. She cleansed the cards and then drew down the energy that she needed to fill them. Opening her eyes, she handed them to Frieda, saying, "Close your eyes Frie; hold the cards, feel them, shuffle them, focus all your intention on them. That's right ... now, I want you to just, 'intend.' Ask questions in your mind; anything you want, 'intending' that the cards give you the answers that you need. If you don't know what to ask, just say, 'anything I need to know' and the cards will know what to do."

"How do the cards know?" Frieda asked. "They're just cards!"

"It's your soul, hun, your soul knows what you need and directs the right cards into your fingers." She watched Frieda concentrate, moving the cards between her fingers.

"And you can talk to my soul?" Frieda asked in surprise, wondering what she'd let herself in for!

"Yes, hun, but only when I'm tuned into you like this. You here, sitting at this table for a reading, it kind of gives me permission to talk to your soul, and maybe your loved ones too, if they are near, and lots of other things." As she said this, she was aware, suddenly, of Miya's presence, and of a man; a youngish man, standing nearby. She was also aware, as she tuned deeper into Frieda's energy, of a heavy tension within her belly, and of a darkness.

She looked at Clarabelle questioningly, but before her angel had a chance to reply, Cassie piped up, "Fear, my dear, lots of! It will all become clear as you begin."

Sarah stared at the cat in amazement.

"It's fine, my dear Sarah, I am only here to help," she grinned. "Tell her about her angel, go on ..." and grinned some more.

"Frie, you have a beautiful angel standing next to you. Her name is Miya, and she is always with you." Sarah said, rather blown away by the energy before her. Miya's light was incredibly bright, and she could feel waves of love coming off her towards Frieda.

"Get away!" Frieda scoffed. "Angel indeed! You're the one with the angels, lady, not me!" She looked to her left, then to her right, despite her protestations of disbelief, and then back at Sarah. "So, what do I do now?" she asked. "Pick some?"

"Yes please," Sarah smiled, adding, "and just place them face down on the table, wherever you want to put them. You can put cards on top of each other, under, over, in groups, whatever you want to do. I just want you to pick the ones you feel that you want, and put them where you want - without looking at the pictures, Frie!"

Frieda was just turning the cards over to look at the pictures on them when Sarah told her this, so she turned them back over to the blank side as instructed. Slowly, she started to pick random cards from the pack, placing them on the table. It was weird! But somehow, it felt right. ...

Miya, Clarabelle and Cassie watched intently. The angels, pouring love and reassurance into Frieda; the cat, pouring information into Sarah! It had begun!

Chapter 11

The first dream had begun last night as soon as her head had hit the pillow, followed by another two in the early hours of the morning. Frieda has woken up shaking, nauseous and afraid, after each and every one of them. Each time, she had run to the bathroom and thrown up; each time, she had had a huge panic attack straight after; and each time, she had prayed for resolution. She didn't know to whom she prayed (she didn't really believe), but at times like these, pray she indeed did!

The dreams were the same ones they always were; images of playing with the man; of him being her 'special friend,' of him tickling her, cuddling her, of her increasingly growing trust in him; trust that grew month by month, until it was totally and completely absolute. It had taken months, many months, for the trust to be where he wanted it to be, for the grooming to be complete, before the abuse began. First, inappropriate touching - but little Frieda did not know that it was inappropriate - because the man had told her that this was what 'special friends' do, and she trusted him, she believed him. So she let him, even when it didn't feel nice, and as time went on, even when it felt awful. She let him because he was her 'special friend' and she loved him. She still believed him when it became painful, when it hurt, and it hurt a lot. She still believed him when he told her it was 'their little secret,' and that 'no one must know,' that she 'must never tell.' She still believed him when it made her bleed, she still believed him right up to the day it stopped ... the day it all ended ... the day the hurt stopped and the pain began ... the day she found her daddy hanging in the garage.

He blamed himself, his suicide note had said. It was his fault, it said. And in his mind, it was. It was his fault that his darling little girl had been put through such horrendous abuse for over two years; abuse at the hands of his closest friend; a friend whom he had trusted, and trusted without question, without hesitation; a friend with whom he regularly and happily left his innocent, beautiful six year old daughter.

The police had come last night with photographs; photographs depicting the most horrific abuse on young girls - many girls - and his darling Frieda was one of those girls; the youngest of the victims of the paedophile ring that his 'best friend' ran. He had been beside himself with grief, with loss, with remorse, with guilt, with shame and blame and anger; so much anger! He wanted to kill him, the man; to rip him from limb to limb, to castrate him, to punish him, to make him suffer, and suffer in the most horrific way imaginable. But the police had told him that the man was already in custody, along with the rest of the ring, and that there would be no need to put Frieda through the trauma of a trial because they had enough evidence without her testimony. The men had already signed confessions, they said, and were pleading guilty, so no messy trial to put any of the survivors of the abuse through.

He should have been pleased, he knew, pleased the man had been caught, but his anger was so all-consuming, so all-powerful and now it had nowhere to go. He couldn't lash out at the man, he couldn't kill him slowly and painfully as he wanted to; he, along with his buddies were all already in custody, safe from his wrath behind prison bars. The anger palpitated around him like an earthquake, shaking him to his core. His anger, his rage, building, building ... and instead of going outwards, out to sweet release ... it went inwards, in to himself. If he hadn't met him, befriended him, trusted him; if ... if ... if ... then his poor Frieda would never have been exposed to this horror.

The detective explained to him how this man had befriended many men, just like him, all with young daughters, and that he had, in fact, groomed the fathers almost as much as he had groomed the children. They said it wasn't his fault, then they had left, taking the disgusting photographs with them; and Frieda's father was left with his pain, his rage, his guilt and his utter self-loathing. He went to his man-shed, his garage; and he drank, and he drank, trying to obliterate the rage, the pain, the hurt, the incredible guilt - but it would not go. It built and it built until he could take no more. In his blinding rage, his blinding pain, he took the tow-rope from its hook, tied it without hesitation from the rafters above, and pulled it into a noose. He stood on the empty box of beer cans with the noose around his neck and threw himself to the floor, breaking his neck in three places instantly.

His wife found him, several hours later. Already in shock from what she had learned earlier in the evening, already hanging on by a thread, she collapsed in a hysterical heap of grief. Her screams awakened the sleeping Frieda, who, following the sounds of her mother's screams, ran to the garage and witnessed the scene of horror before her.

The same dream played over and over for Frieda. If she wasn't dreaming about 'the man,' which she often did, she was dreaming about seeing her father's dead body hanging from the rafters; his neck at a twisted, unrecognisable angle, and her mother's lamenting screams. Her mother had, somehow, managed not to have a total mental breakdown and had, somehow, found the strength in her to keep going, for Frieda's sake. Somewhere, deep inside her, she found the strength to get through that horrific night; to survive, so that she could support her daughter, help her, heal her, be there for her … and she had been doing just that ever since.

Frieda blamed herself for her father's death and for her mother's pain. She always had, and she always would. If she had told … if she had said … if she had … if only … if … if. …

Frieda pulled herself away from the awful memories, and the awful dreams, and refocused. She looked at her closest friend, as close as she'd ever let anyone in, since those childhood days, and she looked at the cards on the table before her; and she prayed, she prayed like never before, "Please, please help me. ..."

And Miya, and Clarabelle, and Cassie, and the whole host of angels and Archangels standing in readiness next to her smiled. "But, of course," they said, "but, of course!"

***

Sarah slowly turned each card over, being careful not to move them from their position. The energy was building as she touched each of the cards that Frieda had laid down, and with each increasing atom that linked within that energy, Sarah was washed with a wave of pain and sadness; a tidal wave of guilt, grief, terror, disgust and shame. She looked up from the cards and at Frieda in alarm, and shock. Frieda was looking at the cards, fear clearly evident on her face. Sarah returned her focus to the cards quickly, careful to hide her shock for fear of frightening her friend even further. She looked at Clarabelle and Cassie questioningly. They both nodded solemnly, indicating that she should continue.

"Trust what you feel, my dear," Clarabelle whispered, nodding to the cloud of dark energy that was pulsing around Frieda, quite clear to Sarah now.

"Trust what you see," Cassie spoke quietly, nodding to the cards.

Sarah continued to turn the cards, and with each one, her awareness grew. With each one, she could see more. The cards spoke, and they spoke loudly; within their silence, they spoke volumes. She saw the past, she saw the present, she saw the immediate future, and now, as she turned the last few over, she could see the longer-term future. She looked up at her friend and smiled gently; a warm, compassionate, understanding smile. A smile that said, trust me. A smile that said, it's going to be alright. And then she began. ...

"These three in the centre, Frie; the ones you've put together in this middle of this outer circle that you've made; these are the 'right now' cards. They overlap each other, which means that they are all affecting each other, they link. The middle one there, the Tower, means that things are coming to a head. It can look scary, it can feel scary, but it is actually really good. It means that all the stuff that has been crap is collapsing, falling away. It can appear to be destructive, but, in fact, it enables you to begin to build something bigger, better, stronger, more stable. The other two cards either side of it; the Death card and the Ten of Swords, they show pain, sorrow, suffering, and it all ending." She looked at Frieda carefully, and continued. "The cards show much suffering, Frie, but they indicate that the suffering is going to end - to die. Do you see?"

Frieda said nothing, just stared at the cards, a glazed look in her eye.

"Give her the Angel cards, Sarah," commanded Clarabelle, pushing the pack towards her. "She needs both, my dear."

"Yes, add some meat on the bones," Cassie agreed emphatically.

Sarah handed Frieda the Angel pack, asking her to

shuffle, and again to pick some cards. "Can you just pick one or two of them for me, Frie, and place them on top of those three Tarot cards in the middle."

It was like she was talking to a robot! Frieda did not respond, or look at her. Instead she just silently took the pack that Sarah handed her, shuffled it, and quietly took the first two cards from the top, placing them over the centre three cards. Archangel Gabriel smiled up from the face of the card, along with Archangel Uriel.

"Can I have another?" Frieda asked, without looking at Sarah. Somehow, she could not meet her eyes. "I feel like I want one more; I don't know why."

"Yes, of course, pick another." Sarah smiled at her friend, although Frieda could not see that smile, so intent was she on her focus on the cards in her hands.

Frieda chose one from the middle, placing it next to the other two Angel cards. Archangel Michael stared up at her. 'Strength,' it said. 'Courage,' it said. 'You are not alone, I am with you,' it said.

Sarah stared at the cards in surprise. *Wow, three Archangel cards in a row! Blimey, there's some stuff going on here!* she thought. She looked at Frieda carefully, beginning to explain their meaning. "Frie, Archangel Michael is with you to give you the courage that you need, in order to deal with what needs to be dealt with ... Archangel Gabriel is here because you need help with communication - there is something, Frie, something really important that you need to talk about, and it's *really* important that you open yourself up and trust, to talk, to share; something that you need to speak about." Sarah's words were coming fast, quick, and they felt like they weren't coming from her mind, or from her thoughts. They felt like they were coming 'through' her, rather than 'from' her. She looked at Clarabelle once again, looking for reassurance that she was doing okay.

"And indeed they are, my dear," Clarabelle smiled. "You are quite right! Those thoughts are not coming from you but through you. You are channelling information from above, from The Higher Realms, and you must trust this information, Sarah. Just say what you feel, speak the truth that pours through you now."

Cassie was nodding her head in agreement. "Just keep going, Sarah; you're doing great," she reassured.

"So what does *he* mean, this Uriel chap?" Frieda asked, still not moving her eyes from the cards. "If this Michael is for strength, what is this 'Uriel' for?"

"Archangel Uriel is the angel for emotional healing, Frie. He is an Archangel and is very powerful; they all are. You clearly need that power to help you let go, or get over something that hurts you inside. Basically, these cards are saying that there is some deep shit going on with you, my friend, and it's time for it all to come out!"

Frieda lifted her gaze from the cards and looked at Sarah directly, straight into her eyes. The pain was clearly visible, and Sarah almost recoiled from its ferocity. *What the hell is going on with her?* she wondered. *She tells me everything, always has, and I don't have a clue what this is about! What on earth is she hiding?*

"So what are these others then? What do these mean?" Frieda questioned, pointing to the circle of Tarot cards she had placed around the centre ones. Each faced up; each meant something different but she didn't know what. She looked at Sarah again, waiting for her to explain.

"This one, the Four of Swords; this means you will soon be able to find some peace, some stability. It means respite from problems. This one - the Six of Swords - this means better times are ahead. That one, the Nine of Swords, is deception, shattered confidence. Blimey, Frie, there are a lot of swords here for you!" she smiled, looking carefully at Frieda for any reaction. There was none. "And a lot of cups!" Sarah looked back at the cards, continuing to explain them to her seemingly frozen friend. "The Ace of Cups inverted, means lost love and despair. The Three of Cups next to it, also upside down, says there has been sex without love, exploitation, and a loss of trust. And the Knight of Cups means deviousness and fraud, also upside down; see?" She looked at Frieda carefully. Frieda's eyes were still on the cards. "Frie, there are a lot of cards upside down here, hun, and a lot of them are saying the same thing, but in different ways. These cards indicate that you have been betrayed and hurt; that trust has been broken and that it has broken you, and broken you badly, hun. These cards are of misery, exploitation, desolation, pain and grief - they are all saying that you are broken inside, hun, and the cards in the middle are saying that NOW is the time to fix that which is broken. Talking about it seems to be key, hence Gabriel; and that you will need strength to face this lot, hence Michael. And that Uriel will help you heal. Do you see, hun?"

Frieda looked up from the cards slowly, staring intently into her friend's eyes. She looked back at the cards, not sure what to say or do.

"But let's look at these now, Frie. These cards here,

further along the circle, are showing the outcome, the result, if you go down this healing path - if you let all the shit out! Look, we have the Two of Cups, showing partnership, and the Eight of Cups, which shows change, good change! That card is about breaking ties, and that one there, that's the Ten of Cups – that's the 'happy ever after' card. *The* best card in the pack, as far as I'm concerned. It's about love; real love, commitment and belonging."

At the word belonging, Frieda's eyes lit up, briefly, then the light went back out. Sarah looked at her carefully. She had used the word 'belonging,' and it had clearly got a reaction out of Frie, so it was important. *Belonging? But that isn't on the pack, it isn't in the book and isn't written into my notes at all! Wonder why I said belonging?* she wondered. *Mind you, the Ten of Cups is about perfect union, perfect love, so I guess belonging is part of that,* she concluded. "We've also got," she continued, concentrating hard on the cards before her, "The Chariot, which is all about success, triumph over adversity; and we have the Wheel of Fortune, which is all about destiny, signalling a new cycle, fresh start, kind of thing. The last card there is Judgement. That's a great card, Frie! It's all about rebirth, absolution - hang on a mo ..." Sarah leaned over to get the Tarot book from the book shelf, opening it to the Judgement card page. "Listen, Frie, I got to read you this bit, you listening?" Sarah felt quite excited, although she didn't know why.

Frieda nodded, looking at Sarah closely.

" 'Judgment in a reading'," Sarah read, " 'urges the querant to move away from the belief that you (or others) have committed a sin and are ultimately a bad person.' Hang on, there's another bit I got to read, wait... here it is, 'put the past behind us, be ready and willing to start afresh ... we can move on and in a sense, be reborn' - hey, that's just the same as the other card, reborn thing ... where was I? Oh yes, 'and then this feeling of absolution can push us towards a specific path, very often one which we dared not follow previously.' See, that's a great card, Frie!"

Frieda looked at the cards and back at Sarah. She was confused! "So, umm ... can you just go through that again, hun. So what does it mean?" she asked.

"Basically, Frie, it means you got to talk about whatever it is that's in there," Sarah pointed at Frieda's heart, "and there," pointing at Frieda's belly, "and in there," Sarah was now pointing to Frieda's lower stomach, "and in there!" The last point was to Frieda's head. "It's all got to come out, hun, and whilst this is gonna be shit to deal with, whatever it is - I can see that, mate - sorry ... and it's shit with a capital 'S'! There's no doubt that this is gonna be tough for you, I can see that too ... Those cards there; they show pain and suffering and the shit of 'what was,' and, 'what will be,' when it comes out ... but those cards there, at the end ... they show a really good outcome, a happy ending. So it's worth it, Frie, really it is, hun!"

Frieda sighed, looking at the cards again, more closely now. She hesitated, looked at Sarah and then at the floor. "So what they are saying - these cards - if I've got this right, is that I have pain and it's locked inside me?"

Sarah nodded.

"That's the past bit yes? And if I talk about it, that's the Gabriel bit, it will all come out, which will be hard and painful to do, but it will be worth it in the end?"

Sarah nodded again.

"And that Michael bloke and that Uriel bloke will help me to get it all out? And then I will get a happy ending?"

"Exactly!" Sarah smiled. "But, Frie, this is all your choice, hun. You don't have to do any of this, none of it! What the cards are saying is this shit that you're holding, this pain that you have inside you, is what is blocking you from real peace, real happiness and real love. And that if it comes out, you have a good chance of finding that peace."

Frieda nodded slowly. "And that card there, that Two of Cups, that's the card of partnership. Does that mean I have a partner coming; a man?" she asked.

"No, Frie, I don't think it does mean that. I think that partnership card means that you're not going to be on your own to deal with this stuff. You have me, I'll help, if you'll let me. And there's your angel, Miya, and the other angels. And maybe there will be other help, stuff we can't see yet. That being said, do me a favour and pull me another card from the Angel pack would you, and put it anywhere you like."

Frieda pulled a card, placing it on the last card in the outer circle, right on top of the 'happy ever after' card, the Ten of Cups. Sarah turned it over slowly. Daniel, the angel of marriage smiled happily up at her.

"There you go, Frie! There is love and marriage for you, the Angel cards confirm it, but it's not yet, mate. You got to go and deal with all your shit before you can get there, alright?"

"Mmm, maybe," Frieda said quietly. "I'll think about

it, okay?" She looked at the cards again, and stood up from the table. "I think I'll go to bed now, Sarah, alright? My heads banging, too much brandy I think," she laughed. It was a fake laugh, a laugh that was practiced. She didn't know any other way than to cover, hide, and mask her feelings. It was automatic, instant, but in that instant, for the first time, she recognised it. She saw the fakeness of the laugh and she stopped. She looked at her friend and cautiously spoke the truth. "Actually, Sarah, if I'm honest," she said quietly, "that's blown me away a bit and I think I need to be on my own for a while, okay, hun?"

"Yes, darlin', of course, it's okay! You go to bed. If you want to talk about it, I'm here, but if you don't, that's cool too. Whatever you need, hun. See you in the morning." And Sarah hugged her friend, trying to inject some love and support into her, as best she could, then watched Frieda quietly leave the room, heading for Sarah's conservatory and the sofa bed that was made up in readiness that waited for her.

As she cleared away the cards, cleansing them carefully before putting them back into their respective boxes, she looked at Clarabelle and Cassie with concern.

"Now you know we can't say a word, Sarah dear. Frieda will tell you when she is ready." Clarabelle piped. "But you did so well, child, so very well. I am so proud of you; we all are!"

"Who was the man, Clar? I mean, I know you can't tell me secrets, but can you tell me who the man was. He stood next to her the whole time!"

"Go to bed, Sarah," Clarabelle smiled. "All will become

clear in time, of that you have my word."

And Sarah went to bed. Exhausted, confused, bewildered; but also, strangely, satisfied! For some reason, she felt that tonight's reading would have a major impact, and one that would help to change the course of a lifetime's pain, and move Frieda onto a happier road ahead. ...

Chapter 12

The early spring's morning sun shone down onto the cottage as the two friends awakened in their respective rooms the following day. Its rays spoke of brighter days ahead; vitality, confidence, a new belief, and a new hope. Frieda woke and felt the hope; the first stirrings deep within her of a new beginning. She stretched, yawned and then felt the punishing headache bearing down on her from last night's brandy. "Oh, Christ!" she yelped, rubbing her temples. "Shit, fuck, bollocks!" She reached for the water next to her and drank it in one gulp, looking around her through bleary eyes at the new conservatory where she'd spent the night. It had been completed just last month and this was the first time that she had slept in it. *Very nice,* she thought to herself. *Very nice indeed!* It had been Simon's idea to have it built; something he had been hankering after since his accident five years ago.

Sarah and Simon's bedroom was on the top floor, up two flights of stairs, and he had struggled enormously with them for weeks after he had come home from hospital following his near fatal accident. Frieda considered their home in more detail. Sarah had lived here for years! Before that, her gran had owned it, leaving it to Sarah in her will. *She's so lucky,* Frieda thought, thinking of her own home; rented, rather than owned. Sarah had no mortgage, no loans; this house was hers and hers outright. *Well, hers and Simon's now,* Frieda knew.

Sarah's house had a nice lounge downstairs, a small dining room, and a functional kitchen with a small table, and a utility room behind it. Upstairs there were two single bedrooms, which the twins occupied, and then the family bathroom. Above that, the top floor housed the large master bedroom with ensuite, occupying the entire floor with windows on three sides; it was light, airy and spacious. The front views from the master suite scanned the small town of Redfields a quarter of a mile away; the side view spanned across the valley with its trees and sloping green hillside, whilst the rear view reached far across open farmland. Frieda knew that Sarah loved this house with a passion. Built some two hundred years before, its old stone walls had faded gently with time. Its large original wooden window frames, long since rotten, had been replaced with modern white double-glazed units since Sarah had taken over its ownership. It was an impressive detached house that sat at the end of a small lane on the fringes of the town where she and Sarah had spent most of their lives. It wasn't an overly large dwelling, but the extra floor at the top of the house made all the difference. It also boasted a large garden, bordered by a tall hedge that separated it from the adjoining fields and which swept gently from the front gate around the sides and across the back. Inside, it had impressive, high Victorian ceilings, with ornamental coving, and beautifully carved wooden spindles on the staircase. Frieda preferred modern, contemporary houses, but even she could see the beauty in this house, this home. She particularly liked the large marble fireplace in the lounge; its black wrought-iron hearth which was usually filled with coals and logs, stood majestically, commanding the attention of the room and all who entered. Its wide French doors used to look beyond the lounge into the cottage garden, which faced the rear of the house, but which now looked directly into the new conservatory, standing proud, beautiful, and, very tasteful, Frieda decided. It had been built 'in keeping' with the style and age of the house; stone walls rather than brick, holding up the lovely double glazed enormous windows. The roof had been built in an apex style, to allow in even more light. All of the windows had blinds especially made and professionally fitted, expensive ones that kept in the heat and, yet, at the same time, kept it cool from the sun's rays. They were all closed now, as were the lounge curtains. The conservatory blinds were closed to protect Frieda from the early morning's sunlight, and the lounge drapes, to give her privacy from the occupants of the house as she slept. She examined the new sofa-bed that she had slept on, and slept well! *Lovely,* she thought, *clearly a good quality one!* She looked around her slowly at the rest of the room. Surrounding her were plants of various sizes and shapes, some hanging from the walls on swirly, fancy brackets and others standing in pots. She didn't have a clue what they were (never green-fingered was Frie!), but they did look lovely!

There was a small table with a large Buddha sitting on it in one corner, and in the other, a beautiful water fountain. Crystals had been placed around the room on the window ledges; various shapes, sizes, colours and materials. Frieda eyed them now, wondering what they were and what they did. She didn't know anything about 'the weird stuff' that Sarah had got increasingly into over the years, but they certainly looked pretty, whatever they were!

She stretched leisurely, noting that her headache was passing, now that she had rehydrated her body somewhat with the water. Reaching out, she picked up the nearest crystal to her on the sofa-bed, holding it in her palm, examining it for clues. It felt warm, nice, somehow comforting. She had no idea what it was but she liked it. She put it back carefully, not wanting to damage it, and rose gingerly out of her bed. Sitting on the side of the mattress, she looked at the crystal again, feeling drawn to hold it once more. "Aw, get on with ya," she said to herself loudly. "It's just a rock! Just a stone! Doesn't mean anything!" She dressed herself quickly, wanting to get into the house and to the wonderful smells that were now emanating from it. *Bacon! Bloody perfect!* she grinned, rushing to finish dressing and get to the kitchen before the smells faded and Sarah cleared up.

"Hurry up, you two," Sarah ordered the twins. They were sitting at the kitchen table behind her, dawdling over their cereals as they argued about school. "Finish your breakfast, come on! It's nearly time to go." She put the finishing touches to the two plates which the cooked breakfasts now sat on, placing a fried egg on each.

"Bloody hell, girl, you're a mind-reader!" Frieda grinned, standing in the kitchen doorway. "Mushrooms and everything, wow, you're a wonder!"

"I know! I am 'Wonder-Woman' and I aim to please," grinned Sarah, placing the buttered toast onto the small plate in the centre of the table. "Bacon, eggs, sausages, beans, tomatoes and yes, even mushrooms." She looked behind her again at the dawdling twins. "Hurry up, you two, you should have been ready by now! Mrs. Blackburn won't be long and you'll be keeping her waiting. Not okay, not okay!" *God, I sound like Clarabelle more and more every day*, she thought with a grin.

She'd woken early, worried about her friend after last night's reading. For some reason, she felt that she needed to be there for her this morning, to try to get her to open up, somehow! She had no clue how! All she knew was that she didn't want Frieda to rush off, so she needed a plan. Food was always a good tempter for Frieda, especially with a hangover, so Sarah had nipped out early to the village shop and bought the ingredients that she needed, rushing back home to create a masterpiece of early morning culinary delights that would tempt Frieda to stay. The wafts of freshly brewed coffee filled the kitchen from the top-rate fresh coffee beans that had been brewing from the machine in the corner of the room, sending waves of caffeinated scented delights over to the awaiting, coffee-addicted Frieda.

Clarabelle beamed at Miya. The two angels were sitting happily on top of the coffee maker as it steamed and gurgled away, using the opportunity the steam presented to preen their feathers and polish their halos. "Such a lovely experience, don't you think, Miya, a steam bath?" Clarabelle grinned. "Although we do need to focus, we have work to do this morning, lots of! Are the others coming?" she enquired. "All sorted is it?"

"Oh yes, dear, they'll be here shortly. I put the call in earlier, you know, just after your Sarah sorted 'the breakfast plan.' The Higher Realms have been notified and the AA's are expected shortly."

"Smashing," Clarabelle beamed. "Just perfectly smashing!" And they carried on enjoying their steam bath while they had the chance.

***

"Sit," Sarah commanded, handing Frieda an empty mug and the coffee pot, now filled to the brim with exquisite Columbian coffee.

Frieda sat, grinning in pure delight. "Yes, Mum," she giggled, sipping the hot coffee happily. "Oh my God, this is fab!" she exclaimed. "What is it? I want some! Where can I get it?" she gabbled, drinking it as fast as she could get it down her neck without scalding her throat.

"And there's fresh orange juice there too, Frie," Sarah said, pointing to the jug on the table.

"Wow! What's all this in aid of?" she asked. "You never normally do us a full English!"

"Yes, well, it's about time I did!" Sarah declared firmly. "Mrs. Blackburn is picking up the kids today; walking them to school with her two, so that you and me can have some 'us' time. She'll be here in a minute." And just as she said those words, the doorbell rang. The next few minutes were a flurry of activity as the twins rushed around grabbing their bags and coats, before being rushed out of the door to the awaiting Mrs. Blackburn and her two young infants on the path. A sudden calm swept over the house as Sarah closed the front door and returned to the kitchen with a grin. "Now then," she smiled, "let's eat!"

Some time later, Frieda loaded the dishwasher as Sarah cleaned down the table and put on a fresh pot of coffee. "Right then, Frie," she said quietly, "are you gonna tell me what that was all about last night, mate?" She smiled gently at her friend, willing her to open up.

Archangels Michael, Uriel and Gabriel stood behind her, quietly injecting energy and love into the surprised Frieda.

"What's this then, an ambush?" Frieda declared, slightly nervously. "Blackmail? You cook me breakfast (a fabulous breakfast I might add), and in exchange I tell you all? That's a bit, umm ... unfair, don't you think?"

"Darlin', I'm not forcing anything, honest! If you don't want to tell me, that's fine, hun, promise! I'm just saying, 'I'm here, I'm listening,' if you want to talk; but only if you want to, okay?" Sarah put her hand on Frieda's arm gently, showing her that she meant it. "I mean, if you have been keeping some big, dark secret from me for all these years, well that's, umm, well it's weird, but it's your choice too, hun."

Frieda looked at Sarah's hand on her arm, and she looked at her friend's face, searching her eyes for something - something that said yes, it was safe; it was safe to open up, to tell her. Sarah's turquoise eyes shone warmth and love, reassurance and care. Frieda sighed deeply. "It's hard, Sarah, really hard," she said quietly. "I've never spoken of it, never! Not to anyone, not even my mum. She knows, of course, but we've never spoken of it. I've never spoken to anyone about it, not ever!"

"But isn't that what the cards were saying last night, Frie?" Sarah said quietly. "Isn't that what they were saying? That whatever 'this thing' is, that it's locked inside you *because* you've never told, *because* you've never spoken. The cards said that if you told, if you got it all out, you would find peace. And, Frie, I got to say darlin', there was a whole load of shit that I could see inside you! It needs to come out, darlin'. Please let me help?"

Frieda considered it carefully. She didn't know how to! How could she tell, what would she say, where would she start?

"Just start anywhere you like," Sarah was saying now, as if she was reading her mind! "It doesn't matter if it's jumbled, darlin', or if it comes out all wrong. We can piece it together bit by bit and we can sort it out; together. And you know I won't say a word, Frie, to anyone, ever; I give you my word."

Frieda looked at her friend and sighed again. *Maybe it is worth it? Maybe I should?* she asked herself silently.

"And whatever it is, I won't judge you either, Frie, never, ever; I promise!"

"Alright, Sar, I'll try," she said quietly, wondering quite how to find the words, or where to start.

With that, all three AA's increased their power, beaming energy into Frieda at exactly that moment.

Archangel Gabriel stood over her, pouring light into her throat. Frieda started to cough; something was tickling her throat, something was irritating it and she coughed and coughed. She felt something shift; as if a block was being loosened from her throat. She coughed uncontrollably for several minutes, needing to run to the sink for a glass of water it got so bad! Just as the coughing had stopped and she had sat back down at the table, her tummy suddenly felt hot and twisted; like a knot was being pulled loose, and her head felt funny, like it was about to explode with pressure - pressure that wanted to come out! She felt sick, seriously sick, wondering if she was going to throw up and waste the lovely breakfast that she'd just eaten! Then she wondered if she was 'coming on'; cramps suddenly starting in her lower tummy. *I'm not due my period*, she thought, *God, don't tell me I've got that as well?* Archangel Uriel and Michael were standing in front of her, beaming light into her stomach and head, focusing on the other blocks in Frieda's body, each one creating a barrier, each one filled with pain and fear.

Sarah watched her friend's discomfort and wanted to say something, to do something, but Clarabelle was shaking her head at her with an emphatic 'no' look, so she stayed put, waiting. She was aware of the light in the room, and the power of it. She was also aware that it was being focused on Frieda, so she sat, and she waited.

Eventually, her friend looked at her, smiling a wobbly smile, and then she began. ...

***

Frieda told Sarah it all; she told her everything. "Well," she said slowly, "it began I guess, recently, with this film, 'The Butterfly Effect'. ..."

At first, it came slowly, disjointed, messy, with no scope of timescale, things in the wrong order, chaotically; but the more she talked, the more the story came together. The whole, awful, horrific story came out. She talked for hour after hour, spilling her memories, her nightmares, her guilt and her shame. The hardest part, the part she struggled with the most, was trying to explain to Sarah about grooming; about how she allowed it, why she allowed it; so very difficult to explain to anyone who had not experienced it, that build-up of trust, a trust that resulted in a willing participant, rather than a screaming victim. It was that 'willingness' that held Frieda's guilt – that, and the responsibility that lay heavily on her shoulders for her father's death.

And Sarah listened. She listened with growing horror ... with growing disgust, and with growing hurt - hurt for her friend; her poor, poor, broken friend. Sarah cried as Frieda spilled her guts; she cried buckets. At one point she didn't think she'd ever stop, that she'd fill the kitchen with her tears and flood it. And Frieda cried too. She cried for what had been, and she cried for what was still held, and she cried for the future that she could never see herself having. She cried for the scars, still so raw, so unhealed; scars that ran so deep, that in her mind, they could never heal, *would* never heal. She cried for her pain that, to her, was just so incurable.

"Nothing," piped up Clarabelle suddenly, "is incurable or un-healable, nothing! 'Incurable' simply means that it needs to be cured from within, that is all! There is no scar that cannot be healed, there is no pain that cannot be released, nothing! Tell her, Sarah, tell her! You must tell her!" she insisted.

And Sarah did. She reassured the crying Frieda that they would heal it, that they would find a way, that there WAS a way, and Frieda began to believe her. She began, in a tiny way, to begin to allow a glimmer of hope; hope that there was a way to freedom; freedom from pain, freedom from shame, freedom from guilt.

"Clarabelle, now you know that's not strictly true!" whispered Miya, frowning. "Sometimes they can be so broken that they can't heal, you know that!"

"Yes, yes, I know that, Miya! Of course, I know that, dear. But those are the ones whose *minds* are broken, along with their spirit. Frieda's is not. They may be a bit bent, a bit dented, but they are not broken! And they can be fixed! Shush now, pay attention."

The angels returned their attention to Sarah and Frieda, sitting at the table together talking. Two friends, joined in their new depth of closeness; a closeness that truth and real trust brings.

They talked for hours, the two friends, and not once did Frieda feel judged, or shamed, or blamed, for her guilty secrets. Not once did Sarah make her feel disgusting, as disgusting as she herself felt. Not once. ...

Another pot of coffee, and a break for lunch (batteries seriously needing to be recharged for both girls), Sarah began the journey with Frieda; the journey to wholeness *for* Frieda. With the angels help, she began to prod, to question, to trigger; to trigger all the beliefs within Frieda, beliefs that held her back so tightly.

"So, Frie," she asked gently, "in this 'grooming' that you talk about, this man made you feel that what you were doing was not wrong, which you clearly believed, yes?" She looked at Frieda and waited, "completely believed, yes?"

Frieda nodded sadly. "Yes I believed. I believed everything he said. I didn't even know it was wrong, this 'inappropriate' touching. Nothing was wrong, nothing was dirty, everything was 'normal' between 'special friends' - or so he said! That's what he told me ..." Her head hung in shame. "Not even the sex ... well," she hesitated, correcting herself, "...the rapes." She whispered the word, poison to her, incomprehensibly difficult for her to say the actual word. "So no, not until I was fifteen and had my first boyfriend. Not till then, no. It was only then that I realised that all that other 'stuff' when I was a kid was ... wrong ... was dirty... was sick ... was *disgusting!*"

"Frie, hun, he was telling you it was normal, and well, back then, back nearly forty years ago, darlin', well, we didn't know! Our mum's didn't tell us about these things! It was all very 'hush hush.' So how did we know? How could you possibly have known? He was there telling you that it was normal, fine, and no one there to correct it. No one to put you right! We didn't have books like they do now, you know the ones, where your parent sits you down and explains about God-awful stuff like 'inappropriate touching' and how you mustn't let anyone do it? And if they try, you are to scream from the roof tops and tell everyone? Frie, we just didn't have any of that in our day, hun. Your mum never warned you, so how *would* you know?"

Frieda considered this, nodding slowly.

"Well then, if you had of known, you would have told, wouldn't you! But you didn't know it was wrong, Frie, so how it could be your fault about your dad? You think that it was your fault that he killed himself, cos if you'd have told, if you'd have said … it would have all come out earlier, and then your dad wouldn't have blamed himself, and wouldn't have died, yes?"

Again Frieda nodded.

"But, Frie, you believed you were not doing anything wrong, so why *would* you have told? Don't you see, hun? You would only have told someone if you'd have believed that it *was* wrong! But this man; this awful, sick, twisted man, he made you believe that it *wasn't* wrong! He made you believe that it was okay! So you wouldn't have told anyone, would you?"

Frieda considered this for a moment. This was new! She was confused now, very confused. To begin to alter a lifetime's worth of beliefs was going to be challenging, and it was going to take time. "Maybe," she said cautiously. "Maybe."

"Did you not ever have any counselling, hun?" Sarah asked, then realised her mistake and corrected herself quickly. "Course not, you never told anyone, did you, so you would never have had the counselling you needed, hun! Well, Frie, I think you need counselling, hun, proper stuff, with experts in this sort of thing! Don't you, darlin'?"

Frieda's head was nodding, realising that yes, maybe she had got a lot wrong, and maybe some of that could be put right. Sarah was going on, saying about all the help that Frieda could access, now that she was talking, now that the secret was out. "There's bound to be some, bound to be!" Sarah was insisting. "Must be! Let's Google it and see what we can find, Frie, aye?"

Frieda nodded slowly, considering this idea. There was no doubt about it, she definitely felt better; much better for talking about it! She felt lighter, stronger, calmer; whilst at the same time, feeling weaker, and if it was possible, feeling even more vulnerable than she did before!

"Well that's because Pandora's Box has been opened ... at last!" declared a happy Clarabelle. "This isn't the end of the journey for Frieda, it's just the beginning - the beginning of the end - the Alpha and the Omega!" she declared. "Tell her, Sarah; tell her what I am saying dear, there's a love," she grinned, beaming at Sarah in delight. "And tell her that her angel is very happy! And yes indeed, she does need help - proper help! I will show you, Sarah, follow me!" and Clarabelle popped over to the top of Sarah's laptop. "Now then," she grinned, "turn it on to your search engine, Sarah, and I will show you where to find the help that Frieda needs. You will find it under 'Rape and Sexual Abuse Clinics,' my dear, or something like that. Maybe centre instead of clinic?" she pondered. "They are all over the country; many areas have them, and each one has expert counsellors in this field, specialists, in it, my dear. We will make sure that the right person is available for her, don't you worry about that!"

"But isn't that for rape victims?" Sarah asked, confused now. "Grown-up rape victims I mean; recent, you know?"

"Oh, not at all, dear," Clarabelle smiled. "Not at all! Their counsellors specialise in all sorts of sexual abuse; including childhood abuse, even if it was years and years ago. There! There's the number, write it down now child, write it down." Clarabelle was pointing to a particular centre, not too far away from Redville. Counselling was listed as being available, with a phone number and helpline alongside it.

And Sarah wrote the number down, handing the scrap of paper to Frieda. "Whatever you decide to do, Frie," she sniffed, wiping another tear away, "you are not on your own. I am here for you, night or day, do you hear?"

Frieda heard. She smiled at her friend, gratitude shining in her watery eyes. "Maybe I'll even sleep tonight?" she suggested hopefully. "Maybe the nightmares are over, at last?"

"Oh, you can bank on it, my dear," chirped up Miya and Clarabelle together, "you can bank on it!"

"Really?" Sarah questioned. "Are you sure?"

Clarabelle turned to Sarah and explained. "You see, my dear, your dreams, or nightmares, are the soul's way of bringing up that which is not seen, that which is denied. Sometimes it is stuff that you do not even know is there, not on a conscious level anyway; it is so far buried that you do not even know that it exists, but it pops up through your dreams, to tell you about it, so that you can sort it! Other times you *do* know, you just aren't dealing with it! Like with Frieda here; she knew, but she has spent a lifetime avoiding, refusing and resisting the very real need to 'deal' with it. That is why her soul kept prompting the dreams, kept bringing them up, so that she would, eventually, face her demons and begin to heal them! Now that she has done just that, faced them I mean, then there is no need for those dreams to keep reoccurring, so they will not - you have my word. Not all dreams are messages from your soul or subconscious, mind you," she added. "Some of them are simply your brain's way of sorting out your day. Many dreams are totally innocent. Frieda's, of course, were not. They were far more than that, but they are over now."

Sarah relayed the message to a relieved Frieda, who was delighted at the concept of a 'decent night's sleep.'

"Do you know what, Sar?" she said thoughtfully. "I don't think I've ever slept properly, not ever. All my exes used to moan about my restless sleep, how I'd keep them awake with my tossing and turning, or that I'd wake them up with my 'lashing about'! I remember waking one boyfriend up, after a particularly nasty dream, with hysterical screaming and sobbing, and even started hitting him, poor thing! As you can guess, he didn't last long! It'd be nice to think I could finally sleep peacefully." And she smiled the biggest, deepest, most genuine smile that she'd ever smiled.

Chapter 13

Andrew laughed. "Really?" he grinned. "Really? A dating site! I don't think so, Miss!"

"But, Dad! You never go anywhere! You can't stay hiding away in here forever!" she implored. "It's not healthy, it's not normal, it's not right!"

"I'm perfectly happy on my own, Miss," he grinned. "And I don't hide! I simply prefer to come home and relax after a hard day at the office! A dating site indeed! I don't bloody think so!" Andrew shook his head with horror at the thought, a thought his twenty year old daughter had brought up more than once over the last ten years since his wife had died. He scratched his head with amusement, fluffing up his short red curly hair as he scratched. He looked at himself in the mirror, hanging opposite to where he was now standing in their lounge, pushing the offending hair back down into place. *Well I guess I'm lucky to still have hair,* he thought to himself. *Most of the men my age are bald, or balding. What is it with red hair,* he wondered, *that it doesn't seem to thin or disappear like many of the men my age who aren't redheads?* It wasn't as bright as it used to be in his youth that was for sure. It had faded significantly over the last few years, tinged now with more than a bit of grey at his temples, the odd spike of grey here and there throughout the top. Carrot top, they'd called him in his younger days. He'd hated it! The incessant teasing that only ginger people know!

He smiled at his daughter. Bless her, she was only trying to help, worried about him being on his own now that she was in university. "I'm fine, Cara, really I am, hun. Don't worry about me," he grinned. "Dating site indeed! Pah!"

"Well I think you should consider it!" she glared. *God, he's so stubborn!* "At least consider it, Dad, pleeeeeaaase!"

"Cara, no! And anyway, by the time I come home from the office, I'm too knackered to even think about going out, never mind dating! I'm happy as I am, hun. Now leave it!" His tone was warning, a tone Cara knew well. "Please!" he added. It was not a request, it was an order, and Cara knew she had failed, again!

"One day," she muttered under her breath. "One day I will get you out there. I promise you that, Mr.!"

She 'humphed' back to her room in disappointment. She'd spent an age, an absolute age, setting up that profile on the dating site that she'd picked, and he wouldn't even look at it! *Fathers! Argh!* She sat down heavily on her bed; her short curly dark hair framing her pretty young face, flopped over her angry green eyes. She stared at the computer screen, examining closely the secret profile that she'd set up for her dad a few weeks ago. His smiling face shone out happily from the profile picture; his headline,

'Ready for Love!' shouted out, 'come and get me,' along with the brief description... 47, 6' tall, blue eyes, red hair ... affectionate (was he? She didn't have a clue! She'd never seen him with a woman and she couldn't really remember much about him and Mum.) ... attentive, funny, GSOH (good sense of humour), likes golf (did he? She didn't know that either, but she'd had to put something for hobbies!). She knew he'd played a couple of times - work meetings and the like, with clients (always with bloody clients - never just for fun!). She couldn't exactly put the truth now could she: watches TV, reads books, and gardening (God, how boring!). Her father was actually really, really boring! He'd never catch a woman with that profile, a real profile! She'd shaved a few years off his age too, putting forty-seven, instead of the fifty that he actually was, and she'd touched up his photo with 'photo-shop,' to remove some of the wrinkles on his face. He'd had loads of replies; replies he, of course, knew nothing about! He'd kill her; that much was clear from his reaction to her suggestion, never mind him finding out that he'd actually already joined!

It wasn't just that he was lonely. She knew he hid it from her, but she was sure that he was. It was just that, in her mind, no bloke as lovely as her dad should be on his own like this. He had so much to offer to the right woman! Not some nutter who'd be high maintenance mind (she'd see to that, make sure that he picked the right one), some lovely lady his age who was lonely too, and then they could be un-lonely together! So okay, he was a bit boring, but he was kind, and solid, and very 'nice.' *Not bad looking for an old fart either*, she thought with a wry smile. *And patient! God, he was so patient!* He'd had to be, bringing her up on his own, especially through those middle teenage years when she'd been such a nightmare! She could see that now, what a pain she'd been, with the benefit of her vast twenty year old experience. That, and two years of her psychology degree, of course, where she'd learned *ever* such a lot about the way people think, what they hide and how they hide it! She was convinced, totally convinced, that her dad was lonely, and *did* need someone. She just had to get *him* to see that too!

Cara turned the computer off with a sigh. *Try again in a few months then?* she thought to herself. She'd wear him down eventually!

Miya grinned at Bart. The two angels were sitting on the bottom of the bed-frame of Cara's enormous bed clapping their hands in glee, watching her disappointed face as she reluctantly closed her laptop. Both beamed at Rena, sitting on Cara's shoulder, who was also clearly very pleased with herself.

"Good job, Rena," Bart grinned.

"Ooh, thanks, Bartholomew! It was easy, easier than I thought! Piece of cake really!" She was more than content with her handiwork of getting Cara to join the dating site, on her father's behalf, in preparation for things to come. "Just planting the seed, my dears," Rena laughed. "At this stage, of course, just a tiny seed."

Bart was Andrew's angel and was now working closely with Miya on the 'get them together plan.' Both angels knew that it was a long-term plan, rather than a short-term one, and that it could be a while before anything 'took off,' but they wanted to be ready. They'd called an inter-angel-cy meeting some time ago to discuss progress and begin to make plans. It had been Bart's suggestion to bring in Rena, Cara's angel, and ask for her help with 'the plan,' which she'd been more than happy to give. Bart knew how much Andrew adored his daughter, and had decided that, if there was any chink in his armour of bachelorhood whatsoever, Cara was the one who could get in through that chink.

"Increase the nagging from Cara a notch maybe?" Miya suggested, although she knew they had months yet, many months, before her Frieda would be ready to join the same site. They hoped it would be right around the same time that Andrew would be finally worn down from his daughter's nagging, worn down enough to finally start thinking about dating.

"Perfect!" they all grinned. "Just perfectly perfect!"

***

"Mum!" Angelica shrieked. "He's being nasty again, Mum! MUM, tell him, tell him!" And then she screamed - a lamented, furious scream. Angelica stomped down the stairs in fury.

"What's he done now?" Sarah grinned, watching her daughter stomp. *God, love her, she looks so mad!*

"It wasn't my fault, Mum, honest!" David appeared suddenly from behind his furious sister, clutching 'Molly' in his grubby hands. The doll's arm hung precariously, twisted at a very strange angle.

"He's bwoked her, Mum; he's bwoked Molly! Look!"

Angelica, with horror in her tearful eyes, pointed at 'her Molly,' still hanging from David's hand.

"Wasn't my fault, Mum, honest! It was an accident, promise!" David handed the battered doll to Sarah, concern in his gentle eyes. "Can you fix her, Mum, can you, can you?" he implored, worried for the doll. He knew how Anj loved this doll. He hadn't meant to break it; he hadn't, really he hadn't! He just got a bit, umm, rough sometimes, and forgot! He really couldn't understand her obsession with dolls at all! What was the point in them if they broke that easy? He much preferred his stuff; his bike for one, that was great! Dad had helped him learn to ride it in the summer holidays, and the stabilisers had come off at last. Yay! David had been screaming up and down the lane for weeks now, and even into the park, learning to do wheelies and skids; great fun! And then there were his toy cars - metal ones - tough, durable, reliable! They didn't break, not like these stupid dolls!

Sarah looked at the battered Molly. *Jes..usss, it's knackered!* Somehow, she would try to repair it, again! Either that or go and get her a new one. Her daughter had had the doll for just six months, but to be fair, that doll had had some use! She looked at Anj and sighed. "Darling, I will do my best, I promise, but I don't know if I can fix her this time, hun. She's in a bit of a state, but I will try. Why don't you play with Cindy, or Barbie, for now, hun, aye? Just while I see what I can do, aye?" Angelica looked at her mother beseechingly, desperation all over her face. "And, David," Sarah added, "stay away from Anj's toys, do you hear me, young man!"

David looked at the floor, shame evident all over his

guilty face. "Sorry, Mum," he mumbled. "Sorry, Anj. Didn't mean it, honest." And he skulked outside to his toy cars that were gathered in the sand pit. He'd created a magnificent race track for them out of the sand, with humps and bumps and all sorts! Sand didn't break, and neither did his cars. He'd be safe there. Not upset anyone!

Fred, of course, followed David out. "Don't worry about it, pal," he grinned. "Dolls is stupid, int they, mate?" His mission clear - to support his best pal (well, second best pal, after Dad), and make him feel better, cheer him up.

Cassie, of course, did exactly the same with Angelica, following her up the stairs to her room and purring all around her, rubbing her tail around the upset child in her efforts and mission - make her feel better too.

Sarah's mission - fix the bloody doll - again!

***

It was early September and all was calm in the Brown household. The late summer sun shone down into Sarah's kitchen as she sipped her tea, gazing out of the open window pondering.

She looked down at Molly, laying on the table in front of her; now 'superglued' to within an inch of her plastic life. The doll had been fixed (again), and peace had once again been restored between her children. They had gone back to school for their second and final year of infant school yesterday, to a new teacher and a new year. Sarah reflected back on the last, wondering quite where a whole year had gone! The children had settled well, loving their school, teacher and friends in equal amounts. Reading was going well, sums coming along nicely, but more importantly, in Sarah's mind anyway, was the interaction it gave them with other children and the opportunities to learn essential social skills. Both children were popular, thank goodness, each with loads of friends. She'd been worried about Angelica, initially, being the diva that she was, but she'd been happily surprised, and relieved, to realise that her daughter actually could share, be patient and even be kind, with other children. Sadly that was not the case with her twin brother! The pair were often at war, or in competition, with each other; arguing and squabbling away most of the time. It drove her nuts! *Maybe it's time to go back to work?* she pondered. *Time to focus on me?* Sarah worked now and then at her store, but it wasn't often, and, she realised with a sigh, it wasn't enough. *Maybe a second store, or expand the one I have,* she thought.

"Yes, well, child, I have a plan to sort your boredom out, don't you worry, my dear," Clarabelle chirped happily. "And it is not related to your store in any way, no, not at all! I have decided Sarah, that it is time for you to 'get out there' with your cards, yes indeed it is!"

"Aye? What? What are you wittering on about now?" Sarah asked in surprise, pulling her gaze from the open window and the wafts of summer flowers from her garden that were trickling through it. "Get out there! Get out where?"

"Ah well, child, I do believe it is time for you to turn 'professional,' as you call it. Get more 'clients'! Do more good with those cards of yours. Yes indeed!" Clarabelle beamed, quite happy in her plan for Sarah; a plan Sarah herself had received no consultation in whatsoever!

"Professional? Get away! Me, professional? You're having a laugh, Clar!" she exclaimed. "I couldn't do readings for people I don't know; never! And I couldn't charge for them; I'm not good enough!"

"Well, Sarah, that is where you are quite wrong, my dear, quite wrong! Now then child, there is a psychic fayre next Saturday in the Town Hall in Redville, and I have taken the liberty of booking you a table. You will find your acknowledgement letter confirming your table within your emails."

Sarah stared at her in total, abject horror! "But..."

"But nothing, Sarah!" Clarabelle grinned. "It is time. Indeed it is! Oh yes, and while I remember, you need to pay the fee, my dear. I couldn't do that bit for you."

Sarah's face was a picture! Her mouth was wide open, her eyebrows up nearly to her hairline, her eyes - just like a rabbit caught in headlights (bright ones!). Clarabelle grinned happily, not at all bothered by her ward's reaction, not a jot! She'd sent the email last night with the completed booking form that she had 'miracled' up, and knew that the confirmation had come through early this morning. She'd tried to arrange the on-line banking to pay the fee too, but, disappointingly, had been unable to get past the bank's very high security firewall. *Most annoying*, she thought. *I had so hoped to have it all sewn up by now, but there we are!*

"Clarabelle!" Sarah's tone was quiet and angry, just as Clarabelle had known it would be. "This is not okay, not okay at all!" she fumed. "Cancel it, immediately!"

"Too late, sorry, dear. It's all sorted; meant to be, my dear, meant to be. Trust me now, child. I promise it is all fine," she chirped, without even a hint of either remorse or concern on her beaming face.

"Un-bloody-believable!"

"What's un-bloody-believable now?" Fred chipped in, plodding into the kitchen looking for his bone, wondering what all the commotion was about.

"Stay out of it, Flopsy," Cassie hissed from under the table. "She needs to do this, so just stay out of it, right!"

"Do what?" *What's going on now?* he wondered.

"Sarah has to go and do readings for strangers at a psychic fayre and she isn't happy, that's what's 'going on,' okay, Flops!"

"Alright, Miss Bossy-boots, I hear ya," grumbled Fred, not quite understanding why he was being so accommodating. Somehow, he knew that the Ninja Cat was right. No idea why, mind you, he just knew! So, ever helpful, he put his paw on Mum's leg and looked up at her lovingly. "Mum," he woofed (Dog, it was so good that she could speak dog!), "you gotta do what Aunty C. says, okay, Mum. It's important."

"Yes, Fred, I realise that, thank you. I'm just a bit nervous, that's all," Sarah said quietly. She also had no idea how she knew that she had to do this fayre thing, but like Fred, she just did!

"Yes, Sarah, it's important," Cassie grinned. "And I'll be there with you, and Clarabelle, and all the others."

"I don't think I can take a cat with me to the Town Hall, Cassie," Sarah smiled, "but thank you anyway."

"Smashing!" declared Clarabelle. "Now then, you will

need a cloth, Sarah, for the table I mean, and some of your lovely crystals, oh, and don't forget a candle; nice big one I think, don't you, child?"

Sarah nodded thoughtfully, contemplating this huge step. There was no doubt about it, her readings really did help people in their own way. She'd done quite a few since that one with Frieda six months ago, and look how that had turned out!

Frieda was now four months into her counselling, and belonged to a support group that she was now quite active in, and was gradually turning her tragic past into a triumphant present.

Sarah had accompanied her on that first visit to the counsellors, holding her shaking hand all the way. By the second session, Frieda had felt able to go alone, and by her third, she was opening up beautifully, so the counsellor had said. There had been many tears, many reactions, many hurts. Hurts that had come out during those sessions and, each time, Sarah was there for her before and after. In time, Angie had been told - the other member of their 'three musketeers' friendship from school. She, like Sarah, had been horrified, then angry, then bitterly sad for her friend, and she like Sarah, had vowed undying support, love and care throughout Frieda's journey. Her children had been told, with Sarah's help, gently and carefully; and through that honesty, they had grown closer to their mother than ever before. Frieda's own mother had joined her in a few of the sessions with the psychologist, exploring the impact together of both the abuse and her father's suicide. It had taken Frieda twelve sessions to get to the point of agreeing that it was not her fault; an incredible release of guilt followed. It had taken another four for her to begin to release some of her feelings of shame, but she was getting there.

Sarah knew that had it not been for the reading that she had done, Frieda may still be locked up inside her pain. Maybe she would have got there without it, but then again ... Sarah looked at Clarabelle and nodded slowly. "Yes, okay then, I'll do the silly fayre. You'd better be there for me though, cos this is well scary!" she declared.

Clarabelle beamed, simply beamed!

And so it began. ...

Chapter 14

"Do you know what, mate, what I find so unbelievable?" Frieda was chomping on a huge bar of chocolate as she sat on Sarah's sofa, slurping her coffee loudly. "Is that some of the parents of these victims, I mean survivors (that's what we're called you know - survivors!), don't even believe them! Can you bloody believe that? How ridiculous! Like you'd make that crap up for God's sake! I was talking with this one woman last week, you know, in the support group, and she said ..." Frieda was shaking her head with disbelief, "... she said that she finally told her father about her shit, you know, what had happened to her when she was a kid, and do you know what he said to her? Do you, do you?"

Sarah shook her head, waiting for Frieda to continue. Her friend was certainly fired up, that was for sure!

"He said, and I can't believe this; he said that she had *a vivid imagination!* Can you fucking believe it! And then he told her that she'd always been 'attention seeking' and to stop making up stuff! And then ... then, he went back to his fucking newspaper, like she hadn't said a word!" Frieda's green eyes blazed with the unfairness, the injustice of this second betrayal, as she saw it. "Forty years old she is, and it's taken that girl her whole life to pluck up the courage to spill her secret, and when she did, she didn't get believed! I tell you, Sar, there are some fuckwits out there! Bastards!"

Sarah was relieved that the children were safely at school and not around. She didn't want them exposed to Frieda's rants, which were often brought on from her support sessions, or to the foul language that filled the air as Frieda ranted. She let her friend vent for an hour, and gradually, her anger passed and she calmed down. It was always the same with Frie; she'd come back from these sessions fired up, but also with a feeling of support and comradery. There was no doubt that she was getting stronger, or that she was feeling better, but it was a journey of ups and downs. On the one hand, she felt understood, supported and far less alone than ever before. On the other hand, she felt even more angry, even more disgusted, it seemed, than she had before! Her counsellor had told her that it was all part of the process, the grieving process.

She would, he said, first go through denial and isolation (tick, done!), then she would go through anger (apparently this always followed denial) - clearly she was now in the 'anger' stage! She'd been told that it would take 'however long it takes,' until it had all worked its way out of her system, and then she would begin to go through the others. The 'stages' they called them; the five stages of grief - the death of innocence, the death of trust, the death of her childhood, and, of course, the death of her father; each to be grieved for in their own way. Each death had never been mourned, they said, had never been healed, and it was that healing which she was now going through. After anger would come 'bargaining' and then it would be 'depression.' Once all this was out and worked through, then and only then, would come acceptance; the last stage. It could take years, they said, for her to come to this final stage, but there was no pressure and no timescale; it would simply work its way through, in its own time.

Clarabelle grinned at Miya, perched on the mantelpiece, watching the two girls chatting. "Years?" she chirped. "Not with our help it won't!"

"Indeed not!" agreed Miya, polishing her halo to perfection. "Months maybe, but certainly not years! Not on my watch!"

***

Sarah laid the cards out carefully on the new golden cloth, placing crystals around them. She surveyed the room nervously. *So many here,* she thought, feeling like a fraud in comparison to the other 'readers.' They were all dressed beautifully in shiny, bright, wonderfully flamboyant clothing; whilst Sarah stood in a blue jumper and jeans, looking like she'd just come back from the school run!

She looked around her at the two hundred year old, very grand Town Hall, wondering, not for the first time, quite what she was doing here! Gazing up at the high, domed ceiling, she gasped with admiration. It stood tall, majestically, commanding attention. High, round stone pillars, spaced evenly around the room, held up the decorative ceiling, where a dozen or more huge glass chandeliers hung, throwing light far down below into the hall, now buzzing with activity. Ornamental coving wound its way around the edges of the ceiling, under which enormous paintings of previous Mayors or Chancellors hung, evenly spaced, each vying to be more impressive than its neighbour.

She looked around her again, this time at the people, the stalls, the activity, curiosity building. Crystal rings and necklaces adorned many necks and fingers around the room, she noticed, even the chaps! Colourful scarves covered chairs and tables, incense burned around the room from, it seemed, every table! Stalls of every description selling various metaphysical goods stood in rows shouting out, in their own way, 'Come to me first'! She saw crystal stalls with jewellery and ornaments, and stands selling drums from various places around the world. There were rattles, gongs, music and books, just about everything anyone into this 'stuff' could possibly ever want! It really was rather wonderful, if not a little bonkers! There were several massage couches laid out, in dark, quiet corners of the room, most with soft, coloured cloths on top, apparently not for a massage, but for 'hands on healing' of various types. There was Reiki healing, spiritual healing, energy healing - *blimey, so many different healings! I wonder what the difference is?* she thought, surprised there were so many. Then there were reflexology areas, as well as many other types of 'ologies.'

It was very confusing!

She left her own table and walked around the room slowly, examining each table, stall or area, trying to understand it all. As she passed the other 'readers,' she noticed with concern, that most of them had proper banners, professionally printed, declaring, 'Clairvoyant to the stars' or 'Medium from so-and-so TV channel,' and suchlike. Sarah definitely felt like a fraud now! "Are you sure about this?" she whispered to Clarabelle, sitting as usual, on her left shoulder. "I don't even have business cards, never mind huge banners!"

"Oh yes, dear, don't you worry about a thing," Clarabelle grinned. "It is all in hand, all sorted."

And then the doors were opening and it was starting. People flocked into the room; women, men and small children. There were buggies, prams and pushchairs, along with the people, clogging up the aisles, some with dogs, and even birds! She was sure that she'd just seen an owl on someone's shoulder! There were people dressed as fairies, with wings and everything (grown-up people!), not to mention the druids in full white gown, accompanied by the obligatory seven-foot tall staff they used like a ginormous walking stick, looking like they'd just stepped out of a 'Moses' film! Then there were the elves (seriously, plastic stick-on-pointy-ears an' all!). They were all ooh-ing and ah-ing at the various wares, touching, smelling, listening, as they moved from stall to stall, curiosity and fascination on their faces, banging gongs and sniffing incense on their merry way around the room. *It may be bonkers,* she thought, *but bloody hell, every one of them is smiling, is happy and is having a perfectly wonderful time! I think I like it!*

Sarah grinned happily to the 'bonkers' people as they passed, especially the elves and fairies, God, love 'em! And then, crashing in through the front doors, came a whole band of 'Arabian Nights,' banging and dancing into the room; bells and rattles and jangly coins from their very skimpy, shiny outfits. *Dear God, belly dancers? No!* But indeed it was, and Sarah watched with amusement and fascination as they meandered their way through the hall, dancing and jangling, up the short stairs at the front of the room and onto the stage in a line. Suddenly loud music struck up from the speakers dotted about the walls and the whole tribe did the most magnificent Turkish/Arabian belly dance that she had ever seen. *Not that I've ever seen one!* she thought with a grin, *only what I've seen on telly in the odd film or two, but God, this is great! Bloody Nora, how do they get their hips to do that?* she wondered in amazement, and then in awe. "Jee…susss, I got to have a go at that!" she giggled. "Maybe not 'Arabian Nights,' maybe 'Turkish Delight' instead!"

Soon after, another band of 'bonkers' people came; all dressed in white tunics and white trousers, and they all had bare feet! *They're gonna catch verrucas!* Sarah worried, *not to mention bloody cold toes!* They did the same as the 'Arabian Nights' people, and made their merry way to the stage, but in a far more sedately manner than the belly dancing girls. Sarah watched fascinated, waiting with bated breath as they took their places. With a 'bong,' new, different music suddenly spouted out of the speakers and the band on the stage began to do a synchronized, 'slow-motion-dance-thing.' It was most bizarre, but at the same time, completely beautiful!

"Tai Chi," a chap next to her said, smiling. "Very good for the soul; very balancing and strengthening. You should try it."

"Mmm, maybe," she grinned, wondering if all those complicated moves were difficult. The music was beautiful; it all was! *Some kind of Chinese music, or Japanese, or maybe Tibetan,* Sarah wasn't sure, but whatever it was, it was lovely!

She watched the 'slow-dance-thing,' enraptured for the next few minutes, hardly noticing the woman hovering nervously by her table, until she quietly touched Sarah's shoulder and asked, "Are you doing readings? How much please?"

Sarah was gobsmacked! Someone actually wanted *her* to do a reading, when there were all these 'experts' here! Wow! "Umm, yes, I am. Umm, how much? I'm not sure! Tell you what; just give me what you feel is fair when I finish, how's that?"

The woman nodded and sat down smiling. She looked at Sarah expectantly. Sarah looked at Clarabelle expectantly. *Shit!*

"Just do what you always do when you've done other readings at home, my dear," Clarabelle grinned. "All is fine, all is well, promise! Just give her the cards and away you go."

Sarah focused and did what she always did. Thirty minutes later she was shocked when the woman handed her several large notes, and asked if she had a card, and where could she find her again? Apparently she was really happy with her reading, saying that she thought it was the best reading that she'd ever had, adding, with a smile, that she'd had loads and knew what she was talking about!

"Tell her she can always find your details through MacKenzie's in Redfields. They will know where to direct her," Clarabelle grinned.

Sarah relayed the information to the happy customer, wondering if she really wanted people at her store to know that she did this kind of stuff!

"It's only temporary, my dear, just temporary. You will have business cards soon enough, and a website too I think, my dear, don't you?"

Just as Sarah was about to argue with Clarabelle about not needing either, another lady sat in the chair opposite her, also wanting a reading. *Blimey,* she thought, *it's all happening!*

Fifteen readings and several hours later, a shattered and knackered Sarah packed away her cards, folded her cloth and headed for the door. She'd had the most amazing day and had loved every minute of it. She'd been shocked initially by the whole thing, the whole experience, the whole *craziness* of it all; but as the day had gone on and she'd chatted to more people, done more readings and got to know more of the other stall holders, she had come to realise just how very liberating, how very easy and contented, how very *wonderful*, these people all were! And now she was one of them!

"Yes, my dear, you are indeed, 'one of them'!" Clarabelle beamed, delighted in her ward's first day 'on the job.' "Many more to come too, many more!" she chirped. "Although I do think that you should review your terminology, Sarah. 'Bonkers' is not quite the most appropriate word to use to describe your wonderful colleagues and customers, hmmm?"

Sarah looked at the floor guiltily. "Well not bonkers as in 'bonkers,' but definitely bonkers strange!" she defended. "These people wear what they want, are 'into' what feels right for them, and none of them give a flying fig about what other people think! In the outside world, the 'rat race' world, that is 'bonkers'; but I tell you what, Clar, it's bloody great! I think they're the ones who've got it right and it's us, I mean the 'rat-racy' ones, who've got it wrong!"

"Perhaps, my dear, it is neither and it is both! It is simply a matter of choice, and as you know, we 'upstairs,' are all for choice." She smiled at Sarah, adding, "It is all about what makes you happy, what 'floats your boat,' so to speak. And, if you could all be a little more tolerant, open and understanding of other's choices, then this world would be a far happier place - far happier!"

Sarah nodded emphatically. She had certainly changed her opinions on a few things after today, wondering if she should join a belly dancing class, and maybe a Tai Chi one too! She made her way to her car, tired, happy and enormously satisfied from the day.

"And," Clarabelle piped up, "you will find when you go home, Sarah, that business cards are waiting for you to pay for on-line, as is your new website - all created and ordered in readiness for you."

"But, I can't afford all that!" she panicked.

"I think you will find the correct and *exact* amount that you need for both will be in your pockets from today's work, so not to worry about that."

Sarah felt the bulges in her jeans from the notes that she'd stuffed into them during the day from each reading. She pulled them out and was shocked to see just how much money was there! "Wow! Bloody Nora!" she grinned happily, counting the money in her hands in wondrous surprise. She had no doubt that Clarabelle was right; it would be precisely the exact amount that she needed for her new marketing. "Wow indeed!"

Chapter 15

Seven candles were flickering on top of the huge birthday cake as the gathered party sang 'Happy Birthday' to Angelica and David in appalling disharmony. New bikes sat proudly outside, their birthday presents, each with a blue or pink bow tied to its handlebars and the essential safety helmet hanging from them. Ten, six and seven year olds sat or stood nearby, each wishing they could be the one to blow out the candles on the lovely cake.

Sarah had allowed the children to invite five friends each to their little birthday tea; she simply couldn't fit any more into the house! That being said, next year she really would have to think about hiring the village hall or something for their eighth birthdays. There'd been Hell up with them trying to decide which of their friends from school was to be invited, just Hell! "Never again," she grimaced, realising, too late, her error. There were eighteen children in their class, and picking just five each had been unbearably difficult for the children. Who to leave out? *Should have just invited the whole bloody lot!*

she thought wryly.

David gazed through the window as they sang, admiring his bike with its shiny, blue and white racing stripes. *So much better than Anj's,* he decided. It was a 'proper' boy's bike this time (now that he was so grown up), with a bar across the middle horizontally; unlike Angelica's pink 'girlie' bike, with its silly bell and pink saddlebag at the back. Its crossbar was angled down, from front to back, so that she could step onto it between the wheels and ride it in a dress. *Daft! Can't do wheelies on that!* he thought in disgust.

Angelica too, was gazing at her new bike. *Beautiful,* she thought, *just beautiful!* She had already strapped Molly into the saddlebag at the back and couldn't wait to get out there and take her for another ride around the garden. *Maybe even into the lane,* she thought with glee.

"Blow out the candles," said Sarah, a big smile on her happy face. *Blimey, seven already! Where do the years go?* she wondered.

It was the middle of March and the spring sun shone in through the dining room window for the birthday tea. 'Happy Birthday' banners hung over the window, balloons tied to each corner of the room (and the front door and gate), and the party, so far, had gone swimmingly. They'd played all the usual; pass the parcel, musical statues, pin the tail on the donkey and, of course, riding the new bikes.

Margaret stood smiling, loving being part of the celebrations for her grandchildren. "Blow hard," she called from the side of the room, wondering if there would be enough cake to go round for all the guests? She felt for her ankles; *swollen again, blast! I'm far too old for all this standing,* she thought with a grimace. *Still, they will all be going outside to play soon and then I can have a chair.*

Ben and Gina were in the kitchen, making tea and coffee for the adults, whilst her other grandson, Joe, was in the living room playing 'play-station.' He had decided that, at nearly twelve, he was far too old for candles and suchlike. He'd argued with his parents all week, saying that he didn't want to go to the 'stupid party,' but they'd insisted, saying that it was his cousins' birthdays and he had to, end of! He'd been sulking ever since! As soon as he'd come reluctantly into the house for the party tea, he had made his way to the living room and plugged his console in immediately. He hadn't spoken to anyone since!

"It's such a shame that Linda and James couldn't make it, don't you think, Sarah?" Margaret said, shaking her head. She'd hate it if she couldn't be there to celebrate her grandchildren's birthdays, and really, for the life of her, couldn't understand why they had not made the effort to fly over!

"Mum, they're getting on now, hun," Sarah replied. "Don't forget, they're nearly ten years older than you, and look how you struggle; and that's just to get you to come from Redville, eight miles away, never mind the two thousand miles from Spain that they'd have to do!"

"Yes well, Sarah, Ben and Gina kindly picked me up to save my ankles from the drive. I really think I shall have to consider getting rid of my little car and using lifts and taxis more often. It is so much easier," she declared, staring at the offending ankles with frustration.

Sarah looked down at her mother's ankles to see how

swollen they were. *She's not doing too badly really, for her mid-seventies,* she thought, comparing her mother's health to that of Simon's parents. Margaret had poor lungs (from the years of heavy smoking), she also had terrible sinuses, suffering badly from headaches as a result. She had cut down on the cigs over the years, admittedly, but still puffed away several each day. Sarah considered her mother's lifestyle. She rarely left her home and had practically a zero social life; it wasn't a particularly healthy existence! Simon's parents, on the other hand, were both non-smokers, lived in Spain in a lovely villa by the sea, and spent most of their time on outdoor living. They played golf regularly and had active social lives with the other British ex-pats in their community. Their health was incredible, especially for a couple in their eighties! They'd been talking recently about moving back to the UK though, now that they were getting older, but kept putting it off because of the British weather. "Just so cold," they'd say. "Bloody freezing!" James would declare, never staying for more than a few days and whenever possible, visiting in the summer months. Mid-March in Britain was not a visit that James wanted to make, even for his grandchildren's birthdays! They'd be over, as usual, in July; spend a week and then hop on the plane back to Spain. They did come over for Christmas every other year though, enjoying the children's excitement of 'Santa Claus' almost as much as the children themselves; but they didn't ever go far from a fire and they didn't stay long!

"Right then, you lot," grinned Simon, grabbing both of his children up and into his arms, "time to go outside and play." Angelica screeched and David giggled as both children were carried out sideways under their father's arms, one hanging each side of his long body.

"Put me down, Daddy!" Angelica shrieked, giggling happily. She was loving the attention that she was now getting from the other children as they stared in amazement at her father carrying her through the door in such a fashion. David flung his arms out in front of him horizontally, singing the theme tune to 'Superman' at the same time.

"Da, da-da-da … da-da-da-da … da-da-da-da!" he sang madly.

The other children all filed out after them, laughing and giggling, leaving Sarah in peace to cut the cake. She covered each slice and placed them inside the ten 'party bags,' along with handfuls of sweets. Joe had insisted that he didn't want one and was far too old 'for all that rubbish'! Concentrating hard on the 'perfect goodie bags' that she was busy creating for the children to take home, she barely noticed the touch on her arm; not until she heard his voice that is!

"Hello, my darling girl. What a wonderful party you've made for my grandchildren!"

Her father's rich, vibrant tone echoed into her mind and she immediately felt his loving presence. "Hello, Dad, how lovely to hear you!" she smiled. "How long have you been here?"

"Och, since the beginning, my dear, but I didn't want to disturb, especially with your mother here."

She was sure she saw him wink, or did she just feel it? She'd been able to sense and feel her father ever since

Simon's accident all those years ago, but in the last year it had become stronger, with him 'popping in' quite often. Clarabelle said that he always had; she just hadn't been aware of it, but now that she was 'opening up' more, as Clarabelle put it, she *was* aware of it, and then some! Sarah chatted away to her father quite happily until, without warning, Ben stuck his head around the door and looked at her in amazement.

"Who you talking to, Sis?" he grinned, with his eyebrows raised and a 'you are being mental again' look!

"Oh hi, Ben, didn't see you there. Just chatting to Dad - he says to say hi, by the way."

Ben scratched his head in amusement. He didn't doubt his sister one jot, especially seeing as he had a Guardian Angel who he could see and chat to himself! He'd just never seen any ghosts, especially his father!

"Och laddie, now you know that's not your path," piped up Clarence (sounding exactly like John, his father), sitting as usual, on Ben's right shoulder. "It is your sister that needs to be able to see those that are in spirit, as part of her work to help and heal those that need her." He added with a chuckle, "and you don't need to do that in the bank, my boy!"

"Too right!" grinned Ben, imagining the chaos if he could see his customers ghostly family members every time he went into a meeting with one. It'd be a disaster! "So, do you see them often, these 'ghosts' then, Sar?" he asked curiously. "Doesn't it scare you?"

"No, hun, not at all. I don't actually see that many, and no, not often. And I only become aware of them if it's important."

"So how's it all going then?" Ben asked, closing the door quietly so that they could talk discretely. "You know, the readings and stuff? I saw your website is getting a lot of hits. Nice web by the way!"

"Thanks, yes, it's been great! I love it! I'm always surprised when I get an email or a phone call, even now. I don't advertise, I don't promote, but people still seem to find out about me. Word of mouth I guess; friends telling friends."

Ben noticed the way that her eyes brightened whenever she talked about her 'work.' He smiled at her, happy that she was happy! "I thought you'd been doing those shows, you know, the psychic fayre things." Sarah was nodding. "Well I bet a lot of people have picked up your business cards there, and probably passed them to friends and stuff," he said thoughtfully.

"Yes, you're right, must be, cos I had to order more last week. Yes, I hadn't thought of that." Sarah pondered the way business had been flowing, increasing and building over the last six months since she'd done her first psychic fayre in the Town Hall. "I've only done a few of those fayres though; it was my fourth one last week. I love them, you know, Ben; they're just so magical and uplifting!"

"And clearly lucrative too!" he grinned, ever the banker!

Sarah considered the financial gain from her work, wondering for the umpteenth time if it was okay to be profiting from helping others. Clarabelle always insisted that it was fine, saying that the universe worked on exchange, and it was only right and proper that she be paid for her time, her energy and her help, just the same as in any other job! She'd also insisted that Sarah set prices, and not continue with the 'pay me what you think is fair' thing that she'd done at the beginning. It had soon become apparent that this generosity (or guilt, as Clarabelle called it), was an open gate for some people to take advantage of her. Instead, on Clarabelle's nagging, Sarah had researched the 'going rate' for readings by examining other people's websites and prices, and had (with prompting), opted for the middle ground between the most and least expensive. She also offered discounts to those on low incomes, in her effort to be affordable to anyone who really needed it. Work flowed gently her way, here and there, generally doing her readings during the day when the children were at school. She'd been aware of 'loved ones' in spirit (those that belonged to her customers), popping in now and again, and she would get some message to pass on; but for the most part, she was there to read the cards, not to work as a medium. Her task was to help people find their way on their path through life. *Should I move?* they'd ask. *Should I leave him? Should I change jobs? Will I have children?* But the biggest and most often requested question was always the same - love! She had been staggered by just how many people had wanted answers to that same question! *When will I find love? Will I ever meet anyone? Is my 'Mr. Right' out there somewhere?* The answer was usually the same; *when you find your way and your peace, then love will come.* So many people wanted a relationship for the wrong reasons - to escape their loneliness, to find their happiness, to find their joy through that relationship! That wasn't love; that was need! It created dependency, and ultimately, unhappiness! Sarah repeated the same message over and over; *when you find your happiness and joy within, then, and only then, will you find that love, real love.* She'd look at them gently, feeling their aloneness, and for many, their desperation. She would say quietly, "When you fall in love with you, then you will find that others will also fall in love with you. Get you happy first, try not to worry about that ... do what you need to do to get you happy ... change that job ... move ... do what you need to do ... work on that confidence ... sort out that esteem ... get out of that stuck space ... unclog your life... stop hiding from life and get out there." She would end with giving hope, if the cards showed it, saying to them, "Once you're happy and no longer stuck, the right one will find you, or you will find them, but it will happen." *When?* they would ask. *When you have found your peace!* she would answer.

Sarah brought her attention away from her work and back to Ben. She smiled. "Yes, it's not bad at all," she said, "the money, you know. But I don't do it for that. I do it cos I love doing it, and I can see the way it helps."

"Like what?" Ben asked, wondering quite how Sarah did what she did.

"Like helping people to make changes, that sort of thing. Do you know what, Ben?" Ben shook his head, waiting for her to continue. "Most people say the same thing to me, when I've finished, that I haven't told them anything that they didn't already know! You know, deep down inside? It's just that they didn't want to see it, or didn't want to face it. When they hear it from me, a stranger, it's like 'confirmation' or something, and then they feel ready to go and sort things out. I don't know, hun, I just know it works and it helps. I can't give you details, you know that. It's confidential; has to be!"

The two siblings continued chatting until Margaret opened the door, saying that their coffee was going cold. She eyed them suspiciously. They'd suddenly shut up as soon as she'd appeared. *What are they up to now?* she wondered, shaking her head. Feeling her ankles swelling, she didn't wait to find out, returning swiftly to the kitchen and the chair that had her name on it - and another slice of the lovely birthday cake!

Chapter 16

The September sun shone down and into the Brown house as the children rushed around, gathering coats, lunch boxes and satchels.

"Come ON, Anj," David implored. "We're gonna be late and I don' wanna be late on my first day in big school, even if you do!" David's blond hair flopped into his blue eyes as he shook his head vehemently, emphasising his annoyance.

God, love him, he looks more and more like his father every day! Sarah thought, grinning at her son.

"Well it's not like it's a whole new school, is it?" Angelica grinned, ignoring her brother's frustration and impatience with equal measure. "I mean, we're only going next door! It's not like when we go to the *really* big school in Redville now is it?" Angelica was completely bemused! The infant school was in the same grounds as the junior school; the first housing the five to seven year olds in the 'infants' section, the second; the seven to eleven year olds in the 'junior' section. Once this stage of their education was completed, they would then go up to the High School in Redville - on the school bus! Angelica couldn't wait! Somehow she would have to still her boredom of this tiny village school and hold out for the wonder of the enormous High School that was four years away. Redfields (where she lived) was a small town/large village and the entire population of the village school was only two hundred or so pupils, and that included both sections! The High School, on the other hand, served the major town of Redville with its huge population (in comparison to boring old Redfields), along with being the catchment school for all the villages within a fifteen mile radius. It had over two thousand pupils and Angelica couldn't wait!

Grabbing her bag and coat leisurely, she grinned at the frustrated David and sighed, "Come on then, grumpy, let's go!"

Fred lolloped alongside them as they walked the short distance to the school. Sarah brought up the rear, chatting away to Clarabelle as she walked.

"Dog, my legs are killing me!" Fred moaned. "Not that anyone cares!" he added with a huff. "Seriously, they bloody do!" he moaned to himself, wondering if he should get Mum to take him to 'Terry-the-Terribles,' down at the vets, and get them checked out. "Na, bollocks," he muttered. "He'll only go and stick another needle in me neck, and probably the stick thing up me bum! Na, sod that!" Fred pondered his day, debating whether to rest up his aching legs or get Dad to take him to the park later. It was his birthday and he'd been given extra doggie chocs for breakie. *Nice!* He was eight now, quite old for a dog, and was feeling his age. He'd even got snappy with

Angelica the other day; most unlike him! Fred sighed heavily, feeling really, really fed up!

"Blimey, Fred, that was a big sigh!" smiled Sarah, watching the dog carefully. He usually loved these walks to school, normally bounding along, but today he was plodding, grumbling away to himself. "What's wrong, hun?" she asked, surprised that he was miserable on his birthday, especially after the doggie chocs! He loved doggie chocs; he was obsessed with them - usually!

"Dunno!" he replied, continuing to grumble to himself. Sarah picked the odd word up here and there, between the sighs and grunts. *What's the point,* mumble, mumble ... *may as well go jump off a bloody bridge* ... mumble, mumble ... *life's shit* ... mumble, mumble, and so it went on; all the way to the school *and* all the way back home again!

Sarah ignored him, deciding to 'sort him out later.' Right now, she needed to focus on her children and getting them to their first day in junior school on time.

***

An hour later, housework done, Sarah sat on the floor in front of Fred's bed in the hall and stroked his head gently. "What's wrong, hun?" she asked quietly. "Tell Mum, there's a good boy."

Fred looked at her slowly. *Maybe she does care?* he wondered.

"Of course, I care, Fred! You know I do!" she exclaimed in horror, reading his mind beautifully. "What's going on with you aye? You've been quiet for days! Has something upset you?"

"Oh, I dunno," he sighed. "I been feeling like this for days now, Mum. All the fun has gone out of life, and … and … I just think life is shit!" A tear rolled dramatically from Fred's eye, showing just how bad it was!

"Clarabelle, I need you!" called Sarah out loud, staring at the ceiling.

Quick as a flash, Clarabelle appeared on her left shoulder. "Yes, dear, you shrieked?" she grinned.

"I didn't shriek, I called!" argued Sarah. "Anyway, can you feel what's going on with Freddie please? He's in a right mood!"

Clarabelle popped onto Fred's head, putting her hands over his head and grimaced with a shudder. "Oh dear!" she exclaimed in horror. "Oh dear, dear!"

"What?" Sarah was scared now! "Is he alright? God, don't tell me he's ill or anything, Clar! Is it serious?" The colour had drained from Sarah's face, her hands began to shake; she felt totally terrified!

"No, not at all, my dear; but there is something wrong, and, I am afraid to say, it is my fault! Most remiss of me, most remiss indeed!"

"Aye? What? What's your fault?" Sarah looked bemused and confused, but also very relieved.

"Freddie, has, unfortunately, become 'contaminated' Sarah, dear. Most unfortunate! My fault; my fault!"

"Contaminated? Is it serious? What's he contaminated with? Can you fix it? You have to fix it!" Sarah was gabbling in her panic, her words tumbling over each other in their rush to get out.

"Contaminated with sadness, my dear. Frieda's

sadness! I forgot, you see, to cleanse the room after her little visit last week. Oh dear, oh me, oh my! How very remiss of me!"

Sarah looked at her in surprise. "Contaminated with sadness? Frieda's sadness? I don't understand!"

Fred looked at them both in disgust and shook his head. "I don't care whose bloody fault it is!" he grumbled. "Just bloody fix it! And soon!"

"Yes dear, of course, dear! Right on it, dear, leave it with me! Won't take a mo, a tick, not long, promise!" And Clarabelle beamed her light from each hand right into Fred's head, pulling her hands back as she did.

Sticking to each hand, like bugs onto a sticky fly-trap, Sarah could clearly see a big, dirty, black, gungy energy. It was like wobbly string, and it was being pulled out of Fred right before her very eyes! She was gobsmacked! "Bloody Nora!" she whispered. "That doesn't look good!"

"Indeed not!" Clarabelle frowned, continuing her job of 'fixing Fred.' Seconds later it was all out, and Clarabelle immediately popped outside with it, removing the offending 'gunge' to the safety of the garden pond, where it was dumped unceremoniously. Returning just as quickly, she beamed at Sarah happily. "All done!" she confirmed. "The water will transmute its nasty energy quick smart! All sorted!"

"Right, Miss, we need to talk!" Sarah exclaimed crossly. "What the hell was that nasty crap doing in my dog?" She was fuming! "And how is it your fault?"

Clarabelle looked at the floor guiltily. She wrung her hands, biting her lip, wondering if she was going to get into trouble 'upstairs' for this appalling oversight!

Fred looked up at the warring pair grinning. He felt marvellous! Bloody marvellous! His aching legs had stopped aching, his headache was gone, and he felt extraordinarily happy! "Yay baby!" he yelled, jumping up in delight. "Fred the Fantastic is back!" and bounded outside to find his favourite bone.

Sarah glared at Clarabelle. "Lounge, sofa, sit, now!" she demanded.

Clarabelle flew quickly into the lounge and perched on top of the sofa, still wringing her hands. "Oops!" she said quietly. "I must admit, my dear, I did rather 'stuff up' there," adding quietly to herself, "big time!" She was pale, and getting paler by the minute; the guilt washing over her in waves. Sarah continued to glare at her, noting Clarabelle's halo dimming significantly under her wrath with each passing second. Clarabelle looked at the floor, mumbling, "You see, my dear, as you know, your Frieda has been very sad lately. She has barely left the house in three months! Three months! Depression is terrible you know, just terrible!"

Sarah nodded. "Go on," she said, still with an angry tone.

She's beginning to calm down, Clarabelle noted with relief, *smashing!* She continued her explanation, the guilt still wracked on her face. "So when I persuaded you to try to get Frieda out of the house, you know, like you did; getting her to come here the other day ... well, I used the opportunity to remove some of that sadness. Miya helped, of course, only we forgot to remove it afterwards, so it must have been hanging around here, and poor Freddie; he must have absorbed it!"

Sarah couldn't believe her ears! "So," she glared, her face going red, the realisation sinking in of the seriousness of Clarabelle's admission, "you pulled this 'stuff,' this 'crap,' out of Frieda; this *contagious* crap, and you just left it in my house?"

Clarabelle nodded, looking even more guilty - if that was possible!

Sarah stormed on. "The kids could have caught it, or absorbed it, or whatever the hell it does to get into other people! Not okay, Clar, not bloody okay AT ALL!" she shouted. If Sarah was mad before, she was bloody furious now! "AT ALL!" she shouted again. She stomped out of the house and into the garden, trying to calm herself down. "In my kids!" she stomped, going in circle around the garden; "in my bloody kids!"

"What's in the bloody kids, Mum?" Fred called, lolloping over to Sarah from his spot under the tree. *Dog, she looked mad!* He plodded back to the tree as she stomped, fetching his second best bone from underneath it. Plodding back to Mum, bone in his mucky jaw, he dropped it at her feet in a show of undying support. "I know it's not much, Mum, but a good chew on that will help those gnashing teeth!" he grinned sympathetically. "And," he added, with total devotion and martyrdom, "if you need it, but only if you *really* need it, I will even lend you, temporarily mind you, my very *best* one!" Dog, he was so clever! He'd sort Mum out in no time! No time at all!

Sarah was trying to calm down, making efforts to reassure herself that her children had not 'caught' the depression left hanging about by bloody Clarabelle, and that they were safe. It took some time, but, eventually, she got there. She sat down heavily on her favourite bench under the apple tree. She loved sitting there; it always brought her back to calmness whenever she was wound up. She thought back to last week when Frieda had come over for coffee. *God, that had been hard!* She hadn't visited for ages, and Clarabelle had told her to nag, bully, push, cajole and do whatever she needed to do to get Frieda out of the house. Sarah had asked why she simply couldn't go over to Frieda's house, as she didn't want to leave, but Clarabelle had said that the energy there was too heavy for any good to come from it. Sarah had agreed, and nagged and pushed Frieda to come over, as she had been asked to do. Eventually, Sarah had worn her down, and a sad and depressed Frieda had turned up for coffee. Her hair was lank and limp, and, Sarah noted, dirty! She hadn't washed it in a week, she'd barely showered, and, she admitted guiltily, most of the time she didn't even get dressed! She was off work, 'on the sick,' and simply couldn't be bothered to do anything.

They had talked for some time, discussing her progress and the overwhelming sadness that Frieda was now going through. Frieda had talked about her childhood, her sadness completely focused on that terrible time years ago. "If only I hadn't been an only child," she lamented. "If only the after-school childcare hadn't broken down, I would never have gone there!"

Frieda had been an only child, born to parents who both worked long hours. Her mum was a nurse, working shifts; her father a sales rep, often away on business. Frieda had been a lonely child, spending a lot of time at childminders, most of whom were too busy with their own, or the other children that they cared for, to pay her much attention at all. When the childminder had become ill, leaving Frieda's parents suddenly in the lurch, her father's 'friend' had offered to look after her. He had worked from home (so he said), so it was no trouble at all. Yeah right! No trouble? He'd revelled in it! The 'so-called-job' had, of course, been his disgusting paedophile work, which included sharing and selling photographs and videos of his 'conquests' with his equally sick friends. Apparently he'd made a fortune! Not that they knew any of that, of course, at the time! Her father had initially thought that he was taking advantage of both their friendship and his friend's luck (working from home), by leaving his daughter there; but as time had gone by, and, it seemed, Frieda was happy to be spending time there, the parents had relaxed and allowed the arrangement to continue, even after the childminder had recovered from her illness.

Frieda had revelled in the one-on-one attention that the man lavished on her; enjoying the praise, the time, the care and the focus that he gave her, and he gave her alone. For the first time in her young life, she had total, focused, undivided attention. At home, it seemed, Mummy and Daddy were always too busy, too tired or not there, to be able to give her anything much at all! So the 'friendship' with her 'special friend' blossomed. The more attention he gave her, the more she responded. She had had no idea where it would lead or what he had planned for her. It was all just so sad! And Frieda had cried some more into Sarah's supporting, loving arms as she'd talked about her past; crying and grieving for her lack of awareness, lack of insight, lack of knowing, lack of resisting! Sarah kept assuring her that it wasn't her fault, and Frieda agreed. No, she said, she knew that it wasn't her fault. She knew she'd been manipulated, she was no longer angry at either the man, her parents or herself. All she could feel now was sadness and pity, and it filled her to her core.

Sarah had asked her if she could 'tune into her,' and see what help could be attained, and reluctantly, the tearful Frieda had agreed. Miya had appeared instantly, explaining to the bewildered Sarah that Frieda was now in stage four of five. The second stage, anger, had apparently taken rather longer than had been expected, nearly a year, delaying progress somewhat. That being said, Miya assured that Frieda had moved through the third stage of 'bargaining' brilliantly, and was now on this next stage of depression. Frieda's permission was asked for the angels to remove what they could, and the willing but apathetic Frieda had acquiesced, letting the angels pull away a huge chunk of abject sadness. Afterwards Frieda had cried some more, and then she had gone home.

Watching her friend's car pull away, Sarah had said to Clarabelle in disappointment that the healing clearly hadn't worked; Frieda was still crying! She had been reassured that the tears were simply the next level of sorrow coming up and out, like an onion, apparently! Lots of layers to be removed and released, but she was getting there.

Frieda was indeed 'getting there'! Over the next six months, under Sarah's, Clarabelle's and Miya's watchful eyes, she completed stage four, depression, finally finished her counselling that had lasted almost two years. She was still an active part of the support group, choosing to remain and help the others that were coming through daily, encouraging them to get to where she, herself, was getting. She was feeling stronger and better every day! There was still some remaining sadness to come out, she was aware of that, but she could finally see the finish line! Acceptance had begun to build inside her. As the depression was leaving her, so, it seemed, it was being replaced with a sense of acceptance that grew every day. The light at the end of the tunnel was shining ahead, and it was shining brightly. She focused on the light and she just knew that she'd get there!

"Indeed," exclaimed Miya happily. "Indeed!"

Chapter 17

The twins' eighth birthday bash this year had been a chaotic frenzy of fun and frolics. Sarah had hired the village hall and invited, it seemed, half the bloody school! Angelica and David had had a whale of a time, and, to their delight, a tonne of birthday presents from the many guests! She'd involved everyone in the family to help organise, plan and create all the necessary food for thirty-five, seven and eight year olds; not to mention the grown-ups, who'd managed to demolish more than their share of kiddies' party food - especially the sausages on sticks! There'd been music and lights (courtesy of Tom, Angie's husband, who knew a 'mate from work with some disco lights'). They had been a huge success and had made the musical chairs go really well! Frieda and Angie, her two closest friends, had helped her, of course, along with Margaret and Gina. It had been great fun. "Definitely the way to go," Sarah had grinned at her helpers, "all the mess in the village hall, instead of in my house!" They'd also used the party as an excuse to celebrate Frieda's 'coming out.' That evening, long after the children and family guests had all gone home, and Sarah's own children were safely tucked up in bed (tired out from their party), the three friends had sat down together exhausted. Sarah opened several bottles of champagne to toast the ending of Frieda's counselling.

"Hell of an achievement, hun," smiled Angie.

"Incredible," grinned Sarah. *God, I'm so proud of her! What that girl has gone through over the past two years has been a rollercoaster! She's hung on by her fingernails at times, wondering if she'd ever 'get there,' but she has!* Sarah was delighted for her. "So what's next, Frie?" she asked, "where do you go from here?"

"Oh, I dunno, mate." Frieda shook her head, pondering this herself. She didn't have a clue! She was back at work now, after several months 'off sick' with depression, and had been trying to refocus her attention on her job at the college in Redville. She had worked in the administration department for many years, and had been supported beautifully throughout the last two years by both her colleagues and her bosses, right up the chain of command. Her counsellor had suggested, from the beginning, that she tell her immediate boss what was going on, and to ask for support. It had taken her a while to do that, worrying about 'losing face' and of being judged, but eventually, she had plucked up the courage and spilled her guts to Mike, her direct manager. He'd been magnificent, to be fair. He'd promised her all the help and support that the large organisation had available, including their own counselling service, which she had, on occasion, used, but only when she was in crisis and couldn't get hold of her own counsellor at the centre. Frieda considered her employers with a smile, feeling so incredibly grateful for their tolerance, and for their 'full sick pay policy.' When it had all got too much for her and she'd gone off sick with depression last summer, they had been patient and understanding, not putting any pressure on her whatsoever to get back to work. She had finally returned last month, stronger and happier, and had been met with hugs from her colleagues, a huge smile from her boss and even a cake! She'd nearly cried, she'd been so overwhelmed by their support.

Where to go from here? Frieda pondered for a moment. "Just my job, for now," she replied to her smiling friends. "I have some making up to do there, although they don't push it, bless 'em, but there is a huge backlog and I just want to catch up with that, and then see where I am after Easter."

"Maybe time to start getting out and about again, Frie?" suggested Angie. Frieda had always been a huge party girl, often out at this-or-that event, and always with a man on her arm! *Mind you, that stopped a while ago now, now I come to think of it. When was it she stopped dating? Maybe ten years ago? Maybe more! She just seemed to have gone right off men altogether!* Angie thought back. She remembered the last time Frieda dated; *yes, ten years or more,* she thought. *He'd knocked her about, that bastard; and badly too! No wonder she'd gone off men! And the one before him had shagged around behind her back, and the one before that had ...* Angie stopped pondering why Frieda had gone off men! It was patently clear why Frieda had gone off men! That being said, she had still gone out a lot, she just hadn't dated. *When did the 'going out' stop?* she wondered, thinking back as far as she could to the last time Frieda had regaled her stories and adventures from her hectic social life. *It's two years! Christ, it's two bloody years! These last two years she hasn't gone out at all! She's practically been a hermit since this counselling stuff started. Blimey, heavy shit!* She sighed, looking at her friend, wondering how she'd survived all the crap she'd gone through! She, herself, had been happily married to Tom for donks! Angie had never known the pain of violence, rejection, abuse, or of betrayal - not like poor Frieda! She smiled at Frieda encouragingly, "Time to start living again now, Frie, aye? Have a bit of fun again, mate, don't you think?" she suggested hopefully, deciding that her friend really needed to get out and have some fun. *Maybe, in time, even a man!* Angie thought. *A nice man, of course, none of the rubbish that Frieda had always attracted to her in the past. Like flies to shit,* she decided. *Only Frieda wasn't shit, or a fly! She was lovely and she deserved better!* Angie considered her new knowledge and understanding about flies and shit; knowledge that she really had hoped never to have! Knowledge shared by Frieda as her own, growing understanding had built, following her many counselling sessions. The trouble was (Angie knew), that Frieda had felt that she *was* shit! For years! For ever, it seemed! So the flies had come! The flies had swarmed; always another one to hurt her and shit on her, making her feel even more like shit than she did before! *Bastards!* Angie shook her head in disgust, wondering just how many 'bastard men' were out there!

She'd had no idea that people could do such things; growing up in her 'safe, secure world,' and going on from there straight to her 'safe, secure marriage.' She had been shocked when Frieda had explained to her, that, for her whole life, she had felt dirty, defiled, unworthy and disgusting (she had explained this after one particularly harrowing counselling session), along with all those other horrible things that you must feel when you've been abused like she was. *Yes, definitely time for a nice man, and one that will treat her with respect, and care, and be gentle!* Angie decided, wondering if Tom knew of any such men. *Maybe I shall have a word? Yes, I shall ask Tom! Maybe set up a dinner party, do a bit of matchmaking?* She looked at Frieda and smiled. "So what about it, hun, you gonna start getting out, mate?"

"Maybe once all the work is caught up, yes. I will see how I feel in a month or two." Frieda looked at her friends closely. She knew that she would never have got through the last two years without them, and as for Sarah ... well, it was all down to her and those cards that all this had started! She grinned at them both. "Sar, Ange, I just want to say," Frieda looked at them with adoration, "that I couldn't have done this without you guys and I ..." (she had tears in her eyes, fighting for control), "I can't thank you enough, either of you ... and, Sar, can you tell my angel, Miya, that I said 'thank you' too, please? If she's there?"

Sarah nodded at Miya, sitting on top of her sofa with Clarabelle. She was beaming happily. "She knows, hun," she said, "she knows."

And both Sarah and Angie threw their arms around

Frieda and hugged her like she was the biggest teddy bear on the planet, all three of them teary-eyed.

"And we," they said in unison, sniffing into their tissues, "are so incredibly proud of you; you wonderful woman!"

***

Cara was studying hard. Her finals were coming up soon and she was beyond panicked! *Will I ever get those damned stats reports right?* she wondered. *Or memorise enough of the biology of the brain to be able to pass the bloody exams?*

Andrew looked at his daughter's anxious face and smiled. He remembered what it was like, those last few weeks in university; the panic, the cramming, the stress. *Bless her,* he thought, *she'll be alright, as long as she stays focused.*

Cara had come home for the Easter break and had barely left her room for the last two weeks, studying late into the night, doing everything she could to pass her degree in this last, final year. Her first exam was in ten days and would be followed by another five over the following two weeks. Then, if all went well, she would be graduating in early July, hopefully with honours! *She certainly deserves it, all the work she's put in,* he thought. He was incredibly proud of his daughter. He stood in the doorway of her bedroom, staring at the plate of cooling food in his hand that he had brought her. "Cara, food! It's been sitting on the dining table for nearly twenty minutes and it's going cold!" he scolded. "You have to eat, love. You can't concentrate properly if you don't eat!"

Cara was sitting at her desk, head down, staring at her laptop with what seemed to be a look of pure terror on her pretty face! She looked up at her father, dragging her gaze away from the diagram of the brain on the screen for a moment. "Sorry, Dad, I forgot. Just need to get this last bit in my head!" Cara looked at the plate of food in her father's hand longingly, feeling the rumbles in her empty stomach.

"What's this then, love? Looks complicated!" Andrew had strolled over to her, plate in hand, placing it next to her on her desk, and was looking at the screen, scratching his head. "I thought you were doing psychology not studying to be a doctor?" he grinned. "Bloody hell, that looks hard, love!"

"Hard doesn't come close, trust me!" she grimaced. "I'm never gonna get it, Dad, never!"

"Yes you will, love. Just stay focused; don't panic, and keep going. You'll get there, I know you will!" He ruffled her hair affectionately, adding, "I believe in you, Car." He looked down and into his daughter's frightened eyes, doing his best to reassure, support, encourage; as he always had.

"Thanks, Dad, you're a star, ta," she grinned. "Now shoo! Go away, working here!"

Andrew left her to it, returning to the kitchen and the stack of dishes that were waiting for him. "Just get this done and then a bit of gardening I think, and my pots," he smiled. "Maybe a glass of wine later too."

After the dishes were done, the cooker wiped and kitchen cleaned, Andrew pottered quite happily in his garden for the next hour. When he was satisfied that all was neat and tidy, weeds removed and paths swept, he returned to the kitchen to wash his hands and pour himself a glass of Merlot. Taking the glass outside, he sat down on the bench and admired his creation; his garden, with satisfaction. It had been a wilderness when he'd first bought this house ten years before; two years after his wife had died. They had lived on the outskirts of a village when she was alive, but it was quite some distance from Redville, where Cara went to school. When it had been the two of them to share the driving, the distance hadn't seemed to matter. Both parents had been able to 'taxi' the growing Cara here and there between them, whenever necessary. But it had all changed once he had become a single parent; the distance becoming a problem for the first time. It just wasn't workable. He had, after two years of trying to make it work, reluctantly sold their lovely home in the country with all its memories, and moved them closer to the large town. It had worked, and they had, eventually, settled.

Andrew surveyed the garden once again, then he examined the back of the detached house in front of him. *Yes, it was all perfect!* Not a huge house, admittedly, but it was nice and it was theirs. It had three bedrooms; two doubles (one each for him and Cara), and a single, which he used as an office. The master bedroom, his, was ensuite, and there was a nice family bathroom which Cara seemed to live in, especially since he'd had a new one put in a few years back, with its flash Jacuzzi bath! *I ruin that girl,* he grinned. He himself rarely used the new bathroom, preferring the shower in his own ensuite, but

Cara loved it, turning the bathroom into her own! Downstairs was an open plan lounge-diner, with a decent kitchen off it, through an archway. There had been a small mortgage left on the village house when his wife was still alive, but that had been cleared from the insurance, following her sad death. She'd had cancer, but had, mercifully, gone quickly. She'd been the love of his life, meeting in university all those years ago. They'd had a strong marriage, a stable life, and life had been very hard without her; especially in those first few years following her death. As time had gone on, the pain had passed, thankfully helped by throwing himself into caring for their only child, the then, ten year old Cara. She would be twenty-two this year, and he couldn't believe how quickly the years had passed!

Andrew surveyed his domain. He was completely content in his world, more so than most, he knew. So okay, he got lonely now and then, but didn't everyone? He had given some thought to his daughter's suggestion of going out more though, and even to joining the silly dating site that she kept on about all the time. She just wouldn't let it rest! He'd dismissed her nagging more than once over the last year or so, but the more she kept on, the more she'd worn him down. He was now at the point where he was allowing himself to consider it, but only a little, and not really in a serious way. Andrew gave it more thought, contemplating the life that would be coming shortly for him. Cara would be flying the nest soon, he knew; his responsibility nearly over. Not that it ever really stopped, of course, just that the main 'growing up years,' when she needed him so badly, were coming to an end. *I really don't fancy the idea of a dating site, no matter how much she nags, or even of dating, but maybe a club?* he thought, wondering if there were gardening clubs in Redville. *Probably not! Maybe a film club?* he pondered. *They had a cinema in Redville, so maybe there's a film club, or a theatre club? I must look into it,* he decided. *Tomorrow....*

***

Frieda was pondering too. She had caught up with everything at work and was at a loose end. *What did I used to do?* she wondered, staring at the television for the eighth night in a row. *Went out with men ... got used and abused (again) ... got pissed ... went to clubs dancing ... Nope! Don't want to do that! What to do then?* Frieda was nearly forty-nine now, and felt far too old for most of the things that she'd used to do 'BC' (before counselling!). None of it appealed anymore!

"Dating!" shouted Miya, sitting on the top of the sofa behind her. "Dating, dating, dating, dating, dating ... but the *right* men, the NICE men," she shouted, continuing her chanting of 'dating, dating, dating' for the next hour.

Maybe I should try dating? pondered Frieda. *Maybe I could find a nice man? A man who will be kind, and thoughtful, and caring, and ... and ... nice! .... Where to find such men? Nice men? That's the problem!* Frieda pondered some more. *None in Redville, that's for sure! Every tosspot, loser, user or abuser, liar, cheat, manipulator and heart-breaker has found their way to my door and/or my bed, and I just can't be going through that again, no bloody way!*

"Ooh, ooh, ooh!" screeched Miya excitedly. "I'm getting through, I'm getting through! How wonderful!" She clapped her hands in glee, shouting even louder now, right into Frieda's left ear, "Dating site, dating site, dating site, dating site ..." And on and on the chanting went, all through the evening, up the stairs to bed, and even into Frieda's deep subconscious as she slept.

Eight hours later, Frieda awoke, with a strange feeling that maybe she should try a dating site to find such elusive 'nice' men.

"Eureka!" screamed Miya, or would have done, had she had any voice left!

Chapter 18

The summer sun hung high in the sky as Andrew snapped photo after photo of his amazing daughter, standing on the university green in front of him. It was July and they had made the trip together to the university that Cara attended, some two hundred miles away. She had passed, and then some! Cara had managed to achieve a 'first' in her degree, and now proudly stood, holding the certificate in front of her as her father snapped away happily. 'BSc Psychology: First Class Honours,' it said. He gazed at his daughter in admiration. She looked fantastic, grinning into the camera, standing in her black cap and gown; the long, green satin dress underneath glimmering in the sunlight, setting off her dark hair wonderfully. He had bought it for her last week in preparation of the event, being dragged around countless shops with her until she had, at last, found the perfect one.

"She's done very well, your daughter," smiled a lady standing nearby. She, too, had been snapping away, taking photos of her own daughter, who had also graduated that day. "Such a shame her father can't be here to see this," the lady was saying. "He'd have been so proud!" She smiled again at Andrew. *What a lovely looking man,* she thought. *I wonder if he's single?* She decided that she wanted to find out, so added, "Your wife not here today either?"

Andrew shook his head, smilingly warmly at the lady. *She seems nice,* he thought to himself. *I wonder where her husband is? Maybe he had to work, couldn't get the day off?* He himself had booked the day off months ago, in preparation for this, determined not to miss his girl's special day! "No," he replied, a warm smile on his lips, "my wife passed some years back. It's just Cara and me, although I'm sure she's up there watching; she wouldn't miss this!"

"Oh, mine too," the woman replied. "My husband, I mean. He passed three years ago now, but I'm sure he's watching too." She smiled at him warmly, wondering how she could get to know him better. Looking over at the refreshment marquis on the other side of the green, she came up with a plan. Nodding towards the huge tent, she grinned at Andrew, fluttering her long eyelashes as she smiled, a twinkle in her brown eyes. "Laura and I are going over there for the free glass of bubbly in a moment. Would you like to join us? Be nice to have a bit of company. I'm Moira, by the way."

Andrew looked at the woman in surprise. He raised his eyebrows quizzically, not sure how to reply or what to say. *Was she just being polite,* he wondered, *taking pity on me because I'm on my own?* He looked around him at the other parents, noting that most were in couples, and, if they weren't, they had a friend or grandparent with them for company. It seemed it was just he and this lady who appeared to be on their own.

Before he had a chance to either or accept or decline her invitation, Cara had stepped in with a, "Oh, what a wonderful idea! Yes, we'd be happy to join you," and she'd grabbed her father's arm, dragging him over to the waiting woman, thrusting him at her like he was an object to be displayed. "This is Andrew," she announced happily, "and I'm Cara. Pleased to meet you!"

Cara had a twinkle in her eye that Andrew couldn't fail to notice. *Oh, God, don't start with the matchmaking / dating thing again,* he thought to himself in panic.

But it was too late, Cara was on a mission! It was the first time in memory that she'd got her father out of the house to anything other than a 'work do,' and here was a woman - an attractive, single woman - who clearly had 'the hots' for him; she was *not* going to let this golden opportunity pass! Cara eyed the woman carefully. *Not too shabby,* she thought, *for an old bird, although she does look a bit predatory for my naïve old Dad. She'll eat him alive!* That being said, Cara decided that it would do him good to get 'some practice,' even if this woman wasn't 'step-mother material,' so carried on with her matchmaking, with what was clearly, the 'merry widow'!

Several glasses of bubbly later, Andrew found himself clutching the woman's phone number, scrawled onto a piece of paper by the meddling Cara, now stuffed into his hand, and agreeing to meet Moira later for a drink. He had no idea whatsoever how that had happened! Cara grinned happily, noticing the startled look of terror in her father's eyes as he sat at the round table in the tent, Moira sitting next to him (with a happy smile), and just plied him with more champagne, grinning at his discomfort. "Just go with it, Dad," she whispered. "How bad can it be? Just give it a go!"

Andrew found himself nodding mutely, still overwhelmed, nay terrified, at the thought of actually meeting a woman for a drink! A real woman! And she clearly was very real! Her perfectly manicured hand rested gently on his knee, and he had no idea how to get rid of it!

"Give him an hour to get back to the hotel and change and he'll be right there, Moira," Cara grinned. "Hotel lobby? Six o'clock okay with you?"

"Oh, yes," Moira smiled, seduction firmly planted in her sparkling eyes, "perfect!"

"Yikes!" yelped Bart, wondering how to avoid this disaster. "And double yikes! Better get some help here! No idea how to sort this, no idea at all!" And he flew upstairs to find Miya and the others, quick smart!

***

Well I'm sure I don't know how to fix this mess you've got yourself into, Bart!" Miya glared. "What do you mean, 'he's got a date'? Who's he got a date with?"

Gosh she was mad! *How had he not stopped this? Silly angel!* Miya couldn't get over it! She'd done her bit - Frieda had joined the dating site - the right one, of course, and Bart was supposed to have sorted his end, to get Andrew onto the same one! But he had failed, and failed miserably! "I shall just have to call Clarabelle for help," she said crossly, "and even Clarence! Clarence knows everything! He'll know what to do!"

"Well actually, I think this is my fault," admitted Rena guiltily. "It was Cara! She was doing her meddling again! I tried, really I did! I tried to stop her, but I couldn't."

Miya sighed. "So who is this 'Moira' woman?" she glared.

Bart and Rena looked at the cloud they were sitting on and said nothing, then stared down at the university below in despair.

"Well? Do we know?" Miya said again, grimly.

Bart and Rena shook their heads sadly. "Well then you'd better find out!" she screeched. "You'd better put in a call to upstairs and get this … this woman, this Moira's angel here … and quick!"

Bart didn't have to be told twice. He flew upstairs as fast as his wings could fly him, rushing into the Angelic temple in a panic. "Clarence! Oh, Clarence, I need you!" he called out desperately.

Quick as a flash, Clarence appeared. "Good grief!" he exclaimed, seeing the ruffled Bart, normally so beautifully composed, all flushed and flustered. "What's gone on, Bart? What's wrong, my friend?" he asked, concern written all over his old face.

Bart relayed the disaster that was 'Andrew and Moira's date,' due in just fifteen minutes, begging for help. "She's on a mission to seduce him, Clar, a mission I tell you! What are we to do?" he implored.

"Ah, well I think the best angel for the job there, is our Nat," Clarence grinned. "He's ever so good with dealing with milfs and gilfs. Learned a lot has our Nathaniel, a lot!"

Nat was duly called, along with Moira's angel, Helena, and all three flew back down quickly to the cloud where Miya and Rena were waiting.

"The trouble with my Moira," explained Helena, "is that she is just so lonely! She can't cope on her own at all, that one! Goes from man to man trying to replace her husband, but, of course, that can't happen properly, not yet! Not until she's dealt with her grief! But she won't listen, not at all! Just thinks she can find her happiness with a new man, and for a while, she is happy, but, of course, it doesn't last!"

"Well get her to go and do her 'vampy man stealing' thing somewhere else!" exclaimed Bart in frustration. "My Andrew is taken! Well, he will be, once we can get him together with our Miya's Frieda!"

"Exactly!" Miya agreed. "He's taken! Hands off!"

"I'll do my best, of course, I will. But I don't know; once she's on a mission she won't give up until she's caught her prey!"

"It's okay, guys!" exclaimed Nat happily, pulling his wand out from his pocket. "I will wave my magic wand and stop his 'man thing' doing its 'boing thing'! Just leave it to me! It worked a treat with my Simon when he had a similar thing going on years ago with his ex; she was a vampy-man-eating milf too, and I sorted her! Just you leave it to me!" And Nat sat down happily, totally convinced that all would be well, polishing his wand in readiness.

Andrew was rather drunk! He hadn't had spirits for ever such a long time, and Moira was ordering yet more cocktails from the bar. Each seemed to get stronger, and each went ever increasingly to his head; the hard alcohol taking its toll. He looked at Moira carefully, watching her as she walked back from the bar; two cocktails held carefully in her hands so as not to spill them. *She really is rather spectacular,* he thought, wondering if he should risk another drink. *I may get silly, get carried away!* He was rather enjoying himself though, more so than he thought he would, and it *had* been a long time since he'd relaxed like this. *Oh, why not?* he thought, *just go with the flow, as Cara had said.* Andrew went with the flow, enjoying the drinks and Moira's hand on his leg in equal measure; a hand that seemed to get higher and higher up his thigh by the minute.

Another few cocktails later, and the hand was now about as high as it could go, in a public place that is! Moira's eyes glazed with delight. *Was that a reaction I just got?* she wondered, looking at Andrew's crotch. *Yes, definitely some stirrings go on there,* she noted happily. She leaned over and into Andrew seductively. "Why don't we take these up to your room?" she suggested. "It's much more comfortable upstairs, don't you think, Andrew?"

And Andrew found himself nodding happily.

Nat just couldn't believe it! He'd waved his wand a hundred times at Andrew's 'boing-thingy,' but nothing had worked. He'd tried to bring in an image of Frieda, but, of course, that had failed - they hadn't even met yet! Then he'd tried Cara, then his deceased wife, but no matter how much he had tried to distract Andrew, he hadn't been able to get through.

"Beer goggles, mate," Bart said in disgust. "Beer goggles!"

"Cocktail goggles more like!" shrilled Miya in horror.

"But it worked with Si!" Nat shrilled. "My magic wand worked perfectly well with Si!"

"But Simon wasn't drunk!" Rena pointed out.

"And you had his love for Sarah to use!" chipped in Miya. "You know, for him to remember and wake him up out of his trance! Andrew hasn't got anyone to use! No one to love! And he's drunk!"

"Oh, dear!" they all said, seeing defeat looming. "Oh, dear, dear!"

Watching Andrew now entering his hotel room with the determined Moira, bottle of champagne in hand, all four angels shrieked. "Noooooo!"

But it was too late! Andrew was too far down the line to return! After nearly thirteen years of abstinence, his body had finally woken up from its long slumber. It, and his normally rational mind, now completely taken over by both desire and alcohol.

And, having bedded the delectable Moira, being the gentleman that he was, it would take him months (many months), to extract himself from the mess that he, the cocktails and the champagne, were just about to get him in to.

"Clarence!" Bart yelled, screaming up to The Realms,

"We're in trouble, Clarence! Helppppppp, Clarence!"

***

Whilst the drunken Andrew was enjoying the delights of passion with the happy Moira, Frieda was perusing the on-line dating site that she'd joined earlier in the day. *He looks nice,* she thought, staring at the picture of Andrew. She read his profile with interest, but then noticed the date of his last 'log in.' *Over a year ago! Well that's no good!* she thought to herself. *He must have found someone and forgot to cancel his profile. Oh, well, never mind, let's have a look at him instead!* And Frieda's attention moved to the next photo on the screen.

Miya sighed heavily. "What do we do now?" she exclaimed. "What in heavens am I to do now. ... ?"

Chapter 19

The four 'fallen' angels stood in front of Metatron nervously.

"Sorry, Sir," Bart said.

"Me too," cried Miya, terribly upset at what was occurring 'downstairs.'

"And me," said Rena and Helena together.

"Hmmm," Metatron replied, shaking his head at the crew. "You have failed majorly," he scowled. "All of you!"

The angels hung their heads in shame.

"Call yourself, Guardian Angels? Guardian indeed!" Metatron practically spat the word 'guardian' at them. "You couldn't guard an open door! Not one of you, never mind guarding a human's destiny!" he said in disgust. "Ashamed of you I am! Ashamed!"

Rena and Helena burst into tears. Bart's lip wobbled and Miya thought she would drown in her tears, she was that upset!

"Sort it out!" Metatron bellowed, "And quickly!"

They flew out of his enormous office, bumping into

each other along the way out of the huge doors, each flying into the hall in a flurry of wings and feathers.

"Oh dear, oh me, oh my!" they cried. "What are we going to do?"

With that, Archangel Michael hurried past, on his way to his monthly briefing with the Boss, calling to them as he passed by. "Wassup?" he smiled, adding, "see me later!" And then he was gone.

"Oh dear, do you think he's cross too?" worried Helena.

"Bound to be," spouted Bart.

"But not as cross as Metatron," said Miya hopefully.

"Well, if anyone can help, it'll be Michael," said Helena, hoping that he wouldn't be too cross with them for their miserably failed mission of getting Frieda and Andrew together.

Miya pondered the problem. Her Frieda had gone on a string of dates with unsuitable men over the last few months, becoming increasingly despondent with each one. She hadn't wanted to see any of them again, not for a second date! Andrew, on the other hand, so Bart had said, had the opposite problem; he just didn't know how to extract himself from Moira! She was clingy and needy, and driving him insane with her need for constant attention. After all his years of being alone, her constant presence was making Andrew feel swamped, crowded and suffocated! She was just too much, but he had no idea what to do, so he did nothing. Miya sighed loudly. Bart had tried his best, she knew. He'd pushed Andrew to end it, but he just wouldn't! Moira hadn't exactly done anything wrong, so Andrew felt that he couldn't just tell her that it was over; not without a good reason! He knew that she wasn't right for him and had begun to realise that if he was going to be any relationship, it just had to be with an independent woman. 'Yes!' the angels had screamed into his deaf ears, 'you need an independent woman; you need Frieda!' But he hadn't listened, hadn't heard, and the months had dragged by. Metatron had been patient, initially, but now he'd had enough. They all had!

"Time to regroup people," Miya said heavily. "Time for Plan B!"

"What's 'Plan B'?" Bart asked nervously.

"I have no idea, Bart! None whatsoever!" replied Miya sadly.

And the angels filed out of the long hall to organise another meeting, and a much needed new plan!

**

Sarah stood just inside the playground gates waiting for her twins to come out from school.

Christmas was coming and she was terribly distracted thinking about all the things that she still had to do. Her mobile phone rang suddenly, pulling her from her thoughts and making her jump. In her haste to answer it, her handbag fell off her shoulder and onto the ground, dropping a whole load of her business cards onto the school playground. She grabbed her bag with one hand and answered the ringing phone with the other, not noticing the spilled cards. "Hi, hun. Yes, Si?" she said into the phone, "Yes, babe, I've got the turkey and yes, I've got the big presents, but … oh, yes, thank you, yes, that would be great, babe, thanks … Love you too, see you later." She breathed a sigh of relief, putting the phone back into her bag. *Thank God for Si,* she thought happily. *He's gonna sort out the other presents after work tonight. Smashing!* It was late night shopping in Redville and Simon would be going with Ben after work to get her present and had rung to ask if she wanted him to get her mum's, and to ask if she wanted him to get anyone else's? He was so thoughtful, bless! He'd brought the Christmas tree last night and they would be decorating it together this weekend with the children. Sarah loved Christmas, totally loved it, but it was exhausting! So much to do!

She didn't notice one of the other mums coming over until she was standing right next to her. "You dropped some cards, Sarah," she said, smiling. Jane bent down to pick them up, looking at them in surprise. "Oh! You do psychic stuff! I didn't know that! Do you do parties? Can I book one?" she asked excitedly.

"Umm, well I do readings but I don't know what you mean by 'party,' Jane," Sarah replied, a little embarrassed by the admission.

"Oh, you know; I get a few of my friends round and you come around to mine and give us all a reading. Do you do that? Can you do Friday?" Jane gabbled, grinning at Sarah.

"Umm, yes, I guess so," she replied, not quite sure about doing multiple readings for a group. *Mind you, I do multiple readings at the psychic fayres, so I guess it's the same as that,* she thought warily.

"Lovely!" exclaimed Jane happily. "I've got your card

now, so I'll text you later with my address. Shall we say seven Friday?" And then she was gone.

Sarah didn't have time to think of the request any further before the children came pouring out of the school doors noisily, banging and shouting their way over to their collectors.

Sarah had almost forgotten about the conversation when her mobile phone bleeped later that night with a message. **Got 6 mates, 7pm is fine. Seen your prices on your web. do u do discount 4 parties? Ta Jane x**. Two seconds later a second text came through with an address and postcode. Sarah considered the question. Should she do discounts for multiple people? What do other people do?

Clarabelle rushed into the room, hugging Sarah. "Ooh, how exciting! A party, I do so *love* parties!" she beamed. "And it will only get better now, my dear. Word of mouth you know, and we both know how very 'chatty' that mouth of Jane's is, don't we, my dear?"

God, yes! Jane is the biggest gossip in town! Sarah being a psychic would be all round the town before bedtime, and probably half the country by morning, if not the world! She looked at Clarabelle in despair. "Everyone will know, Clar! I'll be the talk of the town! I hate gossip, you know I do!"

"Oh, tosh!" grinned Clarabelle. "How do you expect to be able to heal and help all those lovely people if they don't know about you, aye? I had a little word with Gemma earlier, Jane's angel you know? Anyway, you probably didn't know that but I did." Clarabelle was gabbling away happily, completely unaware of Sarah's growing wrath. "Now, where was I? Oh yes, well Gemma and I arranged it all! Your little spill of cards you know ... we are so clever, are we not?" Clarabelle was giggling happily to herself, delighted at her little plan and that it had worked so well! Sarah was, indeed, the talk of the town already, and it wasn't quite nine o'clock! Clarabelle was chuffed to bits! Sarah, however, looked anything but chuffed!

"Clar!" she said in horror to the grinning angel. "What on earth were you thinking? Doing psychic shows and fayres is one thing, but that is separate to my life with Si and the kids, very separate; well, it was! I don't want the village knowing my business. The mums will talk, the kids will hear, and my kids will get bullied and teased, not to mention how this may affect business at the store! You idiot!" Sarah was fuming. She glared at Clarabelle, who, she was pleased to note, had stopped grinning quite so inanely and was looking rather sheepish. "And what about free will? My will? No one bloody asked me!" she fumed.

"Oh dear; oh me, oh my!" Clarabelle blustered. "I hadn't thought of that! Oh, deary-dear! What *shall* I do?" Clarabelle scratched her head in alarm, noticing, as she did, that her halo had slipped somewhat. That definitely meant that she'd stuffed up, again! Big time! "Oops!" she whispered, looking at Sarah cautiously. *She isn't bright red and her hands aren't doing the 'fist thing' that they sometimes do; so she isn't as mad as she can get. Jolly good!* she thought. She smiled at Sarah reassuringly. "Not to worry, my dear. I shall make sure that only the people who need to know find out, and if they don't, I shall buffer you from the storm, don't you fret." And then she was gone; to weave her magic and calm the gossip, as best as she could, leaving Sarah to seethe on her own.

***

"So it went well, in the end, Frie, the psychic party I did last night. I was quite pleased actually. They all seemed happy with their reading, I think I even helped a few."

Frieda sipped her coffee and thought about her friend and her readings. "I'm sure you did, hun," she smiled. "It's very special, this thing you do. And don't worry about the gossip. It'll be yesterday's news by tomorrow and it's not like the kids don't already know about it, is it? I'm sure they can handle it, and anyway, don't they have their own angels to protect them from bullying and stuff?"

Sarah nodded thoughtfully. Yes, Frieda was right. Her children had been brought up with it and understood all the 'weird and wacky' stuff that was around them all the time. They were aware that many children did not know and did not believe, and they felt sorry for them, bless them!

"Yeah, I guess I overreacted," she admitted. "I gave Clarabelle hell, poor thing. She was only trying to help."

Sarah was aware as she talked to Frieda of a man hovering nearby. She'd seen him before, but didn't know who he was. He was clearly for Frieda though, that much was clear. She looked at Frie carefully. "Darlin', I don't suppose you'd be interested in another reading would you?" she asked gently. "Only I think there's stuff you're meant to know, and I can't tell you unless I have your permission."

219

Frieda didn't hesitate. She grinned at Sarah, nodding happily. "Yeah, hun, course!"

They moved over to the table and Sarah tuned in quickly, then cleansed the cards, handing them to Frieda. She chose just a few of the Angel cards that she held, placing four on the table before her.

Sarah turned the cards over slowly. Daniel, the angel of marriage smiled up at her. Next to it, Chantel, the angel of romance - 'New romance is imminent,' it said. Above them sat Shanti, the angel of peace - 'I bring you new tranquillity and a smoother road ahead' it said. Alongside Shanti was Omega, the Victory card.

"Frie, the cards speak for themselves, hun. They are congratulating you on your success, look! The victory card saying you've done it, you sorted your shit, mate!" Sarah laughed. "And look, Shanti is saying it's all behind you now and you can finally have your peace! The other two, those at the top, they both speak of romance and ultimately, marriage. It's coming, hun, look!"

Frieda did, indeed, look. She was grinning, looking at the cards. What a difference! It would be nearly three years since her first reading, and those cards had shown pain, sorrow, suffering and negativity. These cards, now, well! They showed joy and peace and happiness! Frieda was blown away! She looked again at the cards, beaming all over her face. "Just one question, Sar," she asked. "Why are those two above the other two? I mean, did I do that, like, on purpose?"

Sarah smiled. "It means, hun, that like that reading all that time ago, it confirms that you had to 'sort your stuff' and find your victory, and your peace, first, and now that you have, now romance can come in. Do you see, Frie? You couldn't have done it in any other order? You had to sort you first, and I know it's been a lonely, long, old road, but now that you have found that peace within you, now a romance will work and now, that romance can actually last and maybe turn into marriage!"

Frieda's eyes filled with tears, wondering if, at last, she could find that missing belonging.

"And, Frie, I have someone here, someone who wants me to give you a message, hun."

Frieda looked at her in surprise. "What kind of message? Who from?" she asked nervously, adding, "A ghost message?"

"Yes, darlin', it's your dad, Frie. He's here. He was here the first time, and I have seen him around you before, but this is the first time he has come forward and wanted to say something. Is that okay, hun?"

Frieda nodded slowly, not quite believing what she was being told. Her dad was here? Unreal!

"And he says to tell you ... he is sorry, so very sorry, Frie, for bringing that awful man into your life. He blames himself for everything that happened to you and wants you to know he is so very sorry. And, he also wants to apologise to you for his suicide. He says that it was unbelievably selfish of him. He knows that his suicide was wrong, Frie; you needed him, and he is so sorry that he abandoned you and let you down."

Frieda nodded slowly, still getting to grips with the idea that her father was there, talking to her.

"And he says to explain ... this is him now okay, Frie. I'm just saying what he is saying to me. Right, ready? He says that his mind that night, was ... he was ... not 'in his right mind,' if you know what I mean? He says it was broken, snapped, unhinged ... that he wasn't thinking straight. The anger and the shock apparently, well it just knocked his mind sideways, and he went basically, nuts! It was brief, this snapping, it was temporary; it would have righted itself by the morning and he would have found a way to keep going, for you, for your mum and for himself. But he wasn't here by the morning, he was already gone. It was too late, and he bitterly regrets his act, Frie. Bitterly! He says to tell you that he has met many upstairs who took their own life, and each one of them regrets it. God, that's so sad, Frie! Anyway, he says that he knows now, that had he hung on till the morning, his mind would have righted itself, the craziness, the 'unhinged' bit, it would have passed and he would still have been here. It was an impulse; a mad, crazy impulse, and one that he had no way of turning back from. If he could have, he would have, he promises you that. So he has watched over you since, tried to be there for you, from 'up there,' but he knows he's failed you, Frie, and he is asking for your forgiveness. He cannot find his peace until he has it, but he says to tell you that he understands if you cannot give it. He hasn't given it to himself, and probably won't for some time yet! Blimey, Frie, the man is tormented with guilt! Poor lamb! What do you think, Frie? Do you think you can forgive him?"

Frieda looked at Sarah, shaking her head. "Tell him there's nothing to forgive. I never blamed him anyway, I blamed me! For both the abuse and his death. And I forgave myself for both last year. So yeah, tell him I forgive him. Tell him thanks, tell him I'm okay."

Sarah smiled at the man, feeling his guilt and pain. She called out to him, through her thoughts, saying, *time to let go, mate, she forgives you. Time to forgive yourself now, aye?*

The man smiled sadly, then disappeared into the light that was behind him. He'd said what he needed to say. Time to go home now.

Sarah handed Frieda a tissue from the box on the bookcase near the table, letting her wipe her eyes from the emotion that she was now feeling. They were mixed emotions; some sorrow, some hurt and yes, she was surprised to feel, a little anger too. Her counsellor had said that it would be natural for her to feel angry with her father for his suicide, but she never had. Not until now, that is! Frieda allowed the anger to surface, and then, suddenly, when it had come right up and she could feel it all around her, it was like a little balloon had popped and all the anger disappeared. How weird! Now she felt nothing but pity for him. Pity for his wasted life; the life that he could have had, should have had, had he not let his temporary insanity overcome him. But then again, if he was temporarily nuts, crazy, unhinged; well, then it wasn't really his fault anyway, now was it? All these thoughts and more were pouring through Frieda's mind like a train, and, interestingly enough, she was processing each and every one as they came.

Sarah left her pondering, knowing that Frieda was processing what had just happened and went to the kitchen to put the kettle on. By the time the tea had been made and brewed, Frieda was smiling again. "So," Sarah asked with a large smile, coming back into the room carrying two steaming hot mugs of tea and a plate of biscuits, "do I need another new hat then?"

And Frieda grinned.

Chapter 20

"Right gang, what's your 'Plan B' then," Archangel Michael smiled. "I mean, you must have a 'Plan B,' surely?"

They were sitting on Cloud 326, high above Redville, for this *most* important 'Create Plan B' meeting. Bart looked at Miya, Miya looked at Helena, Helena looked at Rena - then all four of them looked at Clarabelle, perched at the end.

"Don't look at me!" she shrieked. "I don't know! I'm just here out of curiosity! Well, maybe also a little bit because my Sarah *may* be able to help *you,* Miya," she admitted, "with the 'Frieda problem,' but I'm sure I don't know how I can be of *any* help *whatsoever* to Bart and Helena!"

"Well I don't know what I'm doing here either," Rena piped up. "I mean, it's not my ward's love life that's involved! Cara is away, anyway; doing her Masters, so it's not even like she can help!"

"Alright, alright!" Michael butted in, interrupting their

squabbling. "You're all here because you may have something to contribute, so pipe down!"

The gathered crew 'piped down' and waited for Michael to come up with something! Anything! It was Easter, again, and still they hadn't solved the problem that was 'Frieda and Andrew,' or rather, 'Not Frieda and Andrew!'

"So what have you tried so far?" Michael asked, waiting patiently for the details of the many attempts that the crew had made to solve their problem. "To split up Andrew and Moira; what have you tried?"

Bart looked at Helena, "Umm ..."

Helena looked at Bart, "Umm ..."

"Umm what?" spat Michael

"Umm ..."

"You are kidding me!" exclaimed Michael, in complete shock. "You haven't tried anything? Nothing at all?"

They both shook their heads solemnly.

"What? You mean you've just let them get on with it, and waited for it to resolve itself?"

Again, they both looked at him, very slowly nodding their guilty heads.

"Well for Goodness sake!" he shouted. "No wonder it's not resolved if you've all just sat on your feathery backsides for the best part of a year! What did you expect, that they would just sort it out themselves?" Michael was horrified! *I thought I'd trained them better than this!* He glared at them. "Well it won't!" he declared firmly. He looked at them in disappointment, shaking his head.

"And you, Rena; you could have done more too! If you'd used your noddle, you could have got Cara to have broken them up easier than anything. Useless, all three of you!"

The angels hung their heads in shame.

"Right then, this is your 'Plan B.' You will try *everything* to keep Andrew and Moira apart, got it?"

They all nodded.

"And if that doesn't work, you will then try *everything* to push them together, right?"

Again, they all nodded.

"That will be your 'Plan C,' but only if 'Plan B' doesn't work, right?"

"Yes, but how will that help? Pushing them together?" Bart asked nervously.

Michael sighed in frustration. "Because," he said slowly, *clearly they need this spelled out!* "Because they are managing to keep their 'relationship' going by spending average time together, so either *more* time or *less* time is the only way to break it!"

"Oh!" all three said. "Hadn't thought of that!"

"And, Miya, what are you doing to sort your Frieda out? Hmmm? Is she still trying to find her 'Mr. Right' on that dating site?"

Miya nodded.

"Why?" he demanded. "Clearly Andrew is not going to use it! Why is she still there? What have you done about it?"

Miya looked at the others, hoping for an answer. They looked away! *Oh well, cheers guys!* she thought with disgust. *Thanks for having my back, not!*

"Really, you lot are rubbish, aren't you?" Michael bellowed. "Maybe you need to go back into training!"

All four looked horrified, until, that is, Michael added, "In transport!" Then they looked terrified *and* horrified!

"Oh, my goodness!"

"Surely not!"

"I'd rather go back to being a car-park angel than go down there!"

"Does that include me?" Clarabelle piped up, extremely worried at this threat. "I mean, this isn't my mess!"

"Not you, no. But I'm watching you! I'm watching all of you!" Michael wagged his finger at the whole crew, the threat clear in his eyes. "I am embarrassed to call you my team! Do you know that? I'm the laughing stock upstairs, do you realise that? You have shamed me, all of you! Now go and SORT IT OUT!" he yelled.

And all four flew downstairs in a flurry of wings and chaos to start putting 'Plan B' into practice.

***

Moira couldn't figure out what was going on. Every time she'd tried to go over to Andrew's house she'd had problems with her car. Either it wouldn't start or there'd been a flat tyre! It had been like this for weeks now! Most inconvenient! It hadn't stopped her, of course. She'd simply rung a taxi, or got a bus, or rang Andrew to fetch her. Mind you, when he'd tried to fetch her, he'd also had a flat tyre or a flat battery, so he'd had to walk instead! It really was most peculiar!

Then there were other problems. When they'd tried to go out to the cinema or theatre, or even for a meal, there had also been issues. One time his boiler broke after a particularly dirty day at work (he had been on-site in his capacity as the architect), so when he'd come home all filthy and grubby, he'd not been able to shower. He had rung to cancel. "Tosh," she had told him, "come and shower at mine!" So he had! There were lots more stories like that. *Weird! It was almost as if the universe were conspiring to keep them apart!*

Andrew too, was bewildered. It seemed that just about every time he had been about to go out with Moira, Cara had rung, needing to talk, or work had rung with a problem that only he could solve. He hated being late (it was rude), but had, on many occasions, been unable to get off the phone and had been forced to be late. Moira had been very understanding, of course, very patient. He thought back over their relationship. He knew that he'd struggled, in the beginning, with her being in his life, but had come to realise as time had gone by that it was just a matter of adapting to being with someone new. He had got used to it, eventually. She really was a good old stick, bless her!

Another week went by, and another. ...

Moira was concerned. She had the most awful stomach, extreme flatulence, and it just wouldn't go! She'd been farting and fluffing all morning! She was due to go over to Andrew's house shortly, and she couldn't be there breaking wind every two minutes, dear me, no!

"High-five people!" grinned Bart.

"Yay!" grinned Helena.

"Naughty," giggled Miya.

"Oh, hang on ..."

Bart looked down in disappointment. Miya was now making her way to the local chemists for some anti-wind tablets!

"Foiled again!" they sighed.

Another week went by, and another. ...

Andrew had a terrible headache. It had just come on suddenly and he felt awful. All he wanted to do was to go to bed. He rang Moira quickly, letting her know their day was off. "Tosh," she had said, "I shall look after you! I'm on my way!"

The angels looked down in disappointment. "Foiled again," they sighed.

Another week went by, and another. ...

This went on, and on, and on. Every block they put in the couple's way had been expertly sidestepped. Every issue overcome. As April turned into May, and May into June, the 'crew' decided that it was time for 'Plan C.'

"So what's the plan, guys?" Bart asked the others, back on their cloud for yet *another* meeting. "How do we push them together more?"

"Well *this* isn't working is it?" exclaimed Miya crossly. *At this rate, they'd all end up 'down in transport'!*

"I think I have it!" grinned Helena. "Yes, I have it!"

And 'the crew' set about putting 'Plan C' into motion.

***

"Oh dear, that's awful. Yes, of course, you can stay at mine," Andrew said into the phone to a distressed Moira. "Yes, bring what you need."

Moira had had the most terrible flood at her house. She had no idea how! All the pipes were really quite new and the house was only five years old, but they'd all burst, and, it seemed, all at the same time! She really couldn't understand it at all. Everything was ruined and it would take days, if not weeks, for it all to dry out. Still, Andrew had come to the rescue and she would be staying with him for the duration. She liked Andrew's house. It was nicer than her own; she was looking forward to staying there, and to being with him properly. If this went well, maybe she should consider selling her own house and moving in with him? It was their one year anniversary next week, and that would be a super time to broach the subject, to move their relationship onto the next level. *Yes,* she decided, *use this as a rehearsal for living together, good plan!*

It had been just five days of Moira being at his house and Andrew was getting really fed up - already! "No peace, just no peace," he muttered to himself, going out to the garden again. *Anything to get away from those bloody soaps!* he grimaced. *Dear God, how many of them were there?* Andrew didn't have a clue. He'd never watched a soap in his life, and he certainly wasn't going to start now!

Moira, though, loved them! Watched them all, every bloody one, hour upon hour of them! And then there were the 'Reality TV' shows. *Jesus, how could people watch that rubbish?* The TV had never been on so much in his house in his life! And his ensuite! Not that he had an ensuite anymore, now that Moira had taken it over completely. It was so filled with her bottles and perfumes, make-up and hair things, not to mention four different dressing gowns (depending on the weather, apparently!), and he just couldn't move in there anymore! And then there was the amount of time she took to get ready for anything! Anything at all! Twenty minutes she'd say, and two hours later she'd come out with a 'ta-da'!

Andrew sat down on his bench, trying to unwind in the peace and quiet of his garden. *At least I have some peace out here,* he thought. But with that, the back door opened and Moira walked out, carrying two cups of tea. *Argh,* thought Andrew.

"I thought, Andrew," she said gaily, looking at the garden, "that we could maybe gravel over that part of the garden and make a nice eating place. (She was pointing to his flower boarder.) Andrew looked at her like she was speaking Japanese, he was that shocked! "A nice table and chairs would look lovely there, don't you think? It's right in the sun; a lovely little sun trap." She smiled at him happily.

Andrew stared at her in horror. *Does she not know me at all?* he thought in disgust. *At bloody all? This garden is my sanctuary, my life, and she wants me to rip it up and put bloody gravel there instead of all those beautiful flowers? Dear God!* He turned to her, his face red, he was so annoyed. "Moira," he spat. "*That* is my flower garden. Those flowers are *that* beautiful *because* they have the sun. I have spent twelve years cultivating this garden, *twelve years,* and I am NOT changing a bloody thing! Gravel indeed!"

Bart and Helena high-fived each other in delight. This 'Plan C' was working a treat!

"But, darling," she was saying, "there is nowhere to eat in your garden, and it's such a shame to waste this lovely sunshine."

Andrew stomped into the house to get away from her, but there was no peace there either. The television blared out the theme tune to one of her soaps, filling the room with its awful sound as he walked into it. "Is she bloody deaf as well as stupid!" he shouted, turning it off with a bang.

"I was watching that!" Moira exclaimed from behind him. "And I am neither deaf nor am I stupid, thank you very much! And don't you raise your voice to me!"

And then, to the delight of the watching angelic crew, the couple had their first row. Andrew shouted, Moira yelled, Andrew stomped, Moira banged. Eventually, Andrew stomped out to his car to get away from her (and from the row), setting off with screeching tyres down the road, leaving Moira to run upstairs to the bedroom and have a good cry.

"Good job!" Miya said happily, watching with Bart and Helena from their cloud.

"Indeed!" agreed the other two.

The following morning, Andrew, having slept on the sofa (when he'd eventually got back from his drive), finally told the tearful Moira what he had wanted to say from the beginning (he had realised this gem of information during his long drive!) - it was over! She wasn't right for him, he said, she didn't know him, she didn't suit him, they weren't compatible, they weren't right together.

With that, Moira's phone rang. She answered it in a daze, still in shock from what she was hearing from Andrew. She listened in surprise to the one-way conversation; overnight, it seemed (so she was informed), the flood in her house had dried up (as if by magic), and the house was now dry enough for her to return. She relayed this conversation to an extremely relieved Andrew, then tried to argue with him that it wasn't over, it was just a row. She pointed out to him that it was their very first row in a whole year of being together, and insisted that that was good; it actually showed how very compatible they were, but he was having none of it. He stated firmly that the last week had showed him just how incompatible they were, and asked her to go; and go she did, assuming that they would 'sort it out' in a few days.

"Please take everything, Moira," Andrew said softly, almost reading her thoughts. "This is done I'm afraid, and you won't be back, so please make sure that you take everything." And then he went to his garden.

By the time he came back in, she was loading her car. She looked at him with pure hatred. "A year I've given you! You, you, PIG!" she cried, then jumped into her car and sped off.

Andrew watched the departing car screaming down

the road and sighed a huge sigh of relief. It was enormous! "Why the bloody hell did I let it go on for so long?" he asked himself. "Just too nice; that's my trouble! Just too bloody nice!"

And Bart, Helena, Miya and Rena sighed an equally big sigh of relief, watching the departed Moira disappear off into the distance, permanently!

***

Whilst all this had been going on with Andrew and Moira, Miya had been working on Frieda, doing her bit to sort out 'her end.' Over the past few months, as Bart and Helena had worked their 'Plan B' and 'Plan C' on their wards, she had been suggesting to Frieda, repeatedly, that dating sites were not the way to go. In the end, she'd had to call in Clarabelle for help.

"Well, my dear, that's simple!" Clarabelle had chirped. "You just need my Sarah! Easy peasy! Why didn't you call before?"

And Sarah had been told to get Frieda off the sites, which she did in one phone call! Ta-da!

Chapter 21

It was September and the twins were going back to school in a few days for their third, penultimate year in juniors. They were nine years old now, and Sarah really couldn't get over where the time had gone!

"Where's me doggy-chocs then, Mrs.?" Fred barked. "Birthday boy here you know! And it's a big one! Double figures; woohoo!"

"Yes, Fred," Sarah grinned. "I know, hun; ten now, blimey!"

The summer holidays had passed quickly; the children got out and about much more, now that they were older and bigger. She'd barely seen them, they'd been out or over at friend's so much! *Mind you, just as well,* she thought to herself. *Work has gone nuts!* Sarah had been doing so many readings that she now had a waiting list. Word of mouth had spread, and she was often surprised just how far people travelled to see her. Her reputation was building, friends telling friends, and they were often friends who lived many miles away. It didn't seem to deter them, the distance. They'd come from miles, sometimes several hours' drive, just to see her! She couldn't get over it!

"Yes, well, when you've finished admiring yourself, lady, I'm still waiting for me doggie-chocs you know!" grumbled Fred.

"Sorry, Fred. And I wasn't 'admiring' myself, cheeky! I was simply thinking how wonderful it is that all these people come all that way, just to see me!"

"I don't give a flying fart if they come all the way from Timbuctoo, just give me my Dog-damn doggie-chocs, woman!" he barked impatiently.

"Fred! Language!" she scolded, but at the same time grinning. *He's so funny, bless him! Flying fart indeed! Where does he get these sayings that he comes out with?* she wondered.

"And I think I should have double helpings too," he added with a grin, "now that I'm in double figures!"

"And watch you throw up from eating too many? I don't think so!" she laughed.

"Umm, excuse me, but I don't get cat treats when it's my birthday," Cassie complained from the kitchen door. "No one gets me anything when it's my birthday!"

"Oh, Cassie darlin', that's cos we don't know when your birthday is, hun. It's not cos we don't care, promise!"

"Well it's not fair!" she cried, doing her best to stamp her paws, but with them being padded, it didn't work too well!

"I know, Mum! Why don't we give Cassie a birthday for the day we got her?" suggested Fred helpfully.

"Do you know what, Freddie, that's a really good idea!

Yes, let's do that!" Sarah looked at Cassie thoughtfully. "It was September, wasn't it?" she asked. "Yes, the day the twins started infant school. Blimey, that's four years ago now! How time flies!"

"Well then, I think I should have four years' worth, don't you, Ma - I mean, Sarah." Cassie corrected herself quickly. That was the second time that she'd done that now! Mind you, with all these readings that Sarah was doing, she was a bit like Ma now. *Yes, she decided, I definitely made the right choice moving in here!* "So where's my cat treats then?" she purred, waiting expectantly at her bowl.

Sarah grinned at the cat, and the dog, reaching into the cupboard for both the doggie-chocs and the cat treats. She was very lucky to have such lovely pets and didn't know where she'd be without them.

"Pet?" grimaced Cassie in horror, reading her thoughts. "*Pet?* I am your *helper*, not your damned 'pet,' madam! As if!" and she stomped out of the kitchen in a huff, but not before she'd eaten all of her cat treats first, of course. Well, that would just be silly, wouldn't it? And as for Sarah being like Ma, well, that was just ridiculous! Ma would never have called her a pet! Pah!

***

Andrew was bored. He'd never really been bored before, not before Moira anyway! He had tried to go back to his old way of life (after she had gone), the life he had quite happily had before Moira, but it had seemed empty somehow. Bit boring as a matter of fact! He didn't want her back, he knew that, but he did need something; that much was clear. Andrew pondered what to do. *Maybe join a club? I was going to do that before, wasn't I, but I never did. Yes, a club I think.* And Andrew went to his computer to look up local clubs.

***

Frieda was bored. She'd had enough of the internet dating thing, and, after a chat with Sarah a while back, had decided to give it up as a bad job and focus on other things. Trouble was, she didn't really have other things!

Frieda stared at the computer, wondering what was around that she could join. She barely went to the support group anymore. It just felt like 'it was done,' and felt wrong somehow, not quite right, to still be there. There was a sense of completion, of finish, and she knew, as she sat there thinking about it, that it was time to let it all go and put it all behind her. *Yes,* she thought, *put it to rest. It's time.* She forgot about looking for clubs to join and rang the support group leader to tell him that she wouldn't be coming back anymore, and then she went for a walk.

"Argh!" screeched Miya from the top of the computer. "Just argh!"

***

Christmas was coming and Andrew was looking forward to their film event tomorrow.

He'd been surprised how much he'd enjoyed the film club that he'd joined in September. *Should have done it ages ago,* he thought. Tomorrow would be the showing of an old classic film, one chosen especially by the group in line with the festivities; a Christmas classic film; 'It's a Wonderful Life.' It would be followed by drinks and discussions about its strengths and weaknesses, although Andrew didn't think there'd be too much of that this week! Usually, they all stayed after they'd watched the chosen film of that week, remaining in the old film theatre that they used for their club. They would all stay after, getting together, chatting about it over a cuppa and a biscuit. They'd discuss the directors, the cut and the awards it may have won. That was the way it had been for the last three months anyway! The group met every two weeks, and the routine was nice. They were a friendly group and Andrew was getting to know a few of them quite well. Tomorrow's club night would be different though. It was Christmas, so the group were all going off afterwards for drinks in a local pub, having it as their club's 'Christmas Party' bash. A large table had been booked in readiness and he was looking forward to it immensely.

***

Sarah looked at the local paper with interest, staring at the advert for the film night at the old theatre the next evening.

Redville Film Club Proudly Presents (it said)
'It's a Wonderful Life!'
A timeless Christmas classic
Open to the Public for this Christmas Special –

Non-Members Welcome
Friday 23rd December, 8pm
The Old Theatre, Redville

"Ooh, ooh, can we go, can we go?" shrieked Clarabelle, jumping up and down on her shoulder excitedly. "It's my favourite, my totally favourite, as you know! And, of course, Clarence's too, seeing as he's in it! Can we, can we, please?"

Sarah grinned at Clarabelle and laughed. "Of course, we can go!" She knew how much Clarabelle loved this film. She did too! "But Simon is out of town, his works do, so I will have to see who I can get to go with me, and to mind the kids," she said, planning their night out in her head.

"Yes, dear, right on it, leave it to me," Clarabelle bustled, popping over to Margaret's quickly to arrange the granny to babysit.

Two seconds later, when Sarah rang Margaret, she was not surprised to hear her agree enthusiastically. She loved babysitting her grandchildren and yes, of course, she'd be there, but could she have a taxi please, as her ankles were very bad at the moment? Sarah grinned, ringing and booking the taxi for Margaret, and then rang Frieda to ask if she would go with her.

"Yeah, of course, I'll come. Not my kind of thing, mind, but I'm happy to come with you to see a boring old film if it makes you happy," she grinned, adding, "but can we go for a drink after, hun? I haven't been out in an age and I could really do with a night out."

"Yes, sure," Sarah smiled, thinking of Frieda and her usual choice of film. 'The Godfather' was more her sort of thing than a mushy Christmas film about angels, but despite that, she reckoned Frieda would enjoy it.

"Can Clarence come too?" squeaked Clarabelle excitedly. "He'll be so cross if he misses it again!"

"Yes sure, why not," Sarah smiled. "Bring them all if you like. I know how you lot upstairs love this film. Yeah, bring 'em all. It's Christmas!"

***

"So we're all going to the cinema tonight, Miya. Would you like to come? Have you seen it? Such a wonderful film!" declared Clarabelle enthusiastically. "And maybe Bart and Helena too. This could be our team's Christmas do! Ooh, how lovely!"

"Bart!" yelled Miya, clear across the sky. "Helena, oh, Helenaaaaaaa!"

"You screeched?" grinned Bart, flying onto the cloud.

"Indeed I did not!" objected Miya.

"Yes?" enquired Helena, joining them with a rustle of feathers.

"Clarabelle's going pictures tonight. Wanna come?" grinned Miya.

"What's 'pictures'?" asked Helena, confused now!

"Pictures? Cinema, silly!" Miya laughed. "Used to be 'moving pictures,' then they brought in sound, and it became 'talking pictures'; ooh, that was ages ago wasn't it? Anyway, now it's just 'pictures'!"

"Ooh, Miya, showing your age now, my dear!" grinned Helena. "No one calls it that anymore! It's cinema now! Really, you are so old-fashioned at times!"

"Tosh! Am not! So, you wanna come or not?"

"Oh, pictures? What to see?" enquired Bart curiously.

"Well, 'It's a Wonderful Life!' of course!" butted in Clarabelle. *As if there was any other film to see! As if!*

"Already going, mate," grinned Bart. "Andrew's going, so I'll be there anyway."

"Andrew's going?" shrieked Miya in shock. "Why do I not know about this? Did you not think to tell me this *hugely* important piece of information?" She glared at him in disgust. *Men!* Had she known this, she would have already arranged it! She'd have had everything in place by now to have Frieda there! *Typical!* She scowled at Bart again. "Had I known this, Bartholomew," she said in annoyance, "I would have had my Frieda there and used this opportunity to get them together. Now, as it is, I have less than six hours! Six hours to plan everything!"

"Oh, sorry, Miya, I didn't think," admitted Bart guiltily. *Yes, why didn't I think of that?* he wondered. *Maybe I do need more training after all?*

"Yes, well, never mind all the 'telling's off,' we have six hours," piped up Clarabelle, "and there are loads of us! And anyway, Frieda *is* going! Sarah has already invited her. So yes, this is a wonderful opportunity to get them together, at last! Someone go and call Rena too. I'm sure if we all work together, we can sort this out between us and make sure it all works perfectly."

Miya heaved a huge sigh of relief, grinning at Clarabelle gratefully. "Oh, thank goodness for that!" she exclaimed. "We could have missed the boat there!"

Clarabelle smiled at them all reassuringly, adding, "There will be no missing of boats tonight, my dear, of that you can be assured. And Clarence will be there, too, of course. He wouldn't miss this for the world, and you know our Clarence ..."

"He's a miracle worker!" they all said together. "A miracle worker!"

"Who's a miracle worker?" piped up Clarence, just arrived from upstairs, joining them on their cloud.

"You are!" they grinned. "You are!"

And Clarence beamed. *So nice to have a bit of acknowledgement,* he thought to himself, *a bit of recognition. So nice!*

Chapter 22

Clarabelle was beyond excited! She loved this film, totally loved it! And not only that; but Frieda and Andrew would finally meet! "Yippeeeeee!" she shrieked, throwing her arms into the air in delight. She was so excited that she nearly fell off the rafters! Alongside her, high up in the 'Gods' of the film theatre, sitting in a row, perched on the beam that criss-crossed the high ceiling, were Clarence, of course, then Rena, Miya and Bart. Helena had decided not to come, being too busy rescuing Moira from her latest disaster, bless! She looked down at Sarah, sitting far below them, next to Frieda, with a grin. They were in the fourth row, and Andrew was in the fifth, sitting directly behind Frieda. He hadn't noticed her yet, he was far too busy chatting to his friend, Steve.

"Not sure this is my cuppa-tea," he said quietly to Steve. "More of a 'Godfather' man myself, but I'm happy to give it a go."

Despite the whispered comment, Frieda, sitting right in front of him, overheard it. "Nor mine," she whispered, turning around to face him. "Part One, Two or Three?" she asked.

"Oh, Part One, definitely!" Andrew replied with a smile.

"Well I think two and three top it, myself, although Coppola did a magnificent job of pulling it all together, didn't he? Mind you," she continued, "he did have Puzo there, right the way through, ensuring that he kept the continuity, don't you think?" Frieda grinned widely.

Andrew was gobsmacked! They were his favourite films of all time! She certainly knew her stuff. He was intrigued, but just as he was about to reply to her comments, the film was starting. The woman had turned back towards the front and his opportunity was gone.

Sometime later, Frieda wiped a stray tear away from her face as the film came to its closing lines ...

"Look, Daddy ... Teacher says, every time a bell rings an angel gets his wings ..."

"That's right, that's right ... (he said, looking to the sky as a bell rang) ... Attaboy, Clarence. ..."

She'd particularly liked the bit in the middle where George had offered to get Mary the moon down from the sky for her. *I wonder if anyone will ever get me the moon?* she wondered quietly. *"Or even want to!"*

Sarah wasn't wondering that! Sarah was wondering what was making her wet? Was it raining in here? She looked up at the ceiling, then burst into giggles, which she tried desperately to stifle. All five angels were sitting on the rafters sobbing their hearts out as the film closed! They were wiping their tears with their feathers, or trying to! They were dripping; positively *dripping* wet! Sarah giggled away, understanding now why Clarabelle loved this film so much. She remembered Clarabelle telling her about the day that she'd got 'her wings,' so to speak. Of course, she already had wings, but she hadn't been able to use them to fly anywhere other than within The Angelic Realms. 'Getting your wings' meant being able to fly down to earth and be a Guardian Angel, and help the earth people and stuff, so it was *HUGE* to get your wings, simply *huge,* for an angel!

Andrew, too, was pondering the film. He was surprised how much he'd enjoyed it, but to be fair, it was a classic. He leaned forward to the lady in front of him, "Don't make 'em like they used to," he smiled. "It was rather good, I enjoyed that! I didn't think I would, but it was very well made, don't you think?"

Frieda nodded, smiling at the man.

"I haven't seen you here before," Andrew said, knowing as soon as he said it that it sounded like a cheap chat-up line. "Sorry, I meant, are you part of this film club too? I thought you might be, as you clearly know about films, but I haven't seen you here before ..." he trailed off, deciding that he was sounding rather foolish, but the lady didn't seem to mind. She simply laughed and said no, she wasn't a member, but yes, she loved films. "Well you should join!" he said firmly. "I'll introduce you to everyone. We're a nice bunch, honest!" And the lady smiled, and she had the loveliest smile he thought that he'd ever seen. And then the lights came up properly, and he could see her wonderful red hair. *Just like mine!* he thought, *only not as much grey as me.* "I'm Andrew," he said, offering her his hand to shake.

Frieda took the man's hand and shook it, and as she did, she felt funny (funny weird, not funny ha-ha!). A tingle had gone right up her arm as soon as she'd touched his hand, like electricity. *Must be static,* she thought as she smiled into his eyes. *Nice man,* she decided, noticing his smile. She nodded thoughtfully at his suggestion. "Maybe, I might just do that," she grinned. "I'll have a think about it. I'm Frieda, hi."

"Hi, Frieda," he grinned, adding, "Well, it would be lovely to see you again. I'd like to find out more about why you think that Part Two and Three are superior to Part One; you know, the 'Godfather'?"

"Happy to oblige," she smiled. "I'm sure we can have a good debate on that one! Not to mention Shawshank, or Citizen Cane, amongst others."

Andrew's smile got bigger. *Blimey, a woman who knows proper films, great films, and I bet she knows who directed and wrote them too! I bet she doesn't watch bloody soaps or reality TV either!* Just as Andrew was about to suggest that she join them for their Christmas drinks, she was being pulled away by her friend. *Shame,* he thought. *I'd like to have got to know her better. I do hope she comes along to the next club,* and then she was gone.

"Blimey, Frie, did you just get chatted up?" Sarah grinned as they made their way to the foyer. "He looked nice! What's his name?"

"Yes, he seems nice. I don't think he was chatting me up though, Sar. We were just chatting. He's a member of this film club. His name's Andrew. He asked me to join, and you know what, hun, I may just do that. I love films! I've watched more films in the last few years whilst I've been in my 'hermit' mode than I've watched in the whole of the rest of my life, and I've got right into them, right into them!" she grinned happily.

"Tell her he IS nice, capital nice, N. I. C. E. NICE!" grinned Clarabelle, flying over to join them, now that she'd finally stopped crying! "Go on then, tell her! ... And he's single!"

Sarah relayed the message to a bemused Frieda, who just looked confused.

"Oh dear," said Clarabelle. "Okay, try this ... she wanted a 'nice' man, and he is as 'nice' as they come. NICE!" she shouted, emphasising the 'nice' yet again. "And stable, and kind, and lovely!" she added, just for good measure. "And you will find him," she looked at the sky, measuring the light, "in approximately three-point-two-five minutes, in that pub, there!" she exclaimed, pointing at the large inn across the road. "And," she added dramatically, "*he* would go and get the moon for you, in about six months, if I have my calculations correct!"

Sarah grinned. *Blimey, this is good!* She relayed the information to Frieda, dragging her friend across the road as she gabbled, insisting that they go to the pub, that pub, and right now!

Frieda didn't argue. He did seem 'nice,' and he looked familiar! She was trying to figure out where she'd seen him before. She was wracking her brain, trawling her memory banks, and then she had it! He'd been on that dating site! She'd seen his profile there, ages ago! *Well, that's interesting!*

Sarah was just getting the drinks in for her and Frieda when Andrew walked in with his group. They were all chatting happily, arguing over who was getting the drinks, when he noticed her at the bar. *That's the woman who dragged that lovely Frieda away! Fabulous! That means she's here, somewhere!* Andrew cast his eyes around the pub and spotted her in the corner, gazing out of the window at the passing traffic. The fairy lights from the Christmas tree next to her in the corner cast sparkles into her red hair, lighting it up. Her eyes shone too. She was beautiful! Andrew found that his breath seemed to have disappeared from his body as he stared at her, and then he realised that he'd been holding it. He let it out quickly. *God, she is gorgeous!* he thought, looking at her with his breath held, yet again! She was slim, elegant, cool; but at the same time, fun, interesting, challenging, and 'hot'! God, she was hot! But then again, she was also cool! Andrew didn't know. His head seemed to be all over the place! What he did know, without any doubt at all, was that he wanted to find out! He walked over to her table quickly, grinning like a schoolboy. "Well, what a coincidence!" he exclaimed. "Well, that's it now, you simply have to join us!" he said, grinning stupidly. He reached out for her hand, which she found herself mutely offering, and walked her over to the rest of his group. "This is Frieda!" he announced, "She'll be joining us."

Frieda looked at him in astonishment. "But, but, but … I'm with my friend!" she finally spurted out. "There, that's my friend, Sarah!" She pointed at Sarah, who was just leaving the bar with the drinks in her hand, heading for the corner table.

"No problem," Andrew said quickly, "She can join us too." And he rushed off to get Sarah, also grabbing her hand, and guiding her to the group and the waiting, and rather gobsmacked, Frieda.

Sarah grinned happily, knowing that this was just perfect and right. Clarabelle had appeared at the bar as she'd waited to be served and told her to take her time, so she had. By the time she'd got served, Andrew had already claimed Frieda, and dragged her over to the film group, where she was already being introduced.

The two girls spent the next hour listening to stories by the club members, before Sarah decided that it was time for her to go.

"But we've got a taxi booked for later," Frieda implored, not wanting to go yet. She was enjoying herself immensely and didn't want the evening to end.

"Sorry, hun, but Mum's texted (courtesy of Clarabelle and Miya meddling), and she needs me home. Apparently she's got 'one of her heads,' so she wants an early night. She's already rung the taxi firm and changed it, so I have to go now. Sorry, mate."

Frieda looked at Sarah; she didn't look sorry. In fact, she was bloody grinning!

"Where do you live, Frie?" Andrew asked, "I can drop you, it's no trouble."

Frieda looked at Andrew carefully, weighing up the offer. Was it safe to get a lift with him? She'd only met him a few hours ago! She looked at Sarah questioningly, but Sarah was grinning, and nodding emphatically.

"Umm, okay then, thanks," she replied hesitantly. "I

live just on the edge of town, by the roundabout."

"Really? Me too! Well that's easy then, isn't it!" he grinned, chuffed to bits that she was staying a bit longer. She was brill! He'd never met a woman so interesting, or so knowledgeable about films. *Not that I've met many I know,* he said to himself, but he didn't care. All he knew was that he was enjoying every second of her company and wanted more!

Frieda was also grinning. She liked him. She liked him a lot! *Happy days,* she thought to herself with delight.

"Oh, thank goodness for that!" Bart said, with relief.

"Fantastic!" screeched Miya, bouncing up and down on Bart's head with excitement. "Just fantastic!"

***

It was Easter and there was a big film night for the club happening this evening. Frieda was getting ready, dressing with extra care for tonight's event. She'd been spending a lot of time with Andrew lately, and they were getting closer, it seemed, every day. He was, without a doubt, the nicest person that she'd ever met, and by far the nicest person that she'd ever gone out with. Not that she was 'going out' with him, not yet anyway.

She'd been waiting for him to make a move for weeks, well months really, but he always acted the perfect gentleman. She had now decided, after the last lift home, that she was going to have to make it clear, obvious, to him, that she was 'into' him. *Perhaps he's too shy?* she wondered. *Perhaps he isn't sure if I fancy him and he doesn't want to spoil the friendship that we have, if I say no?* She'd got to know him pretty well and she knew that he'd only had the one girlfriend since his wife had died years ago, and, apparently, that had been a disaster. *I'll just have to make it clear that I won't say no, if he asks.* Somehow though, she knew that the move needed to come from him, not her. He was old-fashioned, and probably felt that it was down to the man to ask the girl out. She didn't want to emasculate him by stealing his thunder. She'd have to play it carefully.

He collected her at seven and they walked into town together, strolling along, chatting away. After the film, the discussion and the tea and biscuits, he had walked her home, as usual. The moon was full, shining down from the clear sky, stars dotted here and there (as ordered by Miya, of course!). Frieda slowed the pace. "It's a beautiful night, isn't it?" she said quietly, looking up at the stars.

Andrew nodded, saying nothing.

"That moon is huge!" she said, smiling up at him.

Still he said nothing.

"Do you remember that night we met, Andrew; that film, 'It's a Wonderful Life?'" she asked.

"Mmm," he said.

"Do you remember that scene when George wants to get her the moon?"

"Mmm," he mumbled.

"That's a beautiful moon, don't you think, Andrew?" And Frieda stopped walking, gazing up at the moon.

"Dear God alive, woman," he groaned, and pulled her into his arms suddenly, kissing her deeply, with intensity and passion.

Sometime later, Frieda stood back and stared at Andrew in amazement. "Wow," she said. "Well that was intense!"

"Mmm," he said in reply, not taking his eyes off hers.

"Mmm?" she questioned. "Another 'mmm'? What's with all the mmm's?"

"Cos you take my breath away, woman, and there's none left for me to speak any damned words!" he said.

Frieda's jaw dropped open!

"And if I could fly up to that moon in a rocket and bring it back for you, I would!" he declared. "And I'd do anything else you wanted me to do, woman. I am crazy about you! Have been since the night I met you!"

Frieda's jaw dropped even more!

"And I haven't said anything because I didn't think I stood a chance with you, because you're amazing and wonderful and I'm, well, I'm just plain old me and a bit boring, and I didn't want to spoil what we do have, cos if all I can be is your friend, I'll take it. But I'd really like to be more, much more, Frie! If I'm not too boring for you?"

God, love him! Really? Boring? Frieda gazed at him with adoration, and a little amusement. "Andrew, my darling," she said with a grin. "Yes, you are a bit boring, if boring means that you aren't an adrenalin junky. I love boring! I totally love boring! I want boring! I want stable! *I don't* want excitement! Excitement is draining, exhausting, it's a rollercoaster of ups and downs and it's a bloody car crash! I want this, I want you!" And she grabbed him and kissed him hard, just to prove it!

And that was that!

"Oh, thank goodness for that!" exclaimed Miya and Bart, watching from the top of the lamppost. "At last!"

And both breathed an enormous, gigantic, sigh of relief!

"I think that we can safely say that we're out of the woods," grinned Bart.

"Oh yes, me too! No retraining 'down in transport' for me!" shrieked Miya in delight.

"Me neither!" beamed Bart. "Phew!"

Chapter 23

"No, me!" shouted Angelica, running to the door.

"But, Anj, it's my turn!" argued David. *God, she is so annoying!*

The children, were, as ever, arguing about whose turn it was to clean Dad's car.

"But you did it last time!"

"No, you did!"

Simon stuck his head around the kitchen door at the squabbling pair arguing in the hallway. "Right, you two," he said firmly, "you can do it together!"

"But then we have to split the wages!" they both chimed.

"Well maybe, if you do a good job, I *may* pay you a little extra. It depends how shiny and clean you make it. And it's not 'wages,' it's 'pocket money'! Off you go!" Simon smiled at his twins, watching them go running outside to the shed, and the bucket and sponge that were waiting. Fred, as usual, lolloping after them. Cassie, as usual, asleep on the sofa; lazing!

Sarah sighed. "Those two!" she moaned. "Do they ever stop?"

The children would be starting their last year in junior school next week, and throughout the entire six-week school's summer holidays, had not stopped fighting. It was driving her nuts! In an effort to calm it down, Sarah and Simon had given them a series of jobs to do, with the promise of extra pocket money for a good job, and made sure that the jobs were different (and, if possible, in different parts of the house), so as to separate the warring pair. It didn't make any difference; now they just argued about who had the best job! It had been like this for months.

"Don't worry about it, babe," smiled Simon. "It's just a phase. They hate each other now, but it will pass. I bet by the time they get to high school next year, they'll be close as anything."

"Hmmm, we'll see!" she grimaced.

"So, have you heard from Frieda lately?" he asked. He had met Andrew a few times since he and Frieda had become an item and he liked him enormously. Lovely chap! They'd been over for dinner twice and for a barbeque in the summer too, along with Angie and Tom. *It's nice for her to finally have someone,* he thought. He remembered what it had been like for him, before Sarah, when all his mates were married and settled; all except him. He'd often felt awkward at parties, when everyone else was in couples and he wasn't. Oh yes, he'd had girlfriends, casual ones here and there, but nothing 'proper.' Simon was sure that Frieda must have felt the same in the last ten years or so. He couldn't remember a time since he'd known her that she'd even had a boyfriend! Now, though, she seemed really happy and settled, and it looked like they were in it for the long haul. He recognised the signs, from watching his mates, and for himself, once he'd met Sarah, of course.

"Yes, she rang yesterday, raving about a picture that Andrew's bought her. Bless her, Si, she was crying!" Sarah replied, smiling.

"Again?" he grinned.

"No, not that kind of crying! Happy crying, happy tears!"

"Good stuff. So it's going well then?" he asked, pleased for them both.

"Going well? It's going fabulously! Apparently, this picture he got her is of the moon, with a lasso around it. Big full moon, she said, at night, with stars all over, and a big lasso tied to it. She was blubbering her eyes out, bless!"

"Aye?" Simon was bewildered. "Moon? Lasso?"

"Oh, never mind, you wouldn't understand. But it's very romantic and she's over the moon, literally!" Sarah giggled, so chuffed for Frie.

"Is he taking her to Cannes again next year, do you know?" Simon asked. "For the film festival? I thought it might be nice if we went too, have a break in the sun. I like the odd film myself."

"Oh, I don't know, hun, they haven't mentioned anything. Maybe? I think they want to go back again cos they missed so many of the films when they went in May."

Simon nodded. "And that was the whole point of going, wasn't it? To watch films!"

"I know! But they wouldn't have been able to actually

get into the film thingy anyway," she added, "cos that's only for the film people. They were *meant* to be watching all those films on that big open-air screen that they'd set up for 'Joe Public,' you know, on the beach? Imagine that? Sitting on a beach in Cannes, being surrounded by film stars, and all that sea and sun; fabulous!" Sarah thought back to the couple's return and the expected stories they'd have regaled, but no, not one! She looked at Simon and grinned. "They missed every film, you know; bless 'em! Mind you, they'd only been together a few weeks then, so it's hardly surprising that they barely left their hotel room, now is it? Remember what we were like in those first few months?" She grinned at him, a naughty, sexy grin.

"What do you mean, 'first few months'!" he laughed. "We're still like that now!"

"Well, yes, I know," she smiled. "But only when the kids are out of the way; and I'm not knackered, and you're not knackered!"

"I'm not knackered now!" he chuckled, grabbing her wrist and pulling her over towards him.

"Si, Si," she giggled, "kids! The kids are outside!"

"They're cleaning the car, babe," he said, kissing her neck, "they'll be ages yet. Tell 'em Mummy and Daddy have gone for a lay down," and he kissed her some more, sliding his hand under her top and up her back to her bra clasp.

"Behave!" she giggled, looking out of the window at the children. "Oh, bollocks, they won't even know we've gone!"

And the two ran out of the room, giggling up the stairs to their bedroom, where they didn't surface for some time!

Frieda looked at the programme for the Redville Film Club's autumn period with horror. The third film down on the list was the showing of the 'Butterfly Effect'! "Jesus, no!" she exclaimed. "I can't watch that again, not with all those people, and certainly not in front of Andrew! Shit!" Frieda's startled eyes were filled with trepidation. She sat down heavily on her sofa, clutching the programme in her hands. Tears began to form in her eyes, as fear set in. *What to do?*

"What's wrong, Mum?" Jess, her middle daughter, rushed into the room, worrying about her mother, whose loud reaction had been heard in the kitchen, where she'd been sitting with her younger brother having coffee, chatting about the flats they were moving into in a few weeks.

Frieda pushed the programme at her, "Look!" she whispered. "Look what's on in six weeks' time! He'll know, he'll guess, what do I do, Jess? What do I do? I can't go! I just can't! I'll have to be ill, get a headache, be too busy ... shit ... shit ..."

"Alright, Mum; it's alright," Jess reassured, gently taking her mother's hand, trying to calm her down. It was trembling, the fear evident on her face, and within her shaking body. She stroked the hand, holding it tight, trying to help her mum as best she could. "Is it so bad, if he knows, I mean?"

Frieda looked at her daughter in shock. "Tell him? God, no!" she whispered.

"Why not, Mum? Aye? Come on now, Mum, he seems

to really care; I'm sure he'll understand. He's really nice, Mum; I don't think you've got anything to be scared about, really I don't. In fact, I think you *should* tell him. It's been six months now and he's clearly nuts about you. What are you scared about, aye? That he won't want you anymore? That he won't love you anymore?" Jess looked at her mother with concern. She hadn't seen her like this for a long time; at least a year. Seeing this film on the programme had clearly triggered something inside her, though, that much was clear.

"I'd have to watch it in front of everybody," Frieda whispered. "Everybody!"

"Yes, but it's not 'everybody' that you're worried about, is it, Mum? It's him! You're scared of *him* knowing, in case he judges you. Isn't that right, Mum?"

Frieda felt the fear inside her and took a deep breath. *Okay,* she thought, *so what is going on with me here? What's this about?* She dove into the fear, feeling for just what it was that she was just so scared about. Yes, judgment! Jess is right. She looked at her daughter and nodded. "How did you get to be so wise and clever?" she smiled, rubbing her daughter's hand.

"Oh well, that'll be the genes won't it, aye, Mum," and grinned. "You okay then?" she asked.

Frieda nodded. "Yes, I'm okay. I'll give it some thought. I overreacted, I'll be fine. You go have your coffee. And, Jess," she looked at her daughter with gratitude, "thanks love."

Frieda pondered the problem for days, avoiding Andrew while she tried to work out where she was, how she felt, why she had reacted like that about the film. *Should I tell him? How to tell him? What will he think? What will he say? Will it spoil it; spoil what we have? ... I don't want to spoil it! Will he think I'm damaged goods? Will he pity me? ... God, I don't want pity!* On and on the thoughts went, around and around in her head. *Will he think I'm disgusting? Will he think I'm sick?* Eventually, they came back full circle, back to the first thought ... *will he judge me and find me wanting?*

The phone rang for the ninth time that day. Andrew again! He left a message. *Was she alright?* he said. *He was getting worried now,* he said. *Hadn't heard from her, please call,* he said. *Have I upset you?* he said.

Frieda sighed. This wasn't fair. She wasn't being fair! *Poor Andrew! Not a clue, bless him.* She rang him back, guilt eating away at her for blocking him out like this. *Not okay Frie,* she scolded herself.

He picked up the phone as soon as it rang. "Frie?" he asked, hope in his tone.

"Hi, Andrew," she said quietly. "I'm sorry, babe. No, of course, you haven't upset me. How could you upset me; you're perfect!" she grinned, trying to put both the smile and the warmth into her tone, hoping to hide the nervousness, and the guilt, caused by ignoring him for the last few days. She hadn't returned a single text, call or email. She'd just 'gone to ground,' running back to hermit mode, like she did when she couldn't cope.

"Oh, thank goodness for that!" he exclaimed. "Though hardly 'perfect,' my darling, but as long as I haven't upset you; I was sure I must have upset you! So you're alright?" he asked, concern and care in his voice.

"Yes, babe, I'm alright, I promise. I've just had some stuff going on, you know? A lot on my mind, and I needed a bit of space to just work it out. I'm sorry that I worried you, hun, really I am. That was not okay of me and I'm really sorry."

Andrew breathed a sigh of relief. He had been sure he'd stuffed it up somehow. He'd been wracking his brains trying to figure out what he'd done, how he'd annoyed her, but he hadn't come up with any answers.

"It's not you, babe, it's me," Frieda assured. "But," she took a deep breath, "we do need to talk. Can you come over?"

"Of course, I can come over. When do you want me? Now?" he asked.

Frieda heard the fear in his voice. *God, he thinks I'm going to dump him! God, love him!* "Darling," she said quickly, needing to reassure him, "you mean the world to me, you know that don't you? ... I ... I'll see you soon."

"On my way," he replied, and then he was gone.

Frieda stared at the phone in her hand. She'd wanted to say 'I love you,' but couldn't. The words just wouldn't come; she'd felt it, the love, and she'd felt the need and the desire to say it, but she just hadn't been able to. *Why not?* she pondered, realisation immediately hitting as soon as she'd asked herself the question. The answer - *what if he doesn't want me, once he knows this?* That's what had held her back! Not just then, but on many occasions over the past six months when she'd nearly said it; something had always held her back. At first, she had thought it was because she wasn't sure of her feelings for him, but now she realised that was just not true. She was sure! She had been for ages, probably since the beginning, in fact. The reason that she hadn't said it, that she had held back, *the real reason*, was that she was terrified of being judged, of being rejected, of being hurt.

Frieda thought back over her past relationships. She'd never told any of them, not one. It had been a huge wall between them, each of them, she knew - that secrecy. It had prevented real honesty, real truth, real intimacy, and, she realised now, real trust. The counsellor had said that she'd always had issues with control and trust, explaining that all survivors (and he emphasised the 'all'), had the same issues. They needed to feel in control, because in the past, they had had none. They couldn't trust, because in the past they *had* trusted, and that trust is what had led to the abuse. Their way of coping, of handling life, was to be in control at all times and to trust no one! As Frieda pondered, she realised that she had repeated the same pattern of behaviour with Andrew, thereby keeping a wall between them, a distance. It was a distance, a gap; a huge gapping gap, that only she could close, and Frieda knew what she had to do. She had to tell him; she had to trust him and she had to let go of control. If he loved her (and she thought that he probably did), he would support her, he would understand. And, he would understand her in a way that no one ever before had understood her! And through that understanding, would come belonging; the elusive, previously unattainable, 'belonging'!

And so she told him. Nervously, quietly, and, surprisingly, easily; she told him. He listened intently. He did not interrupt, he did not ask questions; he simply sat and listened. With tears in his eyes (by the end), he just listened; and then he held her. He held her so tightly that she thought she might break! And then he cried. Real, sobbing, letting go; unashamed tears. He cried into her hair, he cried into her arms. And she? Well, she cried, too. They cried together, building their bond, their new bond; a bond of trust, of intimacy, and ... of belonging.

At the film club six weeks later, he held her hand tightly all the way through the film, injecting love and support, care and strength into her, all the way from the beginning to the end. He had asked her if she wanted to go, telling her that they didn't have to go, reassuring her that it was okay to miss it, but she had insisted. And she was glad that she did.

Since she'd told him, the bond between them had built, and along with it, trust and intimacy. They had become closer and closer with each and every passing day. She no longer had problems telling him that she loved him, and she told him often. He, who had been holding back from saying the words for fear of frightening her off, also let go, and told her how much he loved her; and he told her often.

And Miya beamed; totally beamed. "Aw," she sighed, feeling all mushy and gooey, "how perfectly perfect!"

Chapter 24

"I wanted to ask your advice, Sarah, your opinion, because you know her the best," he said. Andrew was sitting in Sarah's lounge, staring nervously into her face, looking for clues. He and Frieda were at Sarah and Simon's house for dinner and they'd had a lovely evening. Christmas was coming, and Sarah had been doing her 'hostess-with-the-most-ess' thing, throwing a small dinner party for the two couples in an early celebration. Tom and Angie had been invited but had been unable to make it, Tom's work-do apparently. Andrew looked at the Christmas tree in the corner of the room. *So lovely,* he thought, *especially in here with that open fire. Makes it! I'd love to have an open fire, or maybe a wood burner? Ah well, one day.* He smiled, bringing his attention away from the crackling logs and the tree, looking at Sarah again, waiting for her reaction to his suggestion. "So, what do you think? Do you think it's too soon to ask her to move in with me? I know she's fiercely independent and I'm just not sure if she'll feel smothered, crowded; you know?"

Sarah grinned. "I'm sure if Frie isn't ready, Frie will let you know; and let you know very clearly!" she laughed. "Just ask her, Andrew; just ask her, hun."

"I just feel the need to protect her, you know, to be close to her, to take care of her, but I don't want to suffocate her." Andrew looked at his hands. He'd been wanting to ask Frieda to move in with him for weeks, but he'd been scared to, in case it was 'too much, too soon.' Frieda had gone upstairs to help Angelica wrap her mother's Christmas present after the dinner, and Simon was helping David to do his, so they had the room to themselves. He was using the opportunity that had presented itself to ask her opinion when he'd found himself alone with Sarah. "I know it's silly, this need to protect her; she's perfectly capable of protecting herself. It's just that, oh, I don't know; ever since I found out, ever since she told me, I just do!"

"Hun, it's perfectly natural to want to protect the woman you love!" Sarah laughed. "Simon's very protective of me, and I haven't been through what Frie has, so I can imagine how strongly you feel protective of her. Tell you what, though, mate, you're the first! With all the other men that Frieda's had, it's been the other way around! She's been the protector, taking care of them. Mind you, weak they were, all of them! Losers, mashed up, messed up tosspots, the lot of 'em! That'll have been her need to control, going for weaklings, so that she could feel safe. Of course, it didn't, make her feel safe, I mean. It made her feel worse, but there you go; that's what a need to control does for you. Add to that her inability to previously trust, not that she'd have wanted to trust any of them, mind! I wouldn't trust 'em as far as I could throw 'em! But you're different, hun. You're strong and sorted, and together. And she trusts you; so she doesn't need to control, for the first time, she doesn't need to. She can let go and let herself be taken care of, for a change! So yes, ask her! I bet she says yes!" and Sarah grinned, happy to know that Andrew cared for her friend so much, and that he was so protective of her. It was lovely!

And so he did! When Andrew took Frieda home later that evening, he asked her if she would consider moving in with him. She had looked at him in astonishment. Apparently no one had ever asked her to move in with them before! It had been the other way around (her asking them to move in with her), her need to control, again! She had asked if she could sleep on it, explaining that she wanted to, it was just a bit scary for her to give up her home, to trust him enough to let go of her independence. And then there was her rented property, and, along with it, a lot of her furniture that would have to go. She'd be putting huge trust into both their relationship and into him; and it terrified her. She had explained this, and he had understood.

"You know me," she'd said, "total control freak! I love you, babe, I do. But I need time to think about it, okay?"

And he'd told her to take all the time that she needed; and he meant it! There was no pressure from him, no sulks, and there was also no sense of rejection or insecurity within him. Previous men that she'd known would have felt insecure by her need to consider it and not just say 'yes' straight away, but not Andrew. He just simply accepted it. He accepted her, and he accepted her completely. …

It took Frieda ten days to accept Andrew's offer. Ten days of working on 'letting go.' She let go of control, of fear, and she worked on allowing her trust to build, and to increase. In the end, the day before Christmas Eve, she got there, agreeing to move in with him after Christmas. She took him with her to her letting agents, needing his support as she gave in the written 'one month's notice to quit' on her rental home. Hands shaking, she signed the paperwork, looking repeatedly at Andrew for reassurance that this was safe, that this was okay, that he wouldn't let her down; and he gave it, squeezing her hand reassuringly, smiling at her with love and devotion in his eyes.

After the signing, he took her for a Chinese meal, just about managing to get a table at that time of year. It was Christmas party season and the place was packed. Despite that, right in the middle of the meal, he went down on one knee and proposed. The whole restaurant cheered! Frieda just stared! She stared at both him, perched on the floor, down on one knee, and she stared at the diamond ring, sparkling in its black, velvet box, which seemed to be screaming at her, 'put me on'!

"No, dear," piped up Miya, "that was me!"

Andrew had bought the ring the previous week and had been trying to decide when would be the right time to propose. Christmas Eve? Christmas Day? In the end he'd opted for New Year's Eve the following week, but he'd changed his mind. He wasn't sure when. It may have been the look of terror on her face when she'd signed those papers. It may have been the love that shone out of those beautiful eyes as she'd looked at him like a frightened rabbit in the letting agent's office. He wasn't sure. All he knew was that he didn't want to wait any longer. *No time like the present,* he'd decided, and had pulled the ring box out from his jacket pocket and dropped down on to one knee, there and then, right in the middle of the noodles! He still had the chopsticks in his hand!

Frieda had just stared at him in shock. Then, without any warning, or, it seemed, any prompting from her brain, her head had simply nodded. All by itself!

"No, dear," piped up Miya again, "that was me, too!"

Andrew took the ring, placing it on her finger to rapturous, thunderous applause from the packed restaurant's customers and staff alike. A bottle of champagne was bought, brought, popped and drank, and the happy couple made their way home. Under, of course, a full, round, perfectly shining moon!

"Aw," said Miya, with tears streaming down her face.

"Aw," said Bart, not noticing her tears. He was far too busy wiping away his own!

***

Christmas was fantastic! Sarah threw an enormous surprise (and impromptu) party for Andrew and Frieda's engagement, just two days after Christmas, inviting all the film club, all their friends, and all of the children. They held it in the Crown's function room (their local pub), and it had been a lovely night.

David and Angelica had loved it; being with all the

grown-ups and the older children. They had stopped arguing, finally, being far too busy with their new Christmas presents to be bothered with the distraction of fighting, and had made peace, just in time for the party. They had both been given mobile phones, something that they'd been nagging for consistently for at least the last three years. Both she and Simon had resisted, feeling that they were too young for such things, but at nearly eleven years old now, and with high school looming next September, the parents felt that it was time. Angelica had shrieked with delight at the bright pink case of the new smart phone, whilst David had shrieked with delight at its aps and games! In addition to this, they had both received laptops; for them to improve their computer skills in readiness for the coming years. They had barely left their rooms since!

Fred wasn't happy about it. Not at all happy! He'd had no attention whatsoever from David for days! Simply days! "Oh, my Dog," he moaned. "I am so bored! Beyond bored!"

Cassie wasn't happy either! "Oh, I know, Flops," she said, nodding emphatically. "I'm with you on this one! Angelica's exactly the same! Haven't seen her for days either!"

"Mind you," he admitted, looking at his knee, "in a way it's a bit of a relief. I'm not as young as I used to be and the rough and tumble with David's taking its toll on these old bones."

"How old are you now, Flops?" she asked, licking the offending knee in an effort to help his increasing arthritis.

"Eleven! And not forgetting the three months, old for

a golden retriever, apparently. Maybe I'm on my way out and the laptop for David is his replacement for me."

"Oh, I dunno," reassured Cassie. "I was reading the other day that there was a golden retriever that lived till he was twenty! Although that was a world record. Said so, in the paper. The average life is between twelve and fourteen, though, so Google says; so not to worry, Flops, you've got years in you yet - years!" She grinned at him, trying to cheer him up.

"I wish I could read," he sighed. "I can read pictures, but not newspapers," he admitted, quietly. He wasn't as embarrassed at his failings to read anymore, not since he'd learned that most dogs can't even speak human. He was still a bloody genius, even if his old bones were getting creaky, and David preferred the laptop to him!

"Well let's look at Ma's laptop; oh, I mean, Sarah!" Cassie corrected herself quickly. *Damn, that's three times now that I've called her that. Maybe I'm getting old too!* She shook her head in disgust at the error. "Anyway, let's look at her laptop and do some research on what we can do for that knee, shall we, Flops? Maybe you need some cod liver oil? Yummy!"

"Ooh, yuck!" he screeched. "And double yuck! Fish? No thank you! I don't bloody think so!"

"Well maybe something else then? Something meaty smelling not fishy smelling, although I don't know what the issue is with fish myself," she grinned, thinking of the delights that were, to her, cod liver oil. *Totally yummy!*

And the two went off to the kitchen and Mum's laptop that was sitting on the kitchen table. She, as usual, was in the lounge doing another reading for some lady or other.

Cassie perused various health sites, both animal and human, looking for a solution for poor Flopsy's knee. "She's not bad, for a cat," thought Fred, smiling at her concentration and focus on the screen.

"He's not bad, for a dog," thought Cassie, looking at her old friend with a grin.   And the two pets set about finding the solution to Fred's knee.

***

"What do you mean, 'a prom'? A prom! They're eleven years old! How ridiculous! Whatever is the world coming to?" Margaret spouted.

"I know, Mum. It is a bit daft, but there you are. Another 'Americanism' that we seem to have adopted over here." Sarah shook her head, trying to get her head around it herself.

"A prom to leave junior school? Never heard anything so ridiculous in my life!"

Sarah smiled at her mum, understanding her confusion. She hadn't understood it either! She'd been gobsmacked when the twins had come home with the letter about the 'end of school prom' for the year sixes. There was going to be a disco, photographs, of course, and even a red carpet! All the children were expected to turn up in their finery, at six o'clock sharp, on the last day of school. She'd had to take them into Redville and buy them both outfits, a suit for David, and a prom dress for Angelica, who had, of course, insisted on the most expensive one in the shop.

"Look on the bright side, Mum," Angelica had said,

"we can use these as our outfits for Aunty Frieda's wedding next month."

"Well yes, true. I suppose so," she had reluctantly agreed.

Sarah didn't mind buying new outfits for her children for Frieda's wedding, but she did object to the vast expense that this silly junior prom brought. Madness, total madness! Combining the outfits to double up for the wedding did make sense, so she had gone over to Frieda's to check if it was okay with her.

"Of course, it is, hun!" she'd cried. "Darlin', it's my fourth wedding, so I want it to be a low key affair. I'm not having bridesmaids or anything, and I've only bought myself a cream suit, so whatever they wear is fine with me." Frieda had grinned at her, happiness shining from her eyes. Sarah had never seen her look so well, or so contented, or so peaceful for that matter! There was a kind of 'inner peace' within Frie these days that Sarah could almost touch; it was so strong.

It was to be a small wedding, just close friends and family. Andrew's parents had both passed on and, as he was an only child, it was just him and Cara, plus one or two of his friends and their wives, and a few from the film club, of course. Frieda's own three children would be there, along with her mum. Apart from the immediate family, there was just Sarah and Simon, with David and Angelica, and Angie and Tom and their two children. It was to be held in the register office in Redville, followed by a meal for them all in the restaurant of their favourite country hotel, ten miles away. Then they were flying off to St. Lucia for their two-week honeymoon. By the time they returned, they were hoping the new house that they were having built would be completed. It had always been Andrew's dream, as an architect, to design his own house. He also missed country living a little, and as Frieda had got so into gardening now, with his encouragement, they'd agreed to move out of town. They'd found a nice one-acre plot just three miles away, with planning permission approved for a three-bedroom house to be built on it. Andrew wanted his own design, so had drawn up new plans and resubmitted them. Approval had come relatively quickly, considering the usual red tape (with a bit of help from Miya and Bart, of course, smoothing the way!).

Andrew had loved designing their new home, sitting with Frieda for hours planning the style, the rooms, the layout, the storage, the light, the space, the décor; incorporating everything that they wanted into it. It was to be their 'forever' home, so they'd spent an age on detail, getting everything just right. They'd even designed the garden so that it included a veggie patch and a chicken run (something Frieda had always fancied having a go at), as well as the obligatory flower borders for Andrew, with an enormous lawn. They'd also incorporated a nice patio for an eating area and barbeque, alfresco dining! They'd invited Cara to join in with the design, but she had declined. She had moved out some months back into her own place, and insisted that it was their new home 'for their new beginning,' and to go ahead and not to worry about her and what she wanted. Frieda's children had said the same. They had all moved out some time ago; one into a flat with friends, the other into his own independent space. Frieda's eldest was now married with a young baby, living in Redville with her husband, so it was just her and Andrew to consider really.

Sarah watched her friend as she talked about her new home and the coming wedding, so pleased for her that she'd finally found the happiness that she deserved. She'd really blossomed over the last two years, particularly since she'd been living with Andrew. There was no doubt about it, Frieda was a new woman!

Chapter 25

The wedding had been beautiful! Frieda and Andrew were so in love it was ridiculous (so their children had said), for old farts, that is! They'd just laughed, saying, "Wait till you get to your fifties, cheeky! You won't feel like an old fart, I can promise you that!" The sun had shone; the service was simple, elegant and perfect; then they had all gone to the hotel for the wonderful meal, the speeches and the cutting of the cake. Many photographs were taken, capturing the happy couple's day, and then they were off! St. Lucia beckoned, with its turquoise blue sea, white sand, palm trees and honeymoon suite.

Their new house had been completed just one week before, so it had all been a mad rush moving their furniture in from Andrew's house and over to the new one, before the wedding. His now empty house was already on the market and sold. It had been put up for sale as soon as they'd had a firm completion date for the new-build, and an offer had been accepted within days. It was a relief for Andrew, who had been paying a rather large, temporary loan, secured against his old house. It had paid for the land and the new house which now sat proudly on it. Both Andrew and Frieda had always thought of Andrew's house as 'his,' despite him saying to Frie that it was theirs now, but it had never felt like 'theirs,' for either of them. This though, this new house; this was theirs! They had designed it together and chosen the fittings and fixtures together; Andrew finally felt that it was now a joint home - they both did.

Everyone had helped with the move, of course. A lot of new furniture had been bought by the couple for the new house, all of which had been delivered directly into it by the relevant companies. It was the old stuff that everyone had helped with. 'The picture' (their picture), hung above the new multi-burner that sat in the stone fireplace at the end of the large living room, shining its moonlight from the picture into the room. It had pride of place! *It'll set off the crackling logs beneath it wonderfully; once it's cold enough for a fire,* thought Frieda with glee. For now, it was August and the height of summer, but, Frieda knew, summer or not, it wouldn't be long before that fire was lit!

They'd designed a modern, contemporary house, but had still incorporated into it the character of some country features. There was a large oak beam across the centre of the room; holding up the double height vaulted ceiling with its exposed beams coming down either side at a forty-five degree angle. There was a half mezzanine floor overlooking the living room beneath which Andrew had set up as a reading space. Bookcases had been built into its sloping walls, in the same matching oak as the beams. He was there now, sitting on one of the two new comfy chairs, putting the last of the books onto the new wooden shelves. He looked down through the glass balustrade to the lounge below with a smile, a contented, happy smile. His gaze moved further along down the room, across the lounge area to the other end of the enormous space. Three steps led down to an open-plan kitchen/diner, with its high-gloss ultra-modern kitchen units, and, of course, every gadget known to man! Cream stone slabs were laid throughout, pulling the entire ground floor together, all kept warm by its under-floor heating system. Enormous windows either side of the room (dual aspect, for lots of natural light), looked out onto the various areas of their garden, its view continuing onto the wonderful open countryside beyond. It really was rather spectacular!

He couldn't wait to marry her next week, just couldn't wait! It was going to be a wonderful day, as would be the honeymoon afterwards; then back here, to their wonderful new home and the start of their new life together. He gazed down at Frieda with such love he thought he'd fall over, it was so intense! He watched her now, chatting to Cara as they unpacked boxes of plates and cups, giggling away. *Wonder what they're whispering about?* he thought, happy that his two best girls got on so well.

"You never!" whispered Frieda, a shocked grin on her face.

"Don't tell him," Cara whispered back, "promise? He'd kill me, totally kill me!"

"I won't, I promise. I wondered what that was all about, you know," she giggled. "I saw him, on that site, did I ever tell you that?"

Now it was Cara's turn to look shocked. "No! Wow!"

"Yes, I tried that dating site, the exact same one; must have been for about six months, maybe longer. I saw his profile and thought he looked nice, but I also saw that he hadn't been on-line for over a year, so I just dismissed him, thinking he'd found someone else! So you're saying he never knew? He never even knew that he was even on there?"

Cara shook her head emphatically. "No, and he doesn't know now, and he must never know! He'll kill me! I've taken it down, ages ago, honest!"

"It'll be our little secret, promise!" Frieda grinned. And she gazed up at Andrew, standing on the mezzanine across the room above her, with such love and devotion that she thought she'd pass out. He caught her gaze and returned it, their love beaming across the room like a laser - lighting it up - right up to the rafters!

Miya sighed a contented sigh as she watched them all below. She was sitting on the beam across the centre of the lounge, along with the respective crew of gathered GA's. She laughed at the frenzied activity as furniture was placed and boxes unwrapped by all the helpers. Turning to Bart, she grinned inanely. "Perfect," she chirped, "just perfectly perfect!"

But Bart didn't reply; Bart was crying, again!

Bless, she thought. *Just bless!*

***

"But you got to, Mum, you just got to!" Angelica

implored. "They all wear it! All of them! Every one of them! You got to, Mum; you got to!"

"No, Angelica, you are not having make-up to wear to school!" Sarah argued. *Make-up? To school? At eleven? Ridiculous!*

"But, Mum! You *got to* let me wear make-up!" Angelica's voice was pleading, persistent, insistent. *No way am I backing down on this,* she thought grimly. *No bloody way!*

"Yeah, tell her, Anj," barked Fred. "No bloody way, I agree!"

"Fred, stay out of it!" warned Sarah, feeling very 'ganged up on' by the two now standing before her. Angelica had her hands on her hips, her head cocked to one side, glaring at her. Fred's head was also cocked, standing up for 'madam,' something that he rarely did!

"Well she's right, Mum. I seen 'em! I seen 'em high school kids going to the school bus and it's plastered on 'em. She's gotta fit in! She's gotta!"

"Fred! Enough!" Sarah glared at the pair of them. Her hands, too, were on her hips, her head cocked in defiance. *Here we go,* she thought, *is this when the warring starts between mother and daughter? Already? I didn't expect it for another year or two!*

"Maybe a bit, Mum?" said David, just coming into the kitchen, sports bag in hand, fresh from his tennis practice at the club. "They do all wear it, you know, the girls at our school. To be fair, I think she's the only one without any, apart from the dorky girls, of course, and she is getting teased and stuff from her 'so-called friends.' You know our Anj, she's one of the cool girls, and appearance is everything, Mum, when you're a cool girl, everything! She likes to fit in, be the leader not the follower. And she's so far behind the others she's practically a mile behind, Mum! How about you let her wear a bit, aye, Mum? Just a bit?"

Sarah stared at her son in amazement. *When had this started, him sticking up for her? Mind you, Si had said that they'd probably get close again, once they were in high school. Looks like he's right!* But before she had time to answer him, Cassie chipped in too.

"Well I agree, also," said Cassie, entering the kitchen and winding her tail around Sarah's legs affectionately. "They do grow up quicker these days, and you need to let them, my dear."

Sarah stared at the cat, then the dog, then the children. She turned to Angelica and sighed. "I'll think about it," she said reluctantly. "But only *think* mind! I'm not saying yes!"

"I'm just saying now, Mum, cos it's Christmas next week and you can make it one of my presents, okay? And I prefer Chanel, or ..." She stopped, seeing her mother's face, and decided that she may have pushed it a tad too far!

The children ran upstairs, followed by Cassie and Fred, happy that they'd made a start on the 'wear Mum down' thing. It may take a while, but if they all pulled together, they'd get her to give in, in the end! Enlisting Cassie and Fred's help had been key. She listened to them, did Mum, a lot! Good plan, great plan!

"Told ya it'd work, didn' I?" grinned Fred.

To be fair, he was sick of listening to madam moan.

Months now, just bloody months! All the other girls wear make-up, she'd cried. *Why can't I?* she'd whined. *Mum's so mean,* she'd complained. And on and on the Dog-damn-it moaning had gone, week after dreary week! He'd got so sick of it in the end that he'd offered to help in the 'wear Mum down' plan. "Dog, I hope it works," he sighed to Cassie. "I can't take any more of madam's moaning!"

"Oh, I agree entirely, Flopsy!" scowled Cassie, equally sick of Angelica's moaning. "Although, I do think that we'd better get used to it, Flops, cos it's only going to get worse over the next few years, I can promise you that!"

"Aye?"

"Oh yes, indeed; the teenage years are the worst! The absolute worst! Fights and rows, drama and tears, slammed doors (loads of them!), not to mention the stamping of feet and the verbal abuse! Awful it is, just awful!"

"Verbal abuse? Wassat?" Fred was bemused, having never been exposed to any kind of verbal abuse, ever!

"Oh, Flops, she's going to call her mother every name under the sun over the next six or seven years, and that's if we're lucky! It may go on right up until she's twenty, or even twenty-one!"

"No!"

"Yes! Some of it will be to her face, and that will cause Hell up! Most of it, mind, will be behind her back. She will hate her mother with a passion, on and off, until it passes."

"Until what passes?" asked Fred, even more confused. Angelica screaming and shouting at Mum? And calling her names? And Mum not killing her? Not to mention Dad! Didn't make sense!

"Until the hormones passes, silly. Hormones!"

"Oh, Dog! I remember hormones!" he yelled. "Dog-damn awful things they are! Awful! Oh Dog!"

"Indeed!"

"But it's okay!" he grinned hopefully. "I'll just stay out the way; spend all my time with David, even if he is giving all of his attention to the laptop or play-station."

"He'll be the same, Flops. Not as bad, of course, but still bad!"

"No!"

"Yes! Boys generally aren't as bad as girls. They're bad mind, but not *as* bad! Most of them, that is. It's cos their bodies aren't going through as many changes as the girls, you know, in readiness for having babies?"

Fred was horrified! His lovely David turning into a complaining, nasty, moaning-minny? A mini-Anj? Dear Dog! For the next six-eight years? No! He couldn't get over it! Fred put his head down and prayed for release. "Take me now," he yelled, "I'm too old for this shit! I can't stand it! Take me now!"

"Oh, don't be dramatic, Flops," Cassie grinned. "We'll get through it, somehow!"

But 'upstairs,' Fred's lamented call had been heard ...

Metatron checked his watch carefully. "Oh yes, indeed. Twelve years, three months and eighteen hours," he declared. "That's what the 'All That Is' ordered for our Fred ... Oh, no, wait ... not yet! That's how old Fred is now! We have another year yet! Oops!" Metatron shook his head at his error. *Gosh that was close! Now then, let me think. He was one year old when the Boss gave him that*

284

timescale; that specific timescale, so he has another year yet. Can't be going against the Boss, oh no, not at all! Metatron grinned, looking down on Fred. His paws were over his ears! "Bless him! He'll soon be wishing that he *could* go now! A year of teenage tantrums?" Metatron laughed out loud. "And he thought the terrible-twos were bad! He hasn't seen anything yet!" He set his watch for three hundred and sixty-five days' time, then put his watch back down on his desk with a laugh. "This next year will be a test for our Fred, a big test!" Funny enough, he reckoned he'd pass it though. "Better get the golden halo ready, yes indeed. And speak to Frank; get him ready for collection. Yes, no reason we can't begin the arrangements now. No reason at all!"

Chapter 26

Metatron polished the golden halo carefully. He looked at his watch again. Three hundred and fifty-nine days. *Jolly good!* He'd been watching Fred these last months, and, at times, had wondered himself if Fred would stay the course. It had been tough, very tough! Angelica had, of course, worn her mother down on the make-up argument, but no sooner was that war won, then another would come about. There had been less wars from David, being that much more accommodating than his sister, and much less hormonal, or course, but wars nonetheless. The Brown household had been a tangled web of screaming, shouting, slamming and fighting for the best part of a year. He could feel Fred's exhaustion from all the way up here, high up in The Realms. *Yes, it's time. Time to get him out of there and give him some peace,* he decided.

"So, Frank," he said, sometime later, "I have a *most*

important collection for you next week. *Most* important! You must handle this one with care, much care, do you hear?"

Frank nodded emphatically. *This isn't like the Boss,* he thought, *to call me in to his office about a collection! Not normally, it isn't! I wonder what's going on?* "Yes, Sir," he replied, trying hard to mask his curiosity. "Special delivery, no dropping, handle with care; got it, Boss." In fact, Frank couldn't ever remember a time when the Boss had called him about a delivery, any delivery, ever! *Wow, this must be a really special person!* he decided.

"And ..." Metatron continued, "you are to bring the collection to me, and to me alone. You speak to no one; no one, do you understand? No stopping on the way, no chatting, no dawdling, just me, got it?"

"Yes, Sir," he said firmly. "Got it! No dawdling, bring it straight here!" Frank was confused. Collections were always taken to the Light, not the Boss's office! From there, they were assessed, reviewed and dealt with. He'd never been told to bring a collection here, to the Angelic Temple, to the Boss! How weird!

"Straight from the tunnel of light to my office. No stopping anywhere else. Seven-thirty next Wednesday; p.m., not a.m., got it? Straight here!"

"Got it, Boss, straight here. 19:30 hours. On the dot, straight here, got it!" *I wonder what the others will make of this,* he thought. *Blimey!*

"And, Frank," Metatron added sternly, "you will discuss this with no one! If I hear that any other Grim Reaper knows about this, or any of the AA's or GA's, you will be dismissed, immediately. Do I make myself clear?"

"Crystal, Boss, crystal. Keep my mouth shut, Boss; won't say a word, Boss, promise."

And Frank rushed out of Metatron's office, completely confused about the job, but very clear on one thing; *keep my mouth shut!*

***

Fred was really, really fed up! Angelica was screaming at David, again. Mum was trying to calm it down, again, and he was doing his best to shut out the Dog-damn noise, with his paws over his ears, again! He looked at Cassie in despair. "Dog, give me strength," he sighed, eating yet another packet of doggie-chocs. "Look at me, comfort eating!" he sighed. "It's no wonder I've got so fat! Look at me; I'm bloody huge!"

Cassie looked at Fred's stomach, and sure enough, it was rather large! "Umm," she said, trying to be tactful, "it is, shall we say, rather rotund, Flops; but it suits you!"

Sarah banged into the room, pulling her hair out. "I am going to kill that girl!" she shrilled. "Stone bloody dead! If she survives till she's thirteen, it'll be a bloody miracle!"

"Yes, Mum," Fred said, agreeing wholeheartedly. "Stone dead! Why don't you do it now? Put us all out of our misery!"

"Do you think he's put on weight, Ma, I mean, Sarah?" asked Cassie. Damn, that's four now! "Fred, I mean. I don't think he's put on too much, do you?" She was trying her best to distract Sarah from her 'killing' of Angelica, but she wasn't sure that she'd succeed. She was wound up tighter than a badger's bum!

Sarah looked at Fred's stomach half-heartedly, distracted by her frustration at her daughter, and suddenly snapped out of her anger-trance. *Bloody hell, it's huge!* she realised. *It's really swollen!* She went over to Fred (whose paws were still over his ears), and felt his tummy gently. It was rock solid! "Oh dear, Freddie," she said, trying to hide the alarm in her tone. "That doesn't feel right, hun. I think we need to go and see Terry," she smiled, trying not to worry. It was probably gas or something equally insignificant.

"Oh Dog, no!" yiked Fred, pulling his paws from his ears. "Not 'Terry-the-Terrible'!"

"Afraid so, hun," she grinned. Ten minutes later they were sitting in the waiting room of the village vet. She'd managed to get an emergency appointment and Terry had said to bring Fred straight over. She looked at Clarabelle nervously; sitting next to her stroking Fred's head gently. "Is he gonna be okay?" she whispered to her.

Clarabelle frowned. She was concerned. Very concerned! Fred's energy didn't feel right at all, not at all!

"I *can* hear you, you know!" he moaned. "Dunno what all the fuss is about; I feel fine! Just a bit of weight gain, Mum; stress eating I'll have you know! Too many doggie-chocs, if there is such a thing as 'too many'! Although I can't see it myself," he grinned.

"Are you in any pain, Fred?" they both asked at the same time.

"Nope! Can't feel a thing!" he grinned.

And then the door opened and Terry was calling them in. He smiled at Fred and lifted him gently onto the examining table. Fred sat, nicely for once, allowing Terry to feel his tummy. Terry's face said it all!

Sarah looked at him in horror. She knew! He didn't have to say the 'C' word; she just knew. So did Clarabelle, who was looking at Fred with such love that it shone from her face. A tear slid down both their cheeks simultaneously, silently, followed by another.

Terry looked at her kindly, feeling her distress. "I need to run some tests, Sarah; bloods and a scan, but it's pretty clear, I'm sorry to say. It feels like a large tumour, a very large tumour! Has he been eating okay? Stools okay?"

Sarah nodded, wiping her tears away with the back of her hand. "Yes, both are fine … And, and … he doesn't seem to be in any pain! Wouldn't he be in pain, Terry, if it was such a large tumour? I mean, it may be a blockage, that he's swallowed something, couldn't it?" she asked hopefully, but at the same time knowing that he was right.

"What's a tumour?" grinned Fred, happily laying on the table. For some strange reason he felt rather happy! Extremely relaxed and chilled, in fact! He felt warm and glowy, sort of floaty and free. It was really weird, but really lovely! He looked up at Mum and Aunty C, smiling at them both. Was that a tear in Mum's eye that he could see? He tried to pull himself from his floaty-trance-thing, to see if Mum was crying, but he just felt so sleepy. *Weird or what? Maybe it's a splinter in her eye?* he thought. *Why would she be crying? Daft!*

"Not always, no," Terry was saying. "How old is he now, Sarah? He's over thirteen isn't he? That's really quite old for a golden retriever you know. I think your Fred, I'm so sorry to say, is coming to the end of his time. It's up to you, Sarah. I can run the tests to confirm the diagnosis, but we couldn't operate, not on a tumour of that size; and he is very old now." He looked at Sarah gently. "So what we need to do, is to ask ourselves, do we want to put him through the pain and trauma of all the tests?"

Sarah looked at him, then at Fred, then at Clarabelle, then back at Fred. "Will he suffer?" she asked, looking back at Terry. "If we just take him home, will he suffer?"

"I don't think so, no," he replied quietly. "But if he is in any pain, just call me over and we can give him pain killers, or I can put him to sleep, depending on the severity of the pain. At the moment, he isn't in any pain; so yes, my advice would be to just take him home, Sarah. Let nature take its course, but if you need me, just ring and I will be there to help things along." He patted Fred's head gently, feeling quite upset himself. "Night or day, just ring. I'll be there." He'd been Fred's vet since the beginning, since Fred was eight weeks old, and he was fond of the dog. He looked at Sarah sadly. He knew that she had two children who doted on the dog, particularly the boy. *It's going to be hard on them,* he thought. *Losing your first pet is always the worst, especially for kids.*

Sarah looked at Clarabelle for guidance, but she was shaking her head.

"No tests, no, Sarah. Let's just take him home. I have injected some pain relief into him, to help him you know, although for some reason I did not feel that I actually needed to. Most strange!"

And Sarah took the rather happy Fred home.

They walked out of the vets, through the village and down the lane to their home slowly, both staring at Fred, both knowing that it would be his last walk, ever...

Metatron smiled. He'd been sending pain relief to Fred for some weeks now, wave upon wave. Well, he wasn't going to have his favourite Grim Reaper suffer, now was he? He'd made sure that he'd been there at the vets, of course, with more pain relief. All that poking and prodding wasn't going to be doing that tumour any good at all! As Terry had been feeling the huge tumour, Metatron had been pouring more pain relief into him, although, admittedly, that last lot may have been a bit too much; Fred was stoned! Bless him!

***

Sarah entered the house with a heavy heart. This is going to kill the kids, she thought. And Simon! God, he dotes on that dog!

She looked at the clock; five o'clock. He'll be home soon. He usually finishes on time on a Wednesday, she thought with relief. She looked at Clarabelle, who was stroking Fred. He'd gone straight to his bed when they'd come home, and was now curled up in it, fast asleep. Oh Fred, she cried in her mind, what are we going to do without you? It just won't be the same without you. And Sarah went up to her bedroom quietly and bawled her eyes out for the next hour, which is where she still was when Simon came home and found her.

She told him quietly, sobbing into his arms. She felt his body stiffen, but he did not cry. He just held her silently, staring out of the bedroom window at the fields and countryside beyond. Fields that he'd spent many hours in, walking Fred, playing with Fred, laughing with Fred. He thought back to the duck pond in the park, and Fred's obsession with ducks, an obsession that had nearly got them both killed, and he smiled.

"We need to tell the kids, hun," he said gently. "Come on, darling, dry your tears. We need to be strong for them now; we need to be *extra* strong." And he led her quietly down the stairs to Angelica's room, calling David from his room on the way as they passed by his door.

"Wassup, Dad?" David grinned, coming out of his room and onto the landing.

"I'm busy, Dad!" Angelica huffed, annoyed at the interruption of her favourite TV show that she'd been busy watching.

Sarah called Cassie, who ran into the room, jumping up onto Angelica's lap.

"Sit down please," Simon said softly. There was something in his tone that made both children stop instantly. They looked at their father's face with eyebrows raised, questioningly. They sat down, side by side on Angelica's bed, looking at their parents' faces as they sat together on the small two-seater sofa opposite the bed. Mum had been crying; Dad was pale. Nerves began to rise within each child simultaneously. Something was wrong, very wrong!

Simon spoke quietly, taking the lead, holding tightly onto Sarah's trembling hand. He was firm, calm, and very much in control. It was his job to break this awful news. News that would devastate his children unbearably. News that every parent with pets has to go through at some time, and he truly didn't know how they did it! He took a deep breath, looked into his children's eyes with compassion; trying to share some of his strength with them, to help get them through this. "I need you to be brave, my darlings. I have something very sad to tell you," he took another deep breath. "Our Freddie is very poorly. He is ..." he looked at their faces and into their, now, frightened eyes, "it is his time to go now. He is at the end of his time with us. He's very ill, David, Angelica. He isn't going to make it, I'm so sad to say. But he's not in any pain, he's just old and tired, and ..." Both children had started sobbing. Hands clutched to their faces, they sobbed uncontrollably. Sarah moved from Simon's side to sit between her children; holding each in her arms, clutching them to her chest, she cried with them.

Cassie looked at the floor, a silent tear falling from her grieving eyes.

They sat together for some time. Simon moved over at some point and had joined them; all four of them somehow sitting in a group hug on Angelica's small single bed.

"When will he die? Our Freddie?" Angelica sobbed. "Is it soon?" She looked at her mother with such pain it was almost unbearable.

"I think it is, yes," Sarah replied. She looked at them both. The pure anguish in David's eyes was clear and present. He got up suddenly, running from the room and down the stairs to Fred, who was still sleeping in his bed in the hall. The others all followed him.

Simon picked up the dog's bed, with Fred still in it, and carried it into the lounge. He placed it in front of the fire, laying it down gently. "Light the fire please, Sarah," he said quietly. "Our Freddie likes a fire ... Angelica, go and get all the doggie-chocs out of the cupboard, every single one please, and bring them here ... David, go and get his bones and toys, blanket and whatever else you can find around the house and garden, and bring them here."

All three followed their instructions without hesitation, leaving Simon alone with Fred for a few minutes, apart from Cassie, who hadn't left her friend's side. He stroked his head gently, watching his dog. He looked deep into his eyes; eyes that were now open and awake, just. "I love you, pal," he said, as tears now began to stream unchecked down his face. "I love you so much it hurts! And I will never, ever forget you; never! Thank you for loving me, thank you for being my dog, thank you for saving me, thank you for you. You are 'Fred the Fantastic,' you are a 'bloody genius' and you always have been. I will miss you, Buddy; I will miss you so bloody much!" And he held him. He held him like he'd never let him go, but he did. He had to, because David was now running back into the room with armfuls of Fred's toys, just at the same time as Angelica appeared with dozens of bags of doggie-chocs, and Sarah with the matches to light the fire.

The logs crackled into life quickly, filling the room with a gentle glow. Fred's toys were placed around his bed, doggie-chocs emptied from their packets around him, and then Angelica and David cuddled him, saying their goodbyes. Both were crying and sobbing, both in incredible pain. Sarah looked at the clock on the mantelpiece; seven-twenty-eight. She reached out to Fred, putting her hand on his head, she said simply,

"Never forget how much you were loved, Freddie; are loved! Never ever forget! We will all, every one of us, always love you."

"I love you too," he woofed; quietly, with difficulty. "Always have, always will," he grinned.

Frank watched from the corner of the room. *A dog? I'm here to collect a dog? Don't normally get Grim Reapers collecting dogs! Oh well, the Boss knows best, I guess!* And he reached out his long, shadowy cloak to Fred, covering him with it like a blanket, and pulled it gently to him.

Fred's soul, along with his light and energy, lifted out from his old and worn body easily, smoothly, floating into the shadowy light that was pulling him like a magnet towards it. It felt nice, it felt warm, and above all it felt safe.

And Fred floated away in the blanket without a care....

Chapter 27

Fred floated down the tunnel quite happily. It seemed familiar, this tunnel. The shadowy blanket around him was gentle and safe, and he dozed off into a lovely, dreamy, floaty space of loveliness. ...

Frank carried his collection carefully, just like the Boss had said. He didn't talk to anyone, not a single one! *No dismissal for me,* he grinned. *Nope!* He carried his package all the way down the tunnel, cloaking himself along the way so that he was invisible. No one would see him, no one would distract him and no one would ask any questions.

He arrived at Metatron's office, package intact, not damaged, not dented, delivered on time. He looked at the watch on Metatron's desk as he entered the room. "19:30, just as ordered, Boss," he grinned, putting Fred down gently onto the floor.

"Ah, Frank," Metatron smiled. "Good job."

Frank was just about to leave, having delivered his collection successfully, when surprisingly, Metatron asked him to stay. *Asked? Wow! Wonder what this is about?* he thought.

"And leave the cloak in place," he said, "for now." Frank did as he was told and left his shadowy cloak wrapped around Fred, who was still spark out on the floor.

Metatron placed a call quickly, watching Fred carefully. "Please call GA's Clarence, Clarabelle, Nathaniel, Seraphina and Elijah to my office, immediately," he said firmly into the phone.

The call came quickly. Just as Clarabelle and Nat were giving Sarah and Simon healing for their grief, and Sephi and Elijah were doing the same for Angelica and David, they suddenly had to go.

"But, I am needed here!" they all said together in dismay, looking at their respective ward's crying faces.

"Now, he said, and he means 'now'!" they were told.

So they obeyed. They had no choice!

They rushed upstairs quickly, annoyed at this intrusion and distraction, as they saw it. The four flew into Metatron's office, almost colliding in their haste, just as Clarence arrived.

"Ah," smiled Metatron. "Thank you all for coming. I do appreciate that you want to be with your wards at this time, but," he grinned, "you will soon see why I have called you." He looked at Frank and waved his hand at Fred. "You may unpack your collection now, Frank," he ordered.

Frank did as he was told, pulling his black cloak away

from Fred gently.

Fred jumped, woke up and floated up from the cloak into the room, right in front of Clarabelle and Clarence, who were beaming, positively beaming; so happy to see that the dog had come up to the light, despite all that swearing of his! But before they had a chance to wonder what Fred was doing here, in Metatron's office, he suddenly transformed himself, right in front of them, from 'Fred the dog,' back into his old self, his 'Fred the Grim Reaper self'!

"Oh my!" declared the watching GA's. Clarabelle fell over with the shock!

"Fred!" screamed Frank, running over to him ecstatically; throwing his arms around him in delight. "Oh my goodness, mate, I have sooo missed you!" he screeched, hugging him and hugging him like there was no tomorrow. "Where've you been, buddy? Oh my goodness! You're back, you're back!" Frank was jumping up and down in complete hysteria.

"Well I never!" declared Clarence and Clarabelle, staring at Fred in amazement as they got up from the floor where they had both fallen down in their complete shock.

"Well, I can't get over this!" laughed Clarabelle, running over and hugging Fred, as best she could with Frank in the way, who just wouldn't let go! Then Clarence and the others all joined in, forming an enormous group hug!

Metatron watched the hugging reunion for a little while, allowing the old friends to reconnect, then began to explain to the GA's all about Fred's mission - to kill Simon and bring him back, and that he'd changed his mind, saving him instead. Metatron filled them all in, laughing at their shock and surprise. "And now Fred," he smiled, "it is time."

Fred could have just burst, he was that chuffed! He gazed at the golden halo on its stand in the corner of the room with passion and pride.

Clarabelle and Clarence looked at it too. "Aye?" they said together.

Metatron walked over to the halo, lifting it gently from the stand and walked slowly back to Fred.

"It is with pride," he said, "that I award you this promotion."

Fred dropped to one knee on the floor in front of Metatron, bowing his head.

Metatron placed the halo onto Fred's head, and, as he did, Fred's 'Grim Reaper' black, shadowy cloak, transformed before them into the most beautiful, white feathery angel wings. Bells suddenly rang out across The Realms, marking the huge occasion. Angels from every level stopped what they were doing immediately and stood still as the bells rang out.

"Someone new has got their wings," said one. "That's nice!"

"Oh, how lovely!" said another.

Back in the office, in front of the shocked crew of Guardian Angels, Metatron was performing the ceremony. "I," he said, "Metatron, head of The Angelic Realms, hereby do pronounce you, 'Fred, 'Trainee Third Level Guardian Angel, Class Five'!"

"No way!" whispered Clarabelle. "Fred's been promoted out of transport to be up with us? How very lovely!" And she burst into happy tears!

"Yes, my dear Clarabelle; he has. And," Metatron paused, "you are to be his trainer, Clarabelle. Fred is to remain in the Brown household for the duration."

"Oh, how wonderful!" she shrieked. "Oh, Sir, they will be so pleased!"

"Indeed," agreed Metatron. "He is to return with you now. You are to show him everything that he needs to know, alright?"

"Oh yes, Sir; very alright!" beamed Clarabelle.

"And, Fred, these are your orders." Metatron handed Fred a golden scroll.

He opened it carefully, reading his mission. "Oh, my Dog!" he exclaimed. "I mean, oh my goodness! Oops, sorry, Sir, force of habit!"

"Indeed," grimaced Metatron, looking at Clarabelle. "That needs to go!"

Clarabelle grinned. She wasn't sure Fred would be 'Fred' without his 'oh my Dogs!' but she'd do her best.

Fred was staring at the orders in surprise. He wasn't sure if he was happy or disappointed. "Umm, Sir," he asked, "not that I'm complaining, Sir, but ..."

"Indeed. I thought it rather apt myself," grinned Metatron.

"But a dog, Sir?" Fred showed his orders to the others. "Look," he said to Clarabelle in a whisper, "I'm to be trainee GA to David's new puppy?"

"Yes, well, Fred, we can't have you having a human as a ward just yet; far too soon! It was either that or make you wait the fifteen years until Angelica has her baby, so I thought that this was a rather good compromise. It will be great training for you, help you learn how to guide your doggie ward. And," he grinned, "if anyone can help a puppy it will be you, Fred. You have vast experience in this area now, do you not?"

"Aye? Angelica's baby?" Fred said in horror. "Angelica? Madam? Nightmare madam?"

"Yes, well, I like to 'keep it in the family' so to speak."

"But, but, but ... can't I be David's babies' GA?" he whispered. *Dog, Angelica!* "Please?" he added, hopefully. Very hopefully!

"You have your orders, Fred. If they are not to your taste you can always refuse your mission and go back down to transport?" Metatron glared. *Really, no gratitude! No gratitude at all!*

"Oh no! No thank you, Sir. I'm very happy with these orders," he said quickly. "Very happy indeed!" If anyone noticed the gritted teeth, they didn't mention it.

"Off you go then. You have your own funeral to attend. You don't want to be late!" And Metatron waved them off with a flick of his hand, smiling at the crew as they departed. *Bless, he's done really well, has our Fred. Maybe I should think about promoting more Grim Reapers up to GA?* he thought to himself, and went back to work.

***

The family gathered around the large hole in the ground that Simon had spent the last hour digging under Fred's favourite tree in the garden. It had given him time, time to sort his head out.

The children had stayed indoors with Sarah, all crying around Fred's body (a body that Cassie was guarding and refusing to leave). He'd felt the need to go into practical mode, as most men did at emotional times, and had left them to grieve together. With each dig of the spade, he had done his own grieving, reflecting back on Fred's life. With each dig, he'd begun to come to terms with his loss. He'd miss him; he'd miss him terribly, but he'd gone in peace. He'd not suffered, and he'd had a good life.

When the hole was ready, Simon had gone to his shed, picking up two loose pieced of wood from the back, and looked for the hammer and nails. Ten minutes later, he'd made a cross, ready for Fred's grave. He spent another twenty minutes carving the name 'Fred' into the top piece with a chisel, and then he was satisfied. He called the children and Sarah into the garden, and the family gathered.

They stood silently watching their father place Fred's body, wrapped in his favourite blanket, still in his bed; into the hole. David placed Fred's toys around him, Angelica the doggie-chocs. Sarah placed his lead next to him, and Simon his bowls.

Cassie looked at Fred's body in the grave and cried. She couldn't remember a time, ever, in her whole six lifetimes, that she'd ever been this upset!

Just as they were about to begin saying 'a few words,' they suddenly heard a rustle of feathers behind them.

"Oh, Dog, don't bury me doggie-chocs! That's a right waste, that is!" piped up Fred.

All four, standing over the grave, twirled around in

shock. "Fred!" they screamed in surprise. Cassie jumped in delight! They could all see him, standing there with them, but he wasn't a ghost! He seemed to be half angel, half dog! It was most peculiar! As they watched, trying to get their heads around it, he transformed before them from half dog into full angel, and even had a halo!

"Didn't want to confuse you!" he grinned. "I'm an angel now, Dad; look!" And Fred twirled around proudly, showing off his feathers. "If I'd shown you myself as an angel first, you might not have known it was me, so I did 'half 'n half.' See? I'm a bloody genius! Always knew I was!"

"Fred!" scolded Clarabelle, standing by his side. "You can't swear now that you're an angel! It's not allowed!"

"Oh, Dog! That's gonna be a tuffy!" he grinned. "I'll do my best; but you know me!" And he flew around the garden sniffing, practicing flying with his new feathery wings.

"Fred!" they called. "You're not a dog anymore! You can't sniff!"

"Dog, you're right!" Fred yelled, bending over a stray bone that David had missed. "Yikes! I can't smell anything! Not a Dog-damned thing!" He gave up on the sniffing and flew back to the crowd, still gathered by the open grave. "I'm happy to see that you're burying me under me favourite tree, Dad. That's nice, ta! Crack on then, before I 'go off.' Don't want to be ponging out the garden with mangy old going off-ness, now do I?"

And so Dad had covered his old 'doggie body' up with the soil, patting it down nicely with the spade, then placed the cross at the top, above Fred's head.

Fred looked at them all and grinned happily. "Yeah, that'll do nicely," he beamed. "Smashing!"

All the tears had dried up, he was pleased to see; everyone happy now that Fred was back. "Time for a party then, I do believe!" he grinned. "I got me promotion to celebrate, and I couldn't think of anyone else I'd rather celebrate it with than you lot, my lovely family!" And Fred hugged them all, wrapping them up in his new feathery wings, smiling the biggest, bestest smile that he'd ever smiled!

Epilogue

Ma stood watching the gathered people standing in the church. She was so pleased to see so many people here for her funeral. She examined the casket carefully. *Yes, perfect*. She smiled, a wise, old smile, and yet it shone out of a now, pretty, younger face. The years had fallen away, once she'd got into the light.

She looked down at the body of the old woman lying in the casket before her. The face, old and withered, wrinkles covering every inch. She turned to Pa, grinning. "Don't know how I managed to get to such old age. Ninety! Positively ancient!"

He smiled back. "You were always beautiful, hun, right up to the end. Every wrinkled inch of you!"

Ma looked back at the crowd of people that lined the pews. "Lovely service this will be, hun. I spent an age planning it, an absolute age!" she said to Pa.

He grinned back. "I know, darling. I was watching, always watching. Never left your side, not even for a second."

The couple held hands tightly, waiting for the service to begin. With that, a black cat joined them. Sitting at their feet, she wound her tail around 'her Ma,' lovingly.

"Oh, Cassandra Alexandra the Third! How lovely of you to join us!" Ma said. "I did wonder, when you didn't follow us into the light straight away, whether you were coming at all!"

"Sorry, Ma," Cassie said. "I got a bit confused. I thought I was still alive, silly me!"

"So where did you go then, you know, when you didn't follow us down the tunnel?" Ma asked, bending down to stroke the cat.

"Well, I forgot, Ma. I forgot all about my previous lives when I died on your lap."

"Yes, it was nice, us going together like that, don't you think, Cassie?" Ma grinned. "Although, you took your time going into the tunnel, didn't you?"

"I know! It took me ages to realise that I was dead; but as soon as I did, I made my way back home. I got there in the end, back to your lap; then I jumped into the tunnel just before it closed. I did run to catch you up, Ma, but I couldn't find you. Anyway, I'm here now," she grinned, adding, "I knew you'd be here for this. You wouldn't miss your own funeral now, would you, Ma?" And Cassie purred, a long, contented purr.

"So where did you go? I've been dead a week! We both have!" Ma grinned.

"Oh, well I went for a walk for a while, you know. Then I found myself back in my sixth life. I watched for a while, just reminiscing, and that's when I realised that I was dead, and so I made my way back home, to you."

"Shush now, Cassie," Ma said. "They're starting." And the three stood back quietly to watch the service.

"We are gathered here today," the vicar said, "to celebrate the life of Sarah Brown, or Ma, as she was affectionately known in her later years. Let us begin by singing hymn number twenty-three, 'The Lord is my shepherd …'"

Cassie watched the people singing. As they sang, she reflected on her journey into the past, a journey back to her sixth life, the life where she had revisited her first ever life with Ma, when Ma had been 'just Sarah.' *Blimey, no wonder I kept getting them mixed up!* she thought.

Cassie was 'Cassandra Alexandra the Third' for a reason! This was her third life with Sarah, or 'Ma,' as she preferred to call her (the third life with Ma, but the ninth and final life for the cat). *The first life with Ma had been when she was much younger and the children were little,* she recalled, *just five years old, bless them. I was called just 'Cassie' for that one,* she remembered. That life had gone on until the children were nearly twenty years old. Then there'd been the second life, a year or so later; *another fifteen years, or was it twenty that I had that time?* Cassie couldn't remember. *That was the life when I was called 'Alexandra,' or Sandy for short. That was the life when the children had had children of their own.* Cassie grinned. She'd enjoyed that life! *Why was that one so nice?* she wondered. *Oh yes, I remember; that was the life when Fred became a proper GA, bless him.* She thought about Fred then; her old pal. *It had been nice to stay in touch, to always having him around through these last three lives. Lovely!* It had been nice to see him again on her little visit, though it was weird watching herself as a young cat, joining the Brown house for the first time. She'd been six months old when she'd joined them. She'd run away from the farm where she'd been born (where she'd lived as a rat catcher), and gone in search of a better place. She'd found it, with Sarah. No more rats to catch, no more going hungry the nights she failed; no more being cold, sleeping in the barn. Yes it had been a good life with Sarah. She'd thought, back there on her recent visit, when she'd been lying in the lane that day they'd found her, that it was real, that she was really there! But no, she'd been just a ghost cat, come back from the future, watching an old version of herself from another life. She'd done her best to help her younger self, by sharing her soul energy and knowledge with her, allowing Cassie the First to know what Cassie the Third knew. She'd shared her love of Ma, her love of the Tarot, her love of people, of healing, of helping, and she'd shared it well. Despite Cassie the First never having worked with cards, or any of the energy, and being only six months old, she suddenly had the knowing of nine lives, all of them, past and future, right the way through. Cassie sighed. She wished people had the same ability as cats, the ability to access their past and future selves with all its wondrous knowledge! The world would be a far better place if they could! This last life was the clearest to remember though, the life when Sarah properly became Ma, because it was the nearest, of course, the most recent. That was the life when Ma combined her two earlier names and called her C.A.T. - Cassandra Alexandra the Third. *Ma must have known I was the same cat, clever old thing!* Cassie smiled happily. *She must have been in her mid-seventies when I re-joined her this time, or was she eighty?* Cassie couldn't remember. *Oh, must have been eighty, cos it was after Pa had gone, or 'Simon,' as he preferred to be called.* She looked at the packed church. *Oh, there's David, and Angelica, singing away,* she noticed. *Blimey, they look old! Oh, and there's Fred, sitting on little Sarah's shoulder! How lovely! Not that she's little anymore; gosh, she must be in her twenties now, love her! Nice that they'd named her after Ma, but David was like that. Always a lovely boy!* The hymn finished and the crowd took their seats. All except David. He stayed standing, then made his way to the pulpit. He pulled out a piece of paper; his notes, for his speech.

"Ma went out the way she wanted to," he said. "With her beloved cat, Cassie, curled up with her. It's nice that they went together, and I'm sure Dad was waiting for them both," he smiled, continuing his speech to his mum. "When I found Mum last week, Cassie on her lap, as usual, she had gone peacefully, in her sleep. The cat had died with her, probably from grief," he said. "Always were inseparable those two. Anyway," he wiped away a tear, "I'm sure they're together now." He looked at his sister in the front row. She was wiping away a tear, holding tightly onto her husband's hand. David smiled at Angelica reassuringly, then continued. "Ma always had cats, well, ever since I can remember. Our first was when me and Anj were little, another black cat. That would have been around the time when she first started doing her readings, and as we know now, they have helped many, many people. Ma was a wonder; always helping people she was, right up to the day she died." David's lip wobbled, but as soon as it did, Fred was there, putting his angel wings around him, hugging him and giving him strength and support, along with Elijah, who stood on his shoulder.

"I've got some spare doggie-chocs, if it helps," he grinned.

David smiled at Fred, grateful that he was there to help.

Clarabelle, of course, was also there with them, standing next to Sarah, holding her one hand, whilst Simon held the other. Next to him, stood Nat, waving his wand around, pointing it to anyone who looked upset.

"This isn't a sad day!" yelled Nat. "This is a day of celebration! The celebration of a wonderful life!" He grinned at Sarah and Simon, happy that they were together once more. "You did good, girl," he grinned. "We totalled it up, 'upstairs,' you know, all those people that you've helped over the years. It comes to fifteen thousand, four hundred and twenty-three. Just wanted you to know!" and he went back to his wand-waving.

Sarah and Simon stood together smiling. They watched their children proudly, and their grandchildren, noticing 'little Sarah' as she sat next to her mum, David's wife, and the rather large bump on her lap.

"Uh oh! Looks like great-grandchildren, Fire Girl," he grinned. "Shush now, let's let David finish his speech."

And they did. Sarah and Simon watched as David finished and continued to watch as many other people took their turn at the pulpit, each showering praise on the departed Sarah, each showing how much she had been loved during her life. And she smiled. "It's been a good life," she said quietly, a beautiful smile on her happy face. "A wonderful life, actually!"

And she gazed at them all. A serene, gentle, peaceful smile on her lips; a smile that lit up her face and the room with it. "Goodbye, my darlings," she called to her children as the service closed. "I shall always be close ... be watching over you ... goodbye ... goodbye ... goodbye ..."

As she began to fade into the mist around her, holding Simon's hand tightly, a golden haze glowed brightly as she walked into the light. It filled the church from wall to wall, and from floor to ceiling, making everyone in the room suddenly stop in their tracks. They all looked at the light, and each smiled.

"One of Earth's angels was Sarah Brown," the vicar said, looking up to the heavens. "One of Earth's angels; God, bless her."

And Cassandra Alexandra the Third ran after her. It was her time too, her time to finally go into the light after nine long lifetimes. Lifetimes that spanned one hundred and fifty years. Lifetimes of helping and healing, of comforting and loving, of supporting and guiding. She had been the perfect cat for Sarah Brown. They were two peas in a pod! And as she passed into the light after 'her Ma,' a golden light appeared around the cat too, and she floated into it softly, a serene smile on her furry lips. "Wait for me, Ma, wait for me ... I'm coming. ..."

The End

Angel on My Shoulder
(Sarah's Story)
By
Julie Poole

The first book in the 'Angel' series ...

Sarah is having a bad day! At 37½ life is going nowhere fast. She's been dumped by her latest boyfriend, again! She's lost her latest job, again! And her mother's driving her mad, again! To top it all, she can't even have a moan in peace without Clarabelle piping up every two minutes trying to cheer her up, again! Clarabelle is, of course, Sarah's 'Guardian Angel,' whose job it is to constantly keep Sarah's spirits up - an annoying distraction to say the least! Clarabelle certainly has her work cut out where Sarah is concerned!

Having reached rock bottom, Sarah reluctantly accepts Clarabelle's help, growing gradually from a chaotic, lost young woman into the person she always wanted to be. With the angel's help she is ready at last for her soulmate Simon to enter her life. Throughout her journey a team of angels have regular 'inter-angel-cy' meetings, mapping out and planning Sarah's life for her, often getting it very wrong with hilarious results!

Sarah's story brings hope, magic and inspiration from the beginning right through to its uplifting conclusion; drawing the reader into an emotional rollercoaster that will make you laugh, cry and ultimately leave you with a smile on your face and quite possibly with an empty box of tissues!

Angel in My Heart
(Clarabelle's Story)
By
Julie Poole

The second book in the 'Angel' series …

Following on from 'Angel on My Shoulder (Sarah's Story),' Sarah is finally having a good day! At 38¾ life is now going fantastically! She's just married her soulmate Simon, her store is doing great and she's even getting on with her mother. (Miracles really do happen!) And to top it all, she's pregnant!

Her 'Guardian Angel' Clarabelle is, of course, 'smashingly' happy, but is she risking it all with her crush on Archangel Michael? How will Simon cope with finding out that his new wife has a Guardian Angel that she can see and talk to? Will Nathaniel ever sort out his Gonk hair, and what will Metatron do when he finds out about Clarabelle's crush; will she be banished from The Angelic Realms forever?

In this sequel, 'Angel in My Heart (Clarabelle's Story),' it is Sarah's turn to help her angelic best friend Clarabelle and prevent a disaster. Can she do it? Enter 'Fred the Fantastic' to save the day. Fred is, of course, Sarah and Simon's new dog; a Golden Retriever, who being a genius can speak three languages (dog, angel and human). Whether he can help 'Mum' and 'Aunty Clarabelle' sort the mess out that they've got themselves into, though, is quite another matter!

Angel in My Fingers

(Frieda's Story)

By
Julie Poole

The third book in the Angel series

Clarabelle is on a mission! With the children now at school, it's high time that 'her Sarah' focused! Enter 'Cassie' the cat (much to Fred's disgust), here to help Sarah become the 'Best Tarot and Angel Card Reader' this side of Mars ... Can Sarah do what Clarabelle needs her to do? And can she do it in time?

Frieda has a secret ... a dark, foreboding, sinister secret ... and it is only Sarah who can unlock it ... Can she help Frieda find the peace that she has never known, or is she jeopardising a friendship that has lasted for nearly forty years?

In this sequel - the third in the 'Angel' series - it is time for Sarah to move to the next level. Can she cope with the pressure ... or with what she discovers!

Pain and trauma ... secrets and lies - no one knows what she's been through, and Frieda's determined to keep it that way! With such resistance, can Sarah repair a broken spirit and bring a happy ending, even with Clarabelle and Cassie's help? Clarabelle thinks so, but only Frieda can be the one to determine that!

A Note from Julie Poole

Thank you so much for reading Angel in My Fingers (Frieda's Story). If you enjoyed it, please take a moment to leave a review at your favourite on line store, such as Amazon.co.uk or Amazon.com

    I welcome contact from my readers. At my website you can contact me, leave a review, and find all the links to my social media: www.juliepooleauthor.com

18503321R00193

Printed in Poland
by Amazon Fulfillment
Poland Sp. z o.o., Wrocław